The Sea of Worlds: Gods and Men

By Robert Range

Dedication

To my parents, Roy Neil Range and Patsy Ruth Orren-Range, who passed in 2021. They did well with what life gave them. I look forward to when we meet again.

Table of Contents

Chapter 1: Göttingen, 1925 9
Chapter 2: Nadine Taschner 21
Chapter 3: A Call from the Dark 31
Chapter 4: Inanna 43
Chapter 5: The Council of Seven 54
Chapter 6: Sargon of Akkad 65
Chapter 7: The Ascension of Sargon of Akkad 76
Chapter 8: The Point of Creation 83
Chapter 9: The Secret 94
Chapter 10: The Igigi 102
Chapter 11: The Victory at Ganzir 117
Chapter 12: The *Tiamat* 133
Chapter 13: The Bull of Heaven 145
Chapter 14: The Will of the Genitor 154
Chapter 15: Specified Conception 166
Chapter 16: A House in Kur 177
Chapter 17: The War for Heaven on Earth 188
Chapter 18: Eshumesha 202
Chapter 19: The Nibiru Station 220
Chapter 20: Revelation and Judgement 231
Chapter 21: The Morning Star 243
About the Author 249

Copyright

Copyright 2022© Robert Range
First edition, 2022. All rights reserved.

No part of this publication may be copied, reproduced, stored in or introduced into a retrieval system, or transmitted in any form or by any means (electronic, mechanical, photocopying, recording, or otherwise) without written permission of the author.

Limit of Liability and Disclaimer of Warranty: This is a work of fiction. Names, characters, businesses, events and incidents are the products of the author's imagination. Any resemblance to actual persons, living or dead, or actual events, scenes or dialogues of any person, living or dead, is entirely coincidental. All mention of places or people have been used for dramatic and narrative purposes only in this story. The views and opinions expressed by any of the fictional or real characters in this work do not necessarily reflect or represent the views and opinions held by individuals on which those characters are based or those of the author.

The author has used his best efforts in preparing this book, and the information provided herein is "as provided". This book is designed to provide entertainment to its readers and is sold with the understanding that the author is not engaged to render any type of parental, psychological, legal, or any other kind of professional advice. The content is the sole expression and opinion of its author. No warranties or guarantees are expressed or implied by the author's choice to include any of the content in this book. The author shall not be liable for any physical, psychological, emotional, financial, or commercial damages, including, but not limited to, special, incidental, consequential or other damages. Our views and rights are the same: You are responsible for your chosen actions and results.

ISBN: 9798846698833
Written by Robert Range

Editing and Interior Design by Nita Robinson, *Nita Helping Hand?*
www.NitaHelpingHand.com

Cover by Kelly Martin www.KAM.design

Chapter 1: Göttingen, 1925

Roy Masterson sat at a small wooden table just inside the door of the German tavern. His eyes shifted from the front entrance to the curtained entry to the back storage room behind the bar. He turned up the large tankard to finish the dark German beer. Masterson savored the strong taste of the drink while setting down the empty glass. When the beautiful young fraulein approached with a pitcher of dark beer, he waved her off. Masterson bounced the empty glass on the rough wood of the table as he waited. He looked at his watch, checking his time once again. Masterson's contact walked in, scanning the small tavern.

The man walked to the bar and spoke with the proprietor in a low voice, then louder, "Ein Bier, bitte!" Smiling at the serving fraulein, he turned to sit with Masterson at his small table as they had planned.

Masterson smiled up at the man as he dug a pair of gold-tinted glasses from his coat pocket. He slid the wire-rimmed glasses on then removed them as if satisfied. "Yes, and you are Werner?"

"Yes, I am. They told me you have something for me. You represent the Rockefeller Foundation from New York in America, yes?" The young German seemed excited to meet Masterson as he reached across the table to grasp hands.

Masterson avoided taking the young man's hand, "Yes, I represent the Foundation here in Germany on some of their international projects. They told me you're working on a special field of physics outside Newtonian?" They stopped while the tavern's serving girl brought Werner's pint of beer to the small table. Both men smiled at the girl as they watched her walk away with her hips swinging.

The young German nodded enthusiastically. "Yes, yes, I am. My theory is a re-interpretation of kinematic and mechanical relations at the atomic and subatomic levels. I would like to travel to Copenhagen to continue my research at the Institute of Theoretical Physics at the University. Is that possible?"

"I'm in communications with the Americans in New York. They're very interested in your work and would like to see you collaborate with them. The people I represent believe you're onto something and we can do great things together," Masterson smiled.

As they talked, two brawny men with the look of the *Braune Hemden* walked into the bar. They were looking about as if searching for someone. One of the Brown Shirts had on a pair of gold-tinted eyeglasses, like the ones Masterson carried. When his eyes met with Masterson's, he looked away then tapped his companion's belly, nodding toward the bar. They moved toward the bar, waving for the attention of the tavern's owner.

Masterson slipped on his own glasses as he removed a small envelope and a fountain pen from his inner suit jacket pocket. He glanced up at the two men as he wrote a note on the thick envelope. He pushed it toward Werner. "Contact this phone number late tonight. By then I'll have more information to give to you. Please examine the contents of the envelope. We think you'll be very interested in what we're offering you. We're very interested in your field of work. If you don't hear from me again, the information within the letter is yours to use. I'll relay your interest in the Foundation's educational grant and desire to work with us." Masterson stood, showing the end of their business for today.

Werner stood, nodding his head. Seeing the interest Masterson had in the two large, uniformed men at the bar hastened his departure from the small tavern. He avoided looking at the two men as he exited to the street.

Masterson looked at them through his gold-tinted glasses, their translucent red aura lingering about them like a mist coming off their shoulders and heads. He stepped out from behind his small table and moved toward them, holding his hands up, palms open toward them. Under their heavy wool coats, Masterson could see their ironed military-style shirts with the leather belt and matching diagonal shoulder strap that supported the weight of a holstered pistol on the hip. In flawless German, Masterson addressed the two men, "Hello,

Leader Wolff, Trooper Sauer, good to see you both again. What can I do for you?"

"Who was that you were talking with, Fischer? He had the look of a federal officer." Wolff reached to open Masterson's coat to look at his inner coat pockets.

Masterson stepped back, holding up his hands to block being touched. "Who are you talking about, Wolff? I was here enjoying a beer with an old school friend. You know that place you quit because they were trying to teach you how to read?"

Wolff's face reddened. "You swine, I'll break your neck for talking to me that way." The larger and more muscular man grabbed Masterson's shoulders and shoved him toward the door, surprising not only Masterson but the other people in the tavern and causing the women to gasp.

Masterson turned his body so that his back impacted the door, causing it to burst open. He stumbled out of the tavern onto the sidewalk and street. Masterson looked around for oncoming traffic as he fought to keep his footing on the cobblestones. He turned to face the two brown shirts as they stepped from the single exit like two titans, both focused on him with intense anger. The town street was busy; a small open cab truck had stopped by Masterson who was standing in the road. He turned to cross the street, dodging slow-moving cars and trucks with the two brown-shirted, powerful men in pursuit. Trying to use the sparse traffic to hide his movements, he ducked into a narrow alley between two shops which would only allow one person to pass through, leading to a more open alley behind the row of shops. The two brown shirts were right on his tail; only his quicker speed was affecting his leading them in the chase. As the small alley ended, Masterson threw his back against the wall out of the sight of his pursuers, waiting, his muscles coiled and readying to strike.

Wolff rushed around the corner expecting the attack, drawing his right arm back to prepare for delivering a vicious strike with his fist, but Masterson jabbed the fingertips of his right hand into Wolff's throat just above the breastbone. Wolff collapsed to his knees, grasping his throat with both hands, choking and gasping for air. Right behind him was Sauer, who had pulled a small double-stitched leather bag filled with sand gripped in his right hand.

"Stop!" shouted Masterson, but to no avail; the thug raised his sandbag to pummel him and rushed forward past Wolff. Masterson crossed his wrists above his head, forming an 'X' to block Sauer's downward swing. Their overcoats flared as they fought. Masterson caught Sauer's right arm at the crux of his crossed arms, turning his own right wrist as he scissored his arms, catching Sauer's wrist in his hand. Masterson turned to throw his hip back into Sauer while he pulled his arm and body through the arc of Sauer's intended attack. The momentum of Sauer's downward swing carried the thug up and over Masterson's body, lifting him off his feet as Masterson's back came underneath him. It propelled Sauer into a large jumble of wooden crates and other garbage with a splintering crash. Masterson turned to grab Wolff by the labels of the coat's large woolen collar, thrusting his knee into the larger man's face as he struggled to breathe, shattering the German's nose. The man fell dead weight to the ground in a lump.

Masterson spun on his heels to face Sauer as he climbed from the pile of debris. Rage showed on the man's face as he saw Masterson had put Wolff down. Sauer moved to draw his pistol from his hip holster, throwing his long coattail back so he could clear the weapon from the leather holster. Masterson saw the Luger P-08 pistol flash into view. Masterson planted his left foot and spun clockwise, lifting his right foot to connect with the right cheek of Sauer's face with the heel of his foot. The walls of the alley amplified the bone-crushing crack while they fought. Sauer lay sprawled out on the packed, mud-covered cobblestone. Masterson stepped over Sauer, taking hold of his chin and the back of his head, and with a simple twist ended the man's life. Masterson stood panting for air at his exertion during the melee. He stepped away from Sauer to claim his pistol. Then, with regret, he searched both men for their identity papers, money, and ammunition. The last thing Masterson took was Wolff's set of gold-tinted glasses.

Back on the street, Masterson moved into a store across the way. It was a general store filled with various cast-iron cooking implements, rolls of cloth, and carpentry tools. He moved to look at the items near the large storefront window to watch for the police or more thugs. He watched for several minutes before it satisfied him that there would be no immediate Ejicerce pursuit of him.

"Sir, may I use your telephone?" Masterson asked in perfect German with a slight Saxony accent appropriate for the city of Göttingen on the River Leine. The old man grunted and reached beneath the counter, placing his dial phone on the counter. "Danke," Masterson took the phone in hand and moved off as far as the black, rubber-coated phone wire would allow. He went through the motions of dialing a number while he held the earpiece cradle down so the call wouldn't connect with an operator. This was the agreed procedure he and Valarus had decided upon to activate two-way communications between them while he was in the field. It was a way to let his monitors know he needed to speak to them.

In his mind, he heard the familiar voice of Captain Valarus of the Great House of Salvis, "Report your situation, Roy."

"I think they've compromised me. Two Ejicerce interrupted my meeting with the professor." Masterson looked back over his shoulder, checking the activities of the shop owner who stood watching him from behind his counter.

"Did they harm him?"

Masterson turned away from the proprietor, satisfied he wasn't trying to eavesdrop. "No, I don't think so. I didn't see him or others outside the building. I think the German thugs known as Brown Shirts were there for me. At least, that's the way it appeared to be."

In his mind, Masterson heard Valarus continue, "How do you know they were Ejicerce?"

"I checked them with my visor-glasses. The visor identified them as Ejicerce with a dark aura."

"I see. Did you elude them?"

Masterson nodded then turned back to look at the shop proprietor, "No, they forced me to eliminate them. I figure that will draw out any backup they had onsite."

"Sound tactical move, although the Anunnaki would not approve, you know? But the Ejicerce compromised them. The Anunnaki consider non-Igigi humans a resource."

"I know, I know. I want to be extracted. They compromised this body. The Ejicerce must have tagged me, meaning it compromises the mission. They know the professor's importance to the time stream." Masterson surveyed the near-empty shop, looking for indications he was being watched by others besides the proprietor. "It appears the fight between me and the two Ejicerce wasn't heard. No one has approached the scene of the fight that I can see. Hold on, I'll put on the visor so you can scan the identities of my two attackers. Ready?" Masterson placed his gold-tinted, wire-rim glasses on then pulled out the identity papers of his assailants. He unfolded Wolff's identity paper and read it with the telephone receiver cradled between his chin and shoulder while his visor-glasses scanned what he was looking at. He did the same with Sauer's papers.

"All right, we got their information. You can move to a safe spot for extraction," Masterson heard Valarus' voice say in his head.

Masterson put the papers back in his coat pocket. Then, while removing the gold-tinted glasses and stowing them, he moved toward the counter, placing the telephone within arm's reach of the older man. He withdrew a leather wallet from his hip pocket and fished through it for the local currency. Removing several bills from his wallet, he held them up for the proprietor to see. The man smiled and nodded as Masterson tossed them on the counter before him. "Danke," Masterson said as he folded his wallet and returned to the street outside the store. Pedestrian traffic wasn't heavy, so he moved to a side alley of the store unnoticed as far as he could tell, and sat with his back against the hard brick wall. He removed his gold-tinted glasses and, holding them with the pair taken from Wolff, slammed them into the cobblestone pavement of the alley, shattering the lenses. He tossed the wrecked frames away into the depths of the alley and closed his eyes.

Roy Masterson woke, floating in a non-Newtonian solution that was a tactile connection between his body and the psionic instrumentation. The technology allowed him to possess the body and co-opt the mind of *Walter Fischer*. The liquid goo slithered from his submerged, depilated Dionan body, lowering him to the hard slab surface beneath where he lay. His hairless body allowed the best tactile connection with the projection device. He struggled to move, so he was sitting on the slab rather than laying there like a body on an autopsy table. In his mind, he heard the soothing voice of a famulim as he felt its soft touch on his back.

"How are you feeling, **Veneficus**?" asked the famulim with its telepathic connection to Masterson through touching him, using its tactile-telepathy, an ability referred to as touch-speak to exchange thoughts between them.

Masterson smiled, turning to look at the famulim as it checked him. Its touch was used to check his vital signs through their physical connection. The bald, gray-skinned, androgynous famulim moved its arms languidly as it touched various places on his body to take medical readings. The first beings created by the Genitor when they had arrived in the solar system billions of years ago, the famulim were the caretakers of the other species, created to serve all within the shared reality of the Genitor.

"So, you did not like that body, Roy?" Valarus laughed as he entered the time ship's excursion room.

Masterson gestured to the famulim for a towel, which he wrapped around his loins as he slid off the table. "He wasn't bad, and passive enough that I could concentrate on what I was doing to survive a brawl with two Ejicerce. But he was compromised, if not by being recognized by the Ejicerce then by the Göttingen police as they investigated the murder of the two brown shirts. I'm sure someone had to have seen the pursuit, not to mention the way they greeted Walter in the tavern."

Valarus rubbed his heavy dark beard in thought, "Good point. I agree that the holder-body has outlived its usefulness to us. What do you intend to do next; return to another body and meet with the target again soon, or do we have time?"

"I abandoned the holder very close to the dead Ejicerce. I'm sure the police will pick it up once they investigate the fight. Yeah, we need to move to the second holder-body you selected during the first reconnaissance of the field environment." Masterson moved to retrieve his shipboard clothing while the two men continued to talk.

"Were you able to pass Heisenberg the information before they intercepted you?"

Masterson nodded to the captain as he pulled the light, linen, pastel top over his head and down to his waist. "Yes, and he has the phone number. But we have no way of knowing when he'll call it now that I had to abandon my holder."

"Well, we could activate the alternative holder-body, the female companion of Walter," replied Valarus with a lewd smile.

Masterson smirked, "Good idea. Are you going to possess her?"

Valarus laughed as he stroked his beard. "It would distract me. I will assign Hebeta to the task. She is getting bored with the *Glorious Questor* laying on the bottom of the North Sea. Besides, I do not look as appealing without body hair as you do."

Masterson turned to the famulim as he slid into his linen pants, "How am I, Antuma?"

"You are in perfect health, Chief Adjutant Masterson. You can resume your duties, sir," responded the famulim as it collected the discarded towel Masterson had left on the floor near where his clothing was during his excursion.

Slipping on the non-skid slippers worn on the ship, he followed Valarus into the passageway outside the excursion room. They walked side by side down the cylindrical, pearl, pseudo-ceramic passageway that snaked through the bowels of the ship. "As for my next move, sir, I will need to meet with Werner again as you said, but it would be better to wait, move further down the time stream before meeting with him again. Hebeta can possess Walter's companion and take the call and arrange for another meeting later."

Valarus nodded in agreement, "Yes, and she will enjoy being off the ship, too. The pilots often become bored and then sloppy on missions like this. But we need them. We cannot project into another's subconsciousness and take control without being in both physical and temporal proximity to them. We cannot be further up or down the time stream for such a connection, so we need the time ships."

They stepped into the mission operations center close to the excursion room. Hebeta was already there. She was the ship's senior pilot. But once the time ship was in an operational environment and parked in a secure location, there was very little for her to do. She smiled at the two men as they moved to the large center table. Her ebony skin highlighted her beautiful features. Masterson thought of her as an attractive woman.

Captain Valarus moved to his customary seat at the head of the large geo-morphic table. Adjutant Sumum-Aha stood close to the captain, as was his custom whenever Valarus entered the room. Adjutant Sumum-Aha's three attending famulim entered and stood near him to wait for direction. Masterson and Hebeta moved to take one of several seats circling the table. Valarus tapped the ring on his right hand against the pseudo-ceramic edge of the table. "Hebeta, we've encountered a temporal peculiarity. When Roy was to meet the professor, two Ejicerce appeared to intercede."

Masterson was tapping a stylus against his other hand as the captain spoke until he interrupted, "The two Ejicerce didn't appear to be interested in Werner at all. They asked if he was a German Federal police officer. As Werner was departing, they paid him no attention and focused on me."

Valarus sat back in his chair, stroking his bearded chin while Masterson spoke. The Captain continued, "Although you gave the telephone number to Werner before the Ejicerce Horde intervened, they could compromise it. Hebeta, you will slip into the second holder-body we have set aside as a contingency."

Hebeta laughed at the revelation. "Why me and not Roy?"

"Because the second holder-body is female; it's the first holder's companion," smiled Masterson.

Hebeta laughed aloud, "You are afraid to ride in a female holder, Roy?"

"Let's just say I couldn't pass myself off as authentic, Hebeta."

Valarus and Sumum-Aha smiled at the exchange between the two senior officers. Valarus manipulated the geo-morphic table's controls and a scaled three-dimensional map of the German city of Göttingen materialized. It shimmered into existence, complete with animated water in the Leine River, correct to the point of even showing the locations of present barges moored along the river's edge. Using a beam-pointer, Valarus stood to point out the location where the meeting between Werner and Masterson had taken place only a few hours prior. He moved the red beam to show a location closer to the edge of the city near the river docks.

"This is the domicile of primary holder-body, Walter Fischer. He is a cabinetmaker working in this factory here. He is also a Nationalist, which was an up-and-coming faction within the German government during this period." Valarus deactivated the pointer and resumed sitting in his chair. "Mention of Walter Fischer is not part of our mission profile provided by our patron, thus the temporal peculiarity. He is expendable. So that said, our aim is still to contact the professor, who is a temporal influencer, and pass on the information from our patron."

"I still don't understand why we couldn't just use the professor as a holder and write the paper ourselves," Masterson shook his head with obvious frustration.

Hebeta chimed in quickly, "The easiest way is not the best way. If we planted the information using the professor, he could not explain or recreate the formulas and resulting theories on his own when questioned." She continued, her voice becoming more serious, "To place us in a specific location or time such as the publishing of the paper's exact date can be dangerous to the ship and crew."

Valarus snorted as he listened to his two officers. Hebeta had been with him for several years, but Masterson was a recent addition to the crew, replacing his senior adjutant that had died on an earlier mission Masterson was involved in.

Hebeta leaned forward to look more at Masterson. "The quantum geometry required to place a time traveler spot on their target requires calculations using all twelve dimensions. But the chance of error is high and dangerous. Errors could cause non-reintegration with the perceived reality in the target environment; what some call 'ghosting'. So, we do our calculations using only ten dimensions or fewer. But this places us further from the target. Both in time and location."

"Thus, we are in the right year and even reintegrated close to Europe in the North Atlantic Ocean." Valarus smiled at Hebeta.

Masterson's expression showed he wasn't happy with their explanation of temporal navigation. "All right, I get why we didn't just pop into the day the target published his thesis on quantum mechanics. But why so distant, time wise? We're months, if not years, away from that, aren't we?"

Valarus laughed, "Do you think our professor can quickly understand the complexities of even the basics of the microverse based on one letter? As intelligent as the professor is, this new concept must be fed to him slowly." The captain turned his attention to Hebeta. "So, Adjutant Hebeta, you will enter the field environment using the female companion of Mister Walter Fischer and take that call from the professor to set up their next meeting with our third holder-body choice whom Roy will ride for that meeting."

Nodding, Hebeta asked, "And who is that?"

Masterson spoke up, "*Hans* is an assistant to the leading European member of the International Education Board of the Rockefeller Foundation in New York."

"Questions?" Captain Valarus asked then clapped his hands together. "Let's get to it."

The command team moved from the *Glorious Questor's* mission operations center back to the excursion room. Adjutant Sumum-Aha immediately began preparations for Hebeta's excursion into the German holder-body they had just discussed. This wasn't Hebeta's first excursion into the field in a different place in the time stream than her native point, but this was her first in this location; Germany in 1925. She quickly stripped and lay down on the interface slab. Her body was tense, her face showing apprehension. She didn't enjoy the interface process at all.

Captain Valarus and Masterson stood out of the way of Sumum and his team of four famulim as they worked the consoles of perhaps the most sophisticated controls on the time ship. First, they had to locate and track the holder-body that they had identified for this excursion using the instrumentation of the temporally synchronized ship. The *Glorious Questor* had to be in the same temporal and geographic region as the targeted holder-body. Here, they had set the ship deep in the Baltic Sea off the coast of Germany. Both men watched as the liquid goo of the interface connection rose from the pseudo-ceramic slab on which she lay while the famulim scurried about her, tending to various instrumentations. Slowly, the substance encased her entire body within the translucent pseudo-chrysalis. Contact between the instrumentation and her body was absolute. The two men glanced at each other then retired to the mission operations center to monitor Hebeta's excursion.

Chapter 2: Nadine Taschner

Hebeta felt like she was waking from a dream. She smelled the familiar musty scent of a room not well cleaned. The blanket covering her body felt damp, not wet, but damp. The air was humid; she wasn't comfortable yet realized that this was the norm for where her holder was. Hebeta opened her eyes. The room was out of focus. The fear of failed integration sprang into her thoughts but were tossed aside. Hebeta had done this before, as had most of the senior crew of the *Glory*. She sat up and searched the dim room with her eyes. It was as she had expected based on her pre-excursion review of the time ship's information files for this era. She had been reviewing them since their arrival, as had all the crew the captain could select for fieldwork.

She looked down at her hands, examining them; they were human. Her hands were pale like an Anunnaki Cassidan, but pink rather than blue. She was pleased that she didn't have calloused hands; they were soft. Her holder had a soft life. Hebeta stood, dressed in a heavy cotton dress with a flower pattern. She smiled. It was pretty. Hebeta looked around the compact room. The suppressed mind of the holder was feeding operational information to her consciousness as she explored. She recognized from the holder's memories that she was in a "townhouse". As she gazed out the window by moving a hanging layered cloth, curtains, she realized she was on the upper floor. It was becoming dark outside and had been raining. She remembered something. Where was her companion? He was always home before evening. Hebeta blinked. It always made her uncomfortable when the holder-body pushed something into consciousness. It was like stealing.

The loose wood floorboards squeaked as she stepped barefoot from the bed to a wooden cabinet. It surprised her that she was barefoot until she remembered the holder had been in bed. She lifted her dress to examine the single item of clothing she wore underneath it;

she was wearing a loose-fitting white pantaloon. In the short cabinet, Hebeta found a compact mirror; she smiled as she looked at the image of her holder's face. Bright blue eyes looked back at her from a thin white face. Her hair was wild, short, and blonde, her teeth were... not what she had expected. She closed her mouth, pouting at the discovery. Her attention turned to her body. Her holder wasn't displeasing to the eye, much to Hebeta's relief. The general size was like her own. She worked through a series of quick stretching exercises to familiarize herself with the holder's body, learning its movement, relative strength, and coordination. She paused once it satisfied her. She could control and use the holder's body. She took a deep breath and moved down the stairs to search the lower level of the dwelling.

Earlier in the mission, a team of their gray-skinned famulim had visited this holder's dwelling to take biometric readings to synchronize the excursion instrumentation. That allowed the *Glorious Questor* to locate and place the crew member's consciousness in the selected body for field excursions. They had also placed disposable equipment for use during the excursions in strategic, concealed locations known to the excursion team.

"So, we don't cook – well, good for us," Hebeta whispered. She pulled open a drawer, discovering assorted knives and other cooking utensils. She closed the drawer and searched the other cabinets and drawers, discovering the room was not well-stocked at all. She looked down at the holder's pale hands again. They were soft, the nails painted with red enamel. Hebeta cocked her head to one side then moved on to continue her search of the house's two floors. The upstairs had two bedrooms and an indoor toilet. The downstairs had a family room in the front and a small office and kitchen in the back.

Hebeta searched for the cache left for her use by Adjutant Sumum's site preparation team. She opened the small wooden box left deep in one of the kitchen cabinets. Inside were two pairs of the gold-tinted glasses that would allow her to send and receive telemetry from the time ship. She waited as the scrolling information activated on her lens, showing that the communications linkage was now established. The ship now saw and heard all that she did and could communicate to her in text across her small screens or verbally using low sonic vibration only she could hear. She placed a pair of glasses on her nose then turned her attention to exploring the rest of the kitchen.

Hebeta moved out of the kitchen area with the golden-tinted glasses riding on her nose. She walked back into the large sitting room, taking her time, her senses attuned to the unfamiliar noises she was hearing. The wooden floor creaked as she stepped again and again, not searching for anything in particular. She turned to her right, passing by an office; she smiled at the design and fought off a desire to enter the room and caress the worn velvet cushions lying on the couch. She proceeded deeper into the house, entering an area she really didn't know well at all. Hebeta smiled to herself as the information from the holder was rather transitory or not recalled in its entirety. The holder's information would remain vague and fleeting, missing key points until they fully synchronized. How long that would take was truly a battle of willpower. The stronger the holder's personality, the longer full synchronization would take. But that would also decline with repeated exposures of the holder's mind to the mind of the one conducting the excursion.

She moved back up the stairs to continue her exploration there. She had only been in a sleeping room, not the other two rooms that were also upstairs. At the top of the stairs there were three doors. One was the sleeping room she had emerged from. She opened the door in front of her once she made the stairs landing. A quick examination determined it was just another bedroom. They had slept in one bed based on the way they had left the blanket and sheets tossed about the bed. Hebeta had a sudden holder-based insight, causing her to smile as she closed the door. The next room was a mechanical indoor toilet and bath, poorly kept and in dire need of a cleaning. Hebeta looked quickly about in the room, but found nothing of interest other than to discover her male companion's razor and toiletry kit with the initials "W.F." imprinted on the leather carrying bag.

"Are we expecting this telephone call soon?" Hebeta drew her finger across the dusty windowsill as she spoke aloud. A voice in her head responsed to her question. She was in communications with the ship with the signal relaying a very low-frequency transmission that went directly into her brain from the arms of the gold-tinted glasses she now wore.

"Nope, we don't know when the call will come through or even if it will. But we think it should be tonight, if at all."

She knew it was Masterson answering her question, although the voice in her head was unidentifiable. She moaned, "The captain did not tell me I would have to stay here long!"

"Come on, Hebeta, what are a few days in paradise?"

She growled, knowing the monitor, whoever they may be back on the *Glory*, would hear her frustration.

The voice continued, "Besides, you know we can pull you out if it gets too boring. Just don't die there; the stress on your psyche would be too much for you. Most just up and die for real!"

She giggled, paying more attention to their conversation than to what she was doing in the holder-body. But now she knew it was Masterson working as her controller, as she had for him. No one else on the ship talked with her like that.

The front door to the house burst open, crashing back against the small doorframe. Upstairs, Hebeta stopped speaking as she moved toward the top of the staircase. Quietly, she peeked down the stairs to see who the intruder was.

"Nadine, wo bist du?"

Hebeta cocked her head to the side, concentrating. Realization dawned on her quickly as she tapped into the holder's subconscious, almost realizing the man shouting below was her companion, Walter Fischer.

"Nadine, are you upstairs?" the man shouted again, moving to the foot of the stairs and looking up at her. His hair was wet from the rain, and his overcoat was soaked and dripping water on the hardwood floor.

In Hebeta's head she heard, "Be careful! They should have arrested him at the point where my excursion took place."

She moved into Walter's view, smiling. Drawing on the holder's memories she greeted him, "Welcome home, darling. Are you all right? Is everything okay?"

With a crazed look in his eyes and water dripping down his face from the rain, he charged up the stairs toward her. Outside, the night was falling and the stairwell became a darkened tunnel with little light to see with. Walter flew up the stairs, skipping two steps at a time in his rush toward her.

Hebeta's gold-tinted glasses adjusted to the darkness, illuminating the stairwell for her with a colorless image of Walter rising toward her with a pale rose aura surrounding him.

He stopped with a look of horror on his face. His slap almost broke Hebeta's jaw as he knocked the glasses from her face. "Oh, my god, what are you wearing?"

The impact of Walter striking her spun Hebeta. She fell to her right side, landing on her elbow at the top of the staircase as Walter stood to stare down at her, agitated by seeing her wearing the gold-tinted glasses.

As he moved up the two remaining steps toward her on the landing, she struck out with a vicious kick to his lower belly with her left heel, sending Walter tumbling backward head over heels down the stairs. He replaced his angry look with one of total surprise. He hit the first floor in a tumble of a wet overcoat, and flailing arms and legs.

Hebeta was on him almost the instant he landed. She had landed standing over him as Walter rolled, grasping his belly. Hebeta reached down to grab his coat, pulling him up as she readied her right fist to strike him again.

"No, no! STOP! I beg you," Walter whimpered as he cowered behind his crossed arms, lying on his back under Hebeta.

Hebeta backed off, her chest heaving as the adrenaline rushed through her body, a dark bruise forming on her pale jawline. She stumbled and sat on the lower stair of the staircase. She glared at Walter with angry, tear-filled eyes.

"You nearly killed me!" screamed Walter, moving off his back to sit up, spittle spraying from his mouth as his emotions raced from terror to insane anger. Furious, he dug into his deep coat pocket with his right hand.

Hebeta tensed.

Walter, in his rage, fumbled the Luger pistol from his coat pocket to point at his companion.

Launching herself, Hebeta dove to the right of Walter. He bellowed and fired the pistol without aiming. The noise exploding in the room made their ears ring. She hit the ground hard then rolled toward him while he appeared dazed from the sound of the gun firing. She sprang to her knees beside him, holding his right wrist with her left hand, controlling the gun while delivering a stunning blow to his throat just below the chin. She punched him with pointed fingers; her nails piercing the skin. He gasped, clutching his throat with his left hand. Hebeta shook his right hand violently, sending the Luger clattering across the wooden floor. She released his hand and skittered across the floor on all fours, snatching the pistol into her hands. Hebeta spun to face him, holding the pistol steady in her hands, controlling the aim of the weapon centered on Walter's chest as he attempted to rise.

Walter froze. "Easy, Nadine. You do not want to murder me in cold blood, do you?" He smiled at her, his voice low, hoarse. His neck was very red from the finger jab he had received from her then his gripping it in pain. "Set down the gun, lover. You do not want to shoot me."

Hebeta pressed herself up so she could stand from a squat with her left hand while keeping the pistol trained on Walter. His smile almost took on a serpentine look as she observed him, both of his hands in the air. She could sense the fear and frustration from her holder, although Walter wouldn't see that. "Sit down in the chair."

He moved slowly to sit, his eyes remaining on Hebeta's as he moved. "What are you going to do now?"

"You tried to kill me, Walter." She moved toward the stairs, wanting to retrieve the golden glasses. Pausing at the foot of the stairs she demanded, "Why did you attack me, Walter?"

"You are wearing the demonic." He moved as if he was preparing to rush her but settled back in his chair when she brought her other hand up to grip her right hand to steady her aim.

"You remember the glasses?" she inched her way up the first step, keeping her eyes on Walter as she moved. "Tell me about the glasses." She took another step up.

"They belong to a demon. It takes over your mind, controls you. It caused me to kill two men today." He paused, as if considering something. "The demon made me crush them and throw them away... How do you have them?" Walter moved to the edge of his seat, leaning forward.

Hebeta turned and sprinted up the stairs to the second floor. She fell to her knees as she scrambled to find the glasses knocked from her face when he had slapped her. Hebeta heard Walter thundering up the stairs behind her. "I do not want to kill you!" rolling to her back, she pointed the pistol at the center of his chest.

Walter paused as his hands touched the top stair on the staircase. He stretched his right hand toward her. "Give me back the gun, Nadine, please. I know you do not want to hurt anyone." He smiled at her, his eyes pleading. "Do not put those glasses back on, darling. If you do, you will lose your soul."

Hebeta smiled as she reached for the glasses and shifted the gun from her right hand to the left, allowing her to grope with her right hand along the floor. Walter had coiled like a spring on the upper steps of the staircase, waiting for the moment her gaze strayed from him. Hebeta kept her pale eyes focused on him as she swept her free hand, feeling for the lost glasses. The instant she felt them, she snatched them in her hand. She rolled to her left, scampering out of Walter's way as he lunged toward her up the last step of the stairway.

As Walter sprang forward, he struggled to get ahold of her fluttering dress as she rushed from his grasp. Her bare feet gave her traction on the worn wooden floor, allowing her to escape into the nearest room. She slammed the door, locking it just as his weight crashed against it.

Walter pummeled the door with his fist, making it rattle and shake, but it held. "Open this... open this now!" he screamed.

Hebeta backed further into the room, keeping the pistol pointing at the door. "Masterson, I need extraction from my holder now," Hebeta stated aloud as she listened to the hammering on the bedroom door.

"Patience, Hebeta," replied the androgenous monotone voice from the eyeglasses.

The pounding on the door went quiet. Hebeta lowered the barrel of the pistol. She could hear her own breathing as the silence continued. She lowered the gun that was held in her right hand, standing with her torn dress before the closed door.

"Walter, are you all right?" she ambled toward the door, placing her left hand against it. "Walter?" She unlocked it and stepped back several steps, bringing the pistol back up, aiming center mass at the door. The door handle turned. Her heart raced as she watched the door open. She held her breath and aimed as the door swung back, revealing Walter standing there. He was smiling. "Don't move!" she screamed.

"Better late than never, don't you think, Hebeta?"

Hebeta frowned, "Masterson?"

"In the flesh," Masterson moved into the room, his eyes locked with hers. "We began the excursion procedure to retake control of this holder as soon as he knocked the glasses off you."

"He could have killed me," she whispered as she tossed the gun away onto the bed.

Masterson watched the flight of the pistol to the bed then smiled down at Hebeta as she embraced him. "What set him off – the glasses?" He smiled down at her as they embraced. She seemed reluctant to release her hold on him.

"Yes. I didn't think they remembered events that occurred while they were holding our consciousness on an excursion." Hebeta's body shivered a bit as she held him, his overcoat and suit still soaking wet from the rain outside. "You need to take these off or you will catch a chill."

Together, arm in arm, they squeezed down the stairway to the first floor. Masterson removed Walter's drenched overcoat, hanging it over the back of a chair as they entered the kitchen area. He smiled at Hebeta's confusion about just what to do.

They moved into the kitchen area at the back of the house. "Here, I'll make the coffee and look for something we can eat." He smiled at her as he stepped past her, igniting the gas stove. He stopped after he found the coffee grounds and had poured the right amount into the metal drain on the tin coffeepot. He placed them on the open flame then turned to Hebeta. "You're right, I best get out of these clothes before I get this holder ill."

Hebeta stepped close, breathing, enjoying the scent of the brewing coffee. She wrapped her arms around his waist and hugged. "I agree. I think I can manage down here without you now that you have your coffee cooking."

He laughed and hugged her back tight. "Brewing, not cooking!"

They laughed as she pushed him away to head upstairs and change his clothes. Hebeta had been watching and started organizing a meal for them to ease the hunger pains developing in the bellies of their holder bodies.

Masterson climbed up the stairs. He collected the Luger pistol then made his way into the master bedroom to select fresh clothes for the evening as they waited for the call. Once in the master bedroom, he found the wooden box that contained the stashed visors. He placed a set of glasses on his nose, pushing them back to fit. Masterson continued to search through Walter's closet full of early twentieth-century clothing. He grinned as he admired the three suits hanging in the wooden cabinet. Two needed repairs, but the blue pinstriped one was new. He removed it from its hanger, tossed it onto the unmade bed, and stripped out of his tattered brown suit, letting it pool at the floor. He searched for underclothing in the chest of drawers before donning the pinstriped suit. "Yes," he hissed in satisfaction as he slipped the gabardine cloth over the cotton undershirt and boxers.

"Enjoying yourself, aren't you, Adjutant Masterson?" The androgenous voice in his head startled him.

"Don't do that!" Masterson growled as he continued to slide into the jacket of the pinstripe suit. "So how do I look, Sumum? Presentable?" Masterson stepped over to a full-length mirror in the room to look at himself in the reflection.

"I suppose, sir, but this era's clothing was rather mundane, do you not think?" returned the voice in Masterson's head. The voice always sounded the same regardless of who was speaking, but Masterson had guessed it was Adjutant Sumum rather than his famulim since it was an emergency excursion to help Hebeta.

They cut their conversation short when the sound of a phone's bell ringing started downstairs.

Chapter 3: A Call from the Dark

Both Hebeta and Masterson raced at breakneck speed like children to find the telephone on the first floor of the townhouse. They found it at just about the same time in the compact office room. Masterson snapped up the receiver, bringing it to his ear.

"Hello?" Masterson spoke in German with a natural accent provided by his holder-body's suppressed consciousness.

"Good evening, to whom am I speaking?" responded an equally well accented male German voice.

Hesitating, Masterson answered, "This is Walter Fischer." He looked at Hebeta with a worried expression as he waited for the next question. This was not what he'd expected, and it showed on his face, making Hebeta agitated as she waited quietly near him.

The man on the other end of the phone line spoke slowly, enunciating his words carefully. "We seem to have a common interest, Mister Fischer. The people I represent are not sure that they like the fact that others are interested in their friends. We need to talk about this."

Nervous about what was happening, Masterson adjusted his glasses then placed his other hand over the receiver of the phone. He looked at Hebeta. "Quick, look outside and see if there's anyone watching the house."

"We are monitoring your conversation," came the neutral voice in his head, relieving some of his anxiety.

Masterson slowly returned the receiver to the side of his face to cover his ear. He spoke into the receiver, "What do you suggest then?"

"My friends would like me to meet with you to discuss this common interest we have. They want me to decide if we should intervene or permit your continued contact with our mutual friend."

Masterson paused, waiting for a response from Captain Valarus or whoever was monitoring the conversation on the ship. "Play along, get more information," responded the neutral voice in his head.

"Are you still there, Walter?" interrupted the accented voice on the other end of the phone line.

"Yes, yes, I'm still here. What do you propose?"

"I think we should meet, Walter. I really do. Would you consider meeting with me, Walter?" questioned the man on the phone.

"Yes, say yes," instructed the voice in Masterson's head.

"I would like to meet with you, but I select the location," cautioned Masterson.

"That is fine. I assume it will be somewhere here in Göttingen?"

"Yes, here in Göttingen. I would like to meet you at the Hotel Romantic Gebhards near the city train station on Goethe-Alle Street. There is a hotel restaurant that stays open late. Can you meet me there?" Masterson looked at Hebeta as she slowly slid through the front door from the darkness outside into the living room. She moved closer to him to hear the conversation.

"I will be there in an hour. Wear a red hat for me so I can tell who you are. No red hat, no meeting." Masterson hung up the phone.

Hebeta stared at him in disbelief. "A red hat? Why did you say that?" Hebeta shook her head, trying not to laugh at him.

Masterson shrugged his shoulders, "Something from my previous life." He moved to recover the overcoat he had shed earlier. He stopped at the doorway. "Go fetch something to keep you warm and wear sensible shoes. We may run for our lives here soon."

Hebeta laughed. Then, with a flash of her leg, she swished her dress as she bounded up the staircase back to their shared bedroom. She quickly found an overcoat and some flat-soled shoes that looked worn. Her holder-body seemed to approve of her choices. She quickly bounced down the stairs to find Masterson.

Masterson smiled and pointed back up the stairs, "Get the Luger. It's on the second room's bed. I want you to carry it concealed in a handbag."

"A what?" snorted Hebeta with a look of doubt as she heard his instructions.

"A handbag, a purse." Masterson groaned teasingly and headed up the staircase in search of a purse large enough to carry their captured pistol. He searched the room shared by Walter and Nadine until he found a suitable handbag. They were all cheaply made of patterned cloth, indicative of their holders' meager personal fortune. Masterson smiled to himself, remembering this was the 1920s. The bag he had chosen barely concealed the Luger pistol. He decided to just carry the handgun in his own massive overcoat pocket, as he had before. Masterson moved quickly down the stairs to meet Hebeta at the front door. He handed the purse to her as he opened the door. "Carry this. It's normal for a woman to have such a thing in her hand."

"But it's empty. Why would I carry an empty bag?" she asked questioningly as he guided her out the door.

"Because it's done now. Let's get going or we'll be late for our meeting."

Together in the damp night, Masterson and Hebeta hurried to meet with the man who had called them using the number he had given to Professor Heisenberg earlier in the day. They walked in a light drizzle in the darkness. It was still early in the night with few people on the streets. The sounds of the classic internal combustion engine cars of the era with the accompanying scent of their toxic exhaust were distracting, making them both anxious as they walked. The streetlights along the way created cones of light, making the night seem all the darker.

Masterson put his arm around Hebeta as they hastened down the street back into another residential section of the city. There were no streetlights here. He glanced down at her. Her holder didn't appear to be as strong or physically fit as her own back on the *Glory*. "You are doing all right?"

"I can keep up, do not worry about that," she smiled up at him. It was a new body but with her familiar behaviors. They moved on to Goethe-Alle Street and out of the darkness of the night. The street was one of the main east-west thoroughfares of the city and was busy with traffic and pedestrians, even this late. "How do you know about this place?"

Masterson looked about, "Believe it or not, this street survived until my time. I've walked down this very street before, almost one hundred years from now."

Hebeta stopped and stared at him in astonishment. "You're from this far?" She looked at him with an expression of disbelief, "But this is the beginning of The Decline. How is it possible you are from this time?"

"I'm from the future. The Genitor required my body for something in my time. They told me, but I didn't understand. Now I know how excursions and holder-bodies work. My body, my birth body, was a holder-body for an excursion to someone else. I assume a Dionan. But my consciousness is here with you now." They slowed their pace now that they were on the street where they were to meet their contact.

Hebeta smiled, slipping her arm around him as they walked. "I am an Igigi, a watcher. This world is my birth world, like you. But Captain Valarus rescued me from the Eidin facility before the great purge ordered by the Anunnaki. I was being trained at Eidin to be a worker to assist the Anunnaki's Cassidan and Dionan artisans and technicians in their fieldwork. I caught Captain Valarus' attention, and he arranged for my transfer to him and his ship." She teased Masterson with a bright smile, "I thrill him with the way I pilot his *Glorious Questor*."

Masterson laughed, "I'm sure you thrill him in other ways, too. I've noticed the Dionans are more sensual than the stoic Cassidans." He felt Hebeta tighten her grip on his waist and changed the subject. "You were trained by Valarus to fly the *Glory*?" Masterson looked at Hebeta, remembering that she was a human primitive from Anunnaki eugenics laboratory at Eidin during the last Ice Age and now flew a time ship. "Were you trained to use technology before he rescued you?"

"Yes, I was being trained to be a field assistant. They trained me in the use and maintenance of their vehicles and research equipment."

Masterson slowed their walk then turned to face her in the darkest area between the cones of light. He moved close to her as if they were lovers on a stroll. Looking around to choose when no one was watching them he said, "I changed my mind. Take this gun then stand off a bit. If anything goes wrong, get to a safe place to ask for retrieval and be looking for their lookouts, doing the same thing we are, looking for our backup."

She searched the darkness then looked up at him. "If that is the way you want to do this, but I am not leaving you here." They parted slowly, their bond as two that had been sharing dangers together having grown stronger.

Masterson moved into the Hotel Romantic Gebhards, a four-story structure with an outdoor cafe on the backside of the building, away from the sounds of the train yard on the other side of the north and south running street it sat upon. This late at night, most of the rooms were filled with travelers. The restaurant was open and busy. Masterson slid into the building using the restaurant entrance rather than coming through the hotel lobby door. That wasn't unusual for someone coming from the street to do since the lobby was also on the side of the hotel facing the train yard. He was lucky to find a table that gave him a view of entries into the dining room as well as the access doors to the kitchen. He ordered coffee from the approaching server then settled in to wait.

Masterson looked at his watch. His second cup of coffee had gone cold and he was becoming impatient. He slipped the golden lensed glasses from his nose to massage it when a group of people entering the dining room caught his attention. He slipped his glasses back on and his blood ran cold. Three men had entered the room, each with a translucent pink aura radiating from them, one leading the way, looking about as if searching for someone. He wore sunglasses, and his gaze fixed on Masterson immediately. Behind him were two other men, large men, holding Hebeta bathed in her faint blue aura between them. She tried to divert her eyes from him but couldn't. Her gold lensed glasses were gone. The four of them moved into the diner to make way for two more men to enter. One held the door open for their leader to enter behind the vanguard.

Masterson slowly stood up, moving a step toward them. Hebeta shook her head as if pleading for him to run. He stopped to allow the men to approach him. He held his arms wide at his side, showing no sign he would go for his pockets. He waited.

The voice in his head immediately responded, "We are getting readings from the leader; wait, we will have them for you shortly."

Two of what he now assumed were Ejicerce moved to him quickly while the others searched the dining room for other potential threats. The two beside him weren't subtle in their search for hidden weapons or technology. Once they finished checking his pockets, one reached for his glasses. Masterson batted his hands away, moving back a step to place both men to his front. As the second man moved forward as if to grab him, Masterson planted his fist squarely on the bridge of his nose, making him collapse back to the floor.

"STOP!" the voice of the leader boomed over the room as other patrons gasped or screamed at the sudden outburst of violence. "Stop, there is no reason for this. Calm yourselves, friends." Then, to the surprised patrons, the leader spoke more calmly, "They are old friends, but money is owed. There will be no further problems. Please go back to your meals and have a lovely evening." He smiled as he turned his attention to Masterson.

The leader moved with Hebeta, leading her by her elbow to a nearby table that could seat four. He shoved Hebeta into one chair then seated himself, gesturing to Masterson to take the seat across from him. His four minions orbited the table, gazing at the others in the room to ensure there would be no interference. The one Masterson has punched stood hovering near Hebeta, clutching a bloodied napkin to his face, eyes hidden behind his dark sunglasses.

The leader spoke again, sounding bored, "So, my friend, what brings you to Göttingen? Pleasure or business?"

Masterson looked over to Hebeta and the bloodied henchman. "A little of both."

"We seem to have a common interest in our good friend, do we not? Shall we discuss that common interest?"

"Is he all right?" Hebeta leaned forward, interjecting her question, surprising both men. The concern in her voice communicated honest interest. The leader chuckled then sat back in his chair to appreciate Hebeta at his leisure. Hebeta held her posture and looked into his dark glasses as if she could actually see his eyes.

The voice in Masterson's head reported, "He is a temporal anomaly, possibly an actual Anunnaki. He is not wholly in this location but displaced, possibly in the past and the present, or even future. Exercise extreme caution."

Masterson frowned at the leader. "Who are you?"

"My friend, I might ask the same of you. Why are you here, and again, what is your interest in Professor Heisenberg?" The leader looked at one of his henchmen and ordered coffee for himself and his guests.

"Who are we?" Masterson sat back in his chair, pushing a bit from the table so he could cross his legs. He continued to focus on the leader, not paying any attention to the others orbiting around them.

The leader smiled under his own dark sunglasses then reached into his coat. He drew Hebeta's golden glasses from a pocket and tossed them onto the table with a clatter. "Well, I assume you are Dionan, probably Consortia by the make of those." He leaned forward, swatting the glasses gently toward Hebeta on the table. "If you are Consortia, we do not allow you to be here. This is a cordoned time period, and Professor Heisenberg is specifically restricted access only. You, my friends, do not have access."

Hebeta slid the glasses across the table, pulling them toward her and dropping them into her lap.

"You are Anunnaki?" Masterson lowered his crossed leg and leaned forward, laying his elbows on the table, whispering. "What is an Anunnaki doing in the Twentieth Century? Isn't your time past? Did it not end in ancient Sumer?"

"If you think I am Anunnaki, that tells me you are not or you would know. Tread carefully, my new friend. I have already told you this time is cordoned." The leader sat back. "Again, what is your interest in the professor?"

"He is an important historical figure, sir; I want to know more about him." Masterson remained leaning forward on his elbows, his hands laced together on the table as if to share some secret. "I'm curious where his interest in the subatomic world is rooted. Was he guided in that direction or is it truly a natural desire to understand the unseen world?"

"Who are you to ask such a question?" replied the leader. He turned toward Hebeta, "She is an Igigi, changed to handle the complexities of living in our world."

"How do you know that?" Hebeta's face displayed her shock.

Masterson interpreted Hebeta's surprise as a sign that identification of someone on an excursion in a holder's body isn't a normal ability. They knew she was human and changed to function in Anunnaki society. How?

The voice in his head interrupted, "This is definitely an Anunnaki. You are in danger. We are pulling you out."

Masterson tensed. He had never done an immediate extraction before, and he knew there were dangers in doing it. The leader sensed something was happening. Masterson could see one of them drawing a pistol and pointing it at him from across the table. The leader was saying something.

"Begone, forsaken one! Leave this place before I destroy you," promised the leader with a low, menacing voice.

Masterson's vision turned grey then narrowed to a point of light.

Masterson woke with a start, causing the non-Newtonian fluid they immersed him in during excursions to become hard, which only caused him to panic all the more when it held him still. Masterson caught glimpses of Adjutant Sumum and his technologist moving between his excursion pedestal and Hebeta's. The contact fluid drained away, releasing his body and allowing him some movement. Once his mouth and head were clear and he could speak, he looked toward Hebeta, asking about her condition, but the technologists were busy. Something was amiss.

Masterson glanced at the small team of technologists orbiting around him and Hebeta. Most of them were famulim, synthetic sentient androids. He spotted chiefs Pazemos and Sumum-Aha among them. They were two of Captain Valarus' most trusted members of the crew. They were busy with Hebeta, which raised Masterson's worry that she was in danger. He willed himself to calm, breathing deeply as he tried to ease the tension in his body. Soon he felt the liquid finish draining away from his body, leaving him dry and free to move.

"Is she okay?" he asked as he sat up on the table.

Hebeta laughed, "I am fine. We are alive, Roy Masterson!"

Laughing, they embraced, hugging each other tightly despite their hairless nakedness as the others continued to move about them, turning off their excursion instrumentation and securing their workstations. One famulim gave the couple soft robes to wear as Chief Pazemos ushered them from the excursion room into the adjoining mission briefing room. Captain Valarus, stroking his dark, wiry beard, stood waiting.

As soon as they entered the room, Masterson released Hebeta and pointed his finger at Captain Valarus, "Bastard, you didn't tell me we are the Ejicerce! We're the ones in rebellion against the Genitor and their Anunnaki Order." Masterson moved around the small table, but Chief Pazemos took hold of his right arm to stop him.

"Be careful, servitor. You are on my ship, remember?" Valarus sat down in the nearest seat, keeping his dark Dionan eyes on Masterson. "How could you not have guessed our nature from the beginning? We do not work in opposition to the Genitors' Order, we work despite them. They have their agenda. We have ours, given to us by our circumstance."

"What do you mean?" Masterson slid into a seat near Captain Valarus.

"The Genitor are focused on their projects and their results; we must focus on our survival outside the reality that the Genitor has imposed unfairly on us. We travel time doing the bidding of the Genitor while they arbitrarily decide which of us can continue and which of us are regulated to one particular location on the temporal spectrum."

"Does this include the entire Dionan Consortia?" asked Masterson.

Chief Pazemos interrupted, glancing quickly at the captain, "No, no, the Consortia is a body that represents the desires of all our clans on the world of Diona and our interaction with Cassida and the Genitor; it is not in rebellion against the Genitor or the Cassidans. The Consortia are not allied with the Ejicerce," he paused again, looking at Captain Valarus, "but many members are sympathetic."

"Sympathetic, how?" Masterson searched the faces of the Dionans, now seated at the table with Hebeta and himself.

"Both the Cassidans and the Dionans were seeded on their worlds at the same time by the Genitor, early in this star system's life.

They are cousins, if not brothers, in that they are both the prodigy of the Genitor," explained Captain Valarus.

"As were the Mundus, or humans, on Earth," added Masterson, glancing to his side at Hebeta who was smiling back at him.

"Yes, there are three habitable worlds in this star system: Diona, Cassida, and Mundus," nodded Captain Valarus.

"Or Venus, Mars, and Earth," added Masterson, aggressively leaning forward with his elbows on the conference table, "but when?"

"Shortly after the star first formed, from this point on the temporal spectrum, four billion terrestrial years ago." Captain Valarus sat back in his chair, tapping the table with his massive metal ring on his right hand.

Chief Pazemos spoke up again, glancing at the captain, "Three of the four inner terrestrial planets initially were habitable. They seeded Cassida first, then Diona, and finally Mundus."

"This is all amazing, but we're getting sidetracked here. I want to know why I wasn't told we are an Ejicerce ship." Masterson looked between Captain Valarus and Chief Pazemos before turning to look at Hebeta. "Did you know we were Ejicerce?"

The concern on Hebeta's face said it all. "Yes, I know we are part of the Forsaken. I am honored that they chose me to join Captain Valarus and his crew. They rescued me from certain death where I was from. They rescued you at the Anunnaki city of Kur."

Valarus spoke, "Masterson, you were one of the Forsaken yourself, although you apparently did not realize it. When you came aboard in the city of Kur, the Anunnaki's Seventh Order was pursuing you. You were a renegade. Lady Inanna recognized that from the beginning. We took you aboard without questioning her. Do you not remember?"

Masterson bowed his head, taking a deep breath, "You're right. You took me in when I was being pursued by the Seventh Order." He looked up at Valarus. "But I honestly thought you were an Anunnaki asset, agents working for the Lady Inanna. She is a senior member of the Anunnaki Council. How are you Ejicerce working for Inanna? She is Anunnaki, and they control the Orders of Battle who are sworn to fight you."

"The Anunnaki have different agendas, and each interprets the will of the Genitor differently. Lady Inanna's agenda is similar enough to mine that we have, from time to time, cooperated with each other for our mutual gain." Captain Valarus leaned forward, as Masterson had. "You were one of us the moment you realized you were a tool to them. Actually, I think you were one of us the moment you stepped aboard my ship the first time. That is why I trusted you to become my chief adjutant when we lost Kwonii at Eidin."

Masterson searched Valarus' eyes then said, "You're right, I'm part of this crew. I'm your second in command because of your trust, Captain. If the ship is Ejicerce, then I am Ejicerce." Masterson smiled over at Hebeta and shrugged, "Besides, I have nowhere else to go."

"I am returning us to confer with our patron. Get cleaned up and return to debrief with the other adjutants." Captain Valarus stood looking at Hebeta, Pazemos, and Masterson each before departing for the ship's control room.

Masterson and Hebeta stood as Chief Pazemos turned away from them in his seat, toward his team of famulim standing around the table. They strolled out of the briefing room and up the ramp toward their quarters on the ship's second deck. The ship could reconfigure the *Glorious Questor's* four floating decks itself to adjust to passenger or mission requirements given time; there were no elevators or stairs in the ship for this reason. The ship's corridors were like arteries or veins within a living body, connecting vital components together, using the same technology that allowed the famulim to change their bodies to suit their purpose dependent upon their mission. The *Glorious Questor* was a synthetic sentient, in the same way the gray android famulim were.

Hebeta turned to Masterson as they neared their separate quarters, "You really did not know we were Forsaken?" She cocked her head to the side, smiling as she waited for his answer. Her robe held around her slipped as she relaxed.

Masterson laughed, "No! I truly thought this crew worked for the Anunnaki. I thought they had brought me back from the future, or decline as you call it, to be a courier for them based on what had happened to me since awakening in this new body on Mars, or your Cassida. The way the Ejicerce had been described to me by Captain

Valarus and the Anunnaki woman Inanna, I thought they were crazed, war-mongering demons or something."

Hebeta hip-bumped Masterson as they came to the iris valve doors of their personal cabins. "I am not a demon," she laughed, smiling up at him while quickly hooking his neck with her towel and drawing him down into a lingering kiss.

Masterson whispered, "I think maybe you are!"

Chapter 4: Inanna

The flight crew manned their posts in the control room of the *Glorious Questor*. Captain Valarus hadn't wasted time in ordering the ship to jump out of their present temporal location. The captain and his adjutants were all sure that the Anunnaki in this era were not only aware of their presence but probably by this time had determined their exact location in the depths of the North Sea.

Adjutant Tizar looked up from his instrumentation. "The *Glory* is ready, sir."

The primary officers stood or sat around the central control console, focused on their particular areas of expertise. Adjutant Tizar was their temporal navigator. His responsibility was ensuring the complex mathematics that allowed them to jump from one location within space and time were as correct and as error-free as possible. Their lives and sanity depended upon his computational skills and manipulation of the supporting instrumentation.

"Very well." Valarus moved around the oval console, examining the actual time holographic display of the delta-shaped *Glorious Questor's* exterior that was projected over the center console. He paused then stepped into the small alcove that provided him a view from the bow of the ship. He stared out into the dark depths of the North Sea for what seemed to be an eternity to his staff. Finally, he snapped the command, "Jump the ship!"

Masterson turned and nodded to Hebeta who responded with a smile. She activated the temporal drive, causing the *Glorious Questor* to disintegrate as it converted its molecular profile to information and imprinted on a single atom, which instantaneously passed the information to its entangled twin at the calculated destination. The reintegration of the information instantaneously released a tremendous amount of energy from the fusion of matter according to the ship's molecular profile.

In the *Glorious Questor,* there was no sign or sensation that it had reduced the ship to pure information as energy crossing through space and time then being reintegrated instantaneously somewhere else. Masterson always felt this to be disappointingly boring. But outside the ship, it was an entirely different matter. The *Glorious Questor* was the epicenter of a nuclear fusion release of titanic proportions. The ship was tossed back and forth as it navigated the maelstrom it had created, while most of its occupants were oblivious to the chaos outside their ship. Only the technologists operating the electrostatic drive and external sensors knew just how violently the ship was being tossed around by the temporal typhoon.

"Set a course for *Ganzir.* Inform me when we arrive at the citadel, Protector Adjutant," Captain Valarus looked to Masterson as he left the control room. "I will be in my cabin."

"Yes, sir." Masterson ordered all non-essential watch-standers to begin their post-jump checks, "Tizar, good job. Have your famulim begin their inspection of the ship for anomalies."

Adjutant Tizar smiled and nodded as he stood to stretch his back. "Well, my back is still the same. No change here."

Masterson turned to Adjutant Kikuid, "How are the electrostatic drive plates doing?"

Kikuid, like Tizar, was Dionan. "Operating within prescribed parameters, sir."

Masterson clapped his hands together then rubbed them vigorously, "Good!" He walked around the console to stand beside Hebeta. "How long until we arrive at Ganzir?"

"Oh, I would say about an hour, maybe a little less." Her hands almost mystically swirled about her instrumentation as she verified her information before she smiled up at Masterson. "We'll make it in time, Protector."

Masterson looked down at her where she sat then gently patted her shoulders. "You feeling okay, Pilot? No abnormal thoughts or desires?" He chuckled, "All the parts there?"

Hebeta held up her fingers, wiggling them for his inspection. "All ten fingers, sir!"

He grinned then stepped away from her and moved to the forward alcove to gaze out at the storm raging around them. The energy release from their sudden transdimensional rematerialization had created the storm. The Temporal Drive converted the matter that made up the ship and crew into pure information profiles which were imprinted on a single molecule then, using multidimensional geometry, the molecule was coupled or entangled with a molecule at the desired time and place. The calculations navigating up to twelve non-chaotic dimensions were exponentially complex, even for quantum computations. The more exact the targeted time and location, the higher the probability of error and catastrophe. Twelfth Dimension jumps were only done in dire emergencies. Low tier temporal jumps using four through six dimensional calculations could safely and routinely be made between planetary high orbits in the same planetary system in the same temporal location. Middle tier jumps were used for place travelers most often since they could pinpoint either a location or a time for them to arrive. This created the need for ships to allow movement not only through time but from place to place once the jump had been completed.

The amount of energy needed to entangle molecules and convert matter to complex information reconstituted in another space and time was tremendous. The process required the ability to manipulate more than just the three perceivable dimensions but also other dimensions that cascaded toward a single Point of Creation. The use of the eleventh and twelfth dimensions for high tier calculations become chaotic and unusable, resulting in possible disfigurement or total loss of form for travelers. The total number of dimensional tiers past the chaotic to the Point of Creation was incalculable by all but the Genitor. The dimensional travel itself was the source of cosmic dark matter or *Quintessence* needed to instantly move through space and time, resulting in the powerful release of excess power at the moment of arrival, manifesting as monstrous storms when done within an atmosphere.

Masterson turned back toward the console in the center of the control room. He watched the members of the crew as they methodically checked themselves, each other, and their equipment for distortions or anomalies created by the jump. He smiled. His exposure to being disassembled and reassembled atom by atom and imprinted on a subatomic carrier was very limited compared to the number of times this crew had experienced it. The Genitor limited time travel for travelers because of the changes it could cause both to living and non-living bodies. But once one had experienced the delights of time travel, it was hard to abandon it.

The so-called Forsaken were time travelers: the reassembly of their physical body had altered them. Even slight changes could change a traveler's organ functions, or their body's bone or muscle structure and operation. The changes could be subtle or grossly hideous, such as radical changes in personality or memory, or misplacement or partial reconstruction of vital organs. Time travel was as dangerous as it was exciting. And it was addictive.

Masterson sat down in the chair across from the one used by the captain. Outside the ship, the sky was clearing as the *Glorious Questor* streaked west toward what would someday be known as North America. He picked up one of the portable interface devices from the table to his left, activating it with his touch. He asked for the ship's present location, and the opaque surface of the interface immediately displayed a two-dimensional map as seen from orbit over the Atlantic Ocean with a bright white triangle showing the location of the *Glorious Questor*. Masterson queried for the location of Kur. Instantly, the orbital picture shifted to the western coast of Africa. Centered in the orbital view of western Africa was a clearly artificially built series of rings cascading down to a center circle. "The Eye of Africa," whispered Masterson to himself. He tapped the landmark. The interface zoomed in, centering on the Eye of Africa.

Kur had been the primary command center for the Anunnaki mission on Mundus. They had abandoned the base when the mission commander, Lord Enlil, ordered the destruction of the eugenics research facility at Eidin in a valley that would be known as the Black Sea in Masterson's time. Lord Enlil ordered the bombardment of the Northern Hemisphere's Ice Age glaciers with thermo-reactive bombs. The bombardment resulted in the low radiation fusion reaction explosions melting billions of tons of ice, causing a titanic global flood which destroyed all signs of Anunnaki activity on Mundus.

For the rest of the short flight to Ganzir, Masterson remained seated in the alcove. He watched the *Glorious Questor's* icon on the interface screen traveling at hypersonic speeds as they raced toward the North American coastline. Soon the coast was hundreds of kilometers further east as the ship soared over North America. The *Glorious Questor* slowed to subsonic speed as it began its approach to the Ganzir landing area in what they would know during the Decline as the southwestern United States. The ship slowly landed. Masterson recognized the White Sands location immediately.

"We are here, sir," Hebeta called to Masterson from her station at the control console behind him. She gave the order for the other technologists seated at the console to configure their instruments for ground operations.

Masterson stood looking out at the harsh desert landscape the ship was now surrounded by. Ganzir was his favorite location among the Anunnaki bases that had been reestablished after the Deluge. Being in North America, if even in the distant past, gave him some comfort. Masterson set the interface device on the table near his chair before leaving the control room to inform the captain of their arrival. He realized Valarus already knew they were at Ganzir.

The iris-valved doorway slid open quietly, giving Masterson entry into Captain Valarus' sanctum. The quarters reflected the captain's Dionan ancestry, while also his love of Earth's more diverse history and eclectic culture. The contents of this set of rooms always amazed Masterson compared to his Spartan quarters. But then again, Masterson had fought at the Battle of Thermopylae. Spartan suited him.

"I am having some wine. Would you like some?" Captain Valarus offered as he stood at his sea-desk to move to the oval table he often used for small meetings in his cabin. In the center of the table was a wine tray with fine crystal glasses that were out of place in the high-technology of the *Glorious Questor*. Valarus was a big man by Dionan standards, shorter than a Cassidan but taller than a human because of the slightly lower gravitational pull on Dionan versus Mundus.

Masterson smiled and accepted the offered drink. The wine was excellent, as always. He sat down at the oval table, as was their custom during these meetings. He set the wineglass to the side, folding his hands over the interface device which the captain always made available to him during their meetings. Masterson was learning to wait for the captain to start the conversation.

Captain Valarus made himself comfortable in his chair. He, too, savored the wine as both men sat looking at one another. "Your assessment of the mission outcome, Protector Masterson?"

"I think we screwed up royally, sir. We should have expected interference from either local authorities or the opposition. Although admittedly, my not realizing that we are Ejicerce was a major error; an embarrassing error for myself."

"I still do not understand how someone able to anticipate tactical and strategic situations the way you do did not realize you were no longer a member of the Anunnaki's forces."

Masterson shrugged the question away, "So what's the order of business for our stopover, and how long will we stay?"

"We wait to see what our patron decides." The captain quickly downed the rest of his wine then stood. "Our patron expects you to accompany me."

"We transferred the information to the influencer. What else would there be for us to do, sir?" asked Masterson. "Are we going to go back and verify the influencer survived or used the information passed to him?"

"The influencer received the information. That was a given." The captain explained, "If we remove an influencer from the Tapestry of Time for whatever reason, the Tapestry continues. The flow will continue unimpeded. A new thread will slide into the position and continue on as the influencer. In fact, once we become involved with the influencer, we become part of the Tapestry of Time ourselves. Regardless, the Tapestry of Time continues."

Masterson frowned as he rubbed his smooth chin, missing his beard.

The *Glory*'s androgynous voice interrupted their conversation, quietly announcing an emissary from the Anunnaki Council had arrived. Without speaking, both men stood and headed for the lower decks of the *Glory*. The air outside the Temporal Courier was hot and dry. Masterson smiled to himself, remembering a fantasy movie from his childhood that had a scene of a starship that had landed outside the outskirts of a desert on an alien planet. He glanced over his shoulder at the alabaster cubes, pyramids, and ziggurats of Ganzir that spread toward the far mountains of gypsum. In his own way, like those fantasy characters from the remembered movie, so had he.

At ground level, a few meters from the nose of the *Glory,* stood a trans-dimensional portal. The air swirling around the threshold formed a ball filled with translucent colors reminiscent of soap bubbles. The surface was in constant motion as it appeared to collapse inward on itself at two opposite sides, giving the portal an hourglass on its side shaped appearance. A Cassidan of the Caste of Kishar stood with two famulim waiting for the captain. The Kishar bowed deeply as the captain approached with Masterson at his elbow. Captain Valarus returned the bow, mirrored by Masterson as they came to a stop before their patron's emissary. The taller Cassidan turned with a gesture of welcoming, showing that the pair should lead the way through the portal. Without hesitation, the captain stepped into the swirling maelstrom, moving from where they were to where they were going in an instant. Masterson could see him clearly through the portal somewhere else.

The Kishar followed them through, and together the three stood in a public garden featuring the flora and fauna from Cassida and Dionan, deep in the subterranean central complex. Masterson gazed upward, seeing the limestone dome of the top of the titanic chamber that was an unfathomable distance deep underground below the alabaster city on the surface.

"Will you follow me this way?" The Cassidan turned and proceeded toward a large, multi-tiered ziggurat lush with exotic plants hanging from its layered decks. Both men followed, although they were very familiar with the location of their meeting. They quickly made their way to one of several audience halls within the structure.

"Ah, here are my friends." The Lady Inanna stood in all her resplendent beauty in the center of the small audience chamber. One of the chosen, she was a member of the elite Anunnaki Council of Seven. Purple vines from Cassida surrounded her with beautiful blooming flowers clinging to the walls and columns of the hall. Golden alien insects fluttered between the flowers. Murals of Cassidan landscapes covered the tiled walls of the small audience chamber she stood in.

Standing beside her was her ever faithful famulim, Arra. Masterson had noticed a while ago that the number of the gray skinned androgenous famulim had increased with the departure of the main body of the Genitors' Mundus expedition returning to the *Nibiru* cube-shaped space station. Mission Commander Anu had deployed a much smaller complement of Cassidans and Dionans to the Mundus project, removing all the Orders of Battle. Now there were only fifty Cassidans and Dionans, six hundred famulim, and three hundred uplifted Mundus, not including ship crews. The participation of uplifted Mundus, known as the Igigi, in the Ejicerce Horde revolt at the Eidin Eugenics Center had caused the departure of the *Nibiru* and was the reason they were now closely monitored and supervised. The Genitors' *Nibiru Station* would return to Mundus every 3,600 terrestrial years as it made its roaming tour of the Solar System.

Lady Inanna, or Anna as Masterson knew her best, was radiant. Her pale bluish-white skin sparkled and glittered with a golden sheen that was produced by the application of lotion to protect Cassidans from the glaring Mundus sun. Her ash blonde hair was piled high around the traditional cone-shaped headpiece worn by the Anunnaki for communication. She wore a light gossamer robe that curled around her lithe form. She smiled at the two shorter Dionan men as they approached her.

"I bid you welcome, Captain Valarus and Protector Dumuzid," she smiled, causing both men to return the smiles, suggesting their familiarity with her. Protector Dumuzid was the name the Anunnaki ground commander had awarded Masterson for service rendered to Lady Inanna during her failed espionage mission to the lost citadel of Eidin. Inanna towered head and shoulders above the two men as they bowed in greeting to the youngest member of the Anunnaki Council of Seven. "Come, let us be seated." Inanna motioned for them to join her on the plush seats available for their use near a small water fountain containing colorful aquatic creatures from Cassida. The three made themselves comfortable, Masterson sitting closest to Inanna.

"Thank you for the delivery, Captain Valarus. You confirmed what I already suspected," began Inanna.

"And what was that, Lady Inanna?" queried the captain.

"That the Watchers from that area of the Temporal Spectrum aggressively executed their duties," she replied.

Masterson furrowed his brow, displaying his confusion. "I don't understand."

Inanna reached over to caress his hand with her own, "My Dumuzi, only the Genitor possesses the ability to perceive all along the Temporal Spectrum. We, their servants, only see what is immediately before us, even though our essence may span several years or even centuries within it."

"Our essence? You mean our soul?" Masterson moved his hand to slide over hers, squeezing to show his affection and joy at being reunited.

Valarus snorted.

"Yes, Dumuzi, what you would call your soul. Most of us perceive reality only using the three spatial dimensions. Although some can see using more, like those that are clairvoyant or claircognizant. But even they see the dimensional spectrum at specific points. The Genitor alone can see the Temporal Spectrum in its whole and understand what they see."

Masterson's face showed understanding as he gazed at her. "So for an Anunnaki to know the future, they must travel there themselves or send a representative, an observer, to report back."

Inanna smiled, "Yes, and you, my Dumuzi, are just that person for me." She laughed then looked toward Valarus, "As are you, my Captain!"

Valarus spoke next. "What have you learned, Lady Inanna?"

"My Captain, you must enlighten me! Tell me what you have learned from your excursions into our future."

"I must defer to your chosen observer. Everything appeared as it should according to the famulim records of that era," responded Captain Valarus as he accepted dark tea from the platter Arra presented to him as they spoke.

Arra moved to serve Masterson as their attention all shifted to him. He nodded to the famulim, smiling at it. He whispered, "Thank you," earning a smile from the android.

He looked at Inanna as Arra stepped away from the group, returning the tray to the counter. "I learned the Anunnaki are active right until my time, the time my soul is from. The time I am most aware of, where most of my memories come from. It surprised me that there was no sign of Anunnaki activity in that era in the famulim records available on the *Glorious Questor*."

Inanna cocked her head to the side with a most alluring smile that made Masterson smile. "Why does that surprise you? Did the Genitor not seed this world with the help of the Cassidan Hosts and the Dionan Consortia of Clans? Aren't the Mundus the creations of the Genitor?"

"Yes, but remember, Lady Inanna, my consciousness is from that era, what the famulim call The Decline. I don't remember there being an Anunnaki presence." Masterson looked between Inanna and Valarus. "In my time, some believed there were aliens from other worlds or maybe other times, but they were legends, myths. Not regarded as factual beings that really existed."

"Intriguing that our presence at the time of The Decline was not recognized by the Mundus. That is a curious development," mused Inanna aloud.

"Lady Inanna, may I ask what starts The Decline?" Masterson frowned as he leaned more toward her.

She thought for what seemed to Masterson like an eternity then answered her protector's question in a low voice, "The return of *Nibiru Station* to Mundus."

"That doesn't happen!" She had surprised Masterson by the revelation that the Genitor and their Host of Castes, Clans, and Orders of Battle would return to Earth in the twentieth or twenty-first centuries. "That just didn't happen."

"Yes, it does, Protector Dumuzid," corrected Inanna. "The Decline begins when the *Nibiru* returns to Mundus, and Lord Enlil discovers the descendants of the creatures he had ordered destroyed had succeeded after they had been ordered to leave by Commander Anu."

"I don't understand." The pain in Masterson's face was clear.

"Do you remember that Lord Enlil ordered the destruction of all the hominids?" she asked softly.

"Yes?"

"Some of us disagreed with him," she smiled.

Masterson's confusion ceased as he looked at Inanna. "What must I do?"

Lady Inanna extended her hand to him again as she stood towering over the two men seated beside her, "Come with me, my Dumuzi, my protector. I will tell you."

Chapter 5: The Council of Seven

Inanna walked hand-in-hand with Masterson to the center of the audience hall. She turned to take his other hand, looking down at him. Her light gray eyes searched his dark blue eyes before she turned to speak to Captain Valarus. "I have a need for this man, Captain. He can return to you when it is finished." With that, Inanna released Masterson's left hand and turned her hand palm up. A small liquid sphere appeared in the cup of her hand. She smiled. The sphere glided to the ground a few meters away from them to the center of the audience hall and expanded, forming a portal. With Masterson's hand in hers, she led him through the portal to another location only a heartbeat away.

Inanna's personal temple was on the surface; uncharacteristic for a Cassidan, and particularly for an Anunnaki. She loved Mundus. She occupied a large ziggurat near the center of the surface citadel. They arrived on one terrace of her temple, stepping through the portal into the hot desert sunshine. They smiled. Inanna took him there where they stood. Their lovemaking was intense, almost bestial in ferocity. Her telepathic abilities enabled her to enter his mind and take them into levels of intimacy not experienced by others as they became one, both physically and emotionally. As the evening fell, they lay together on one terrace under the starry sky, deeply embracing each other as they lay exhausted.

"You are my goddess," chuckled Masterson as he lay with the Cassidan giant in his arms. "I prefer when we lay together so I don't have to look up to you."

She laughed then pretended to be offended before she devoured his mouth, stretching one more time over his body, pinning him to her sleeping pallet. "Although I may be taller than you, my Dumuzi, I will never look down on you."

"How long do I have before I must return to Valarus?" His hands roamed over her sensual body as they talked.

"For the Captain, he will believe you were only gone a day, perhaps two. Shorter, and he would suspect we are up to something," she smiled down on him as her ash blonde hair cascaded down around his face.

"What are we up to?" laughed Masterson despite the sensations her body was giving him. He fought to remain focused on the task at hand and not to slide into another bout of lovemaking.

She smiled as only she could. "I have a short time to prepare this world to take its place among the Host of the Genitor." She plucked at his lower lip with her fingernail as they spoke.

"You have a short time? I thought Enlil was still the mission commander," questioned Masterson.

She laughed her musical laugh then rolled him atop her. "He is the mission commander, but this world is mine. I have claimed it. It belongs to me. Lord Anu has taken the seven Orders of Battle back aboard *Nibiru* and has left us with only the minimum of castes, clans, and famulim to form this world to the Genitors' Will before his return." She giggled then continued, "I intend to raise my Order of Battle using the Mundus."

"What?" Masterson pushed himself off her supple body, looking down into her eyes, "You're staging a coup while Lord Anu is away on *Nibiru*?"

She smiled up at him seductively. "This is your world, my Dumuzi, but I helped create it. I do not want to see it exploited until it is a shell of its former self, like Cassida and Diona. I want it to thrive, and so do you." She kissed him passionately before he reluctantly pulled his lips away.

"If you fail, what will happen to you?" he asked, caution and concern clearly in his voice.

"I will be returned to *Nibiru* or Cassida and be spurned by the Anunnaki, something I can endure if that is the cost of elevating Mundus to the level of Cassida," she whispered, her breath warm on his face.

"And what will become of me?" he whispered against her lips.

She paused before kissing him deeply. "*They* will remember you."

The next morning, Masterson woke sleepily. He smiled and stretched, looking to see Inanna standing in the bright morning sun, admiring the sky on the terrace. Her naked beauty rivaled the sun in the sky. He just watched her in awe until Arra, Inanna's personal famulim, interrupted, offering him dark tea and fruit. Masterson laughed, accepting both then moved to stand beside the goddess on the terrace. Laid out before them was the city of Ganzir, shining white in the desert's morning sun.

"The Mundus here don't look like the ones that were outside Eidin. They are ruddy like I am. How is that?" Masterson took a large bite of the fruit offered to him by Arra as he watched the citizens of Ganzir going about their business several tiers below them.

Inanna turned, looking at him with an arched eyebrow. "After the Battle of Eidin, we provided support to those that survived the Deluge as they migrated eastward into the subcontinent, then on across the great ocean to arrive here."

"Some survived the Deluge? I thought Enlil killed all humanity except the few aboard the ARC carrying the knowledge cylinders." Masterson frowned as he continued to watch the Mundus walking and working below.

"No, not at all. The Deluge was regional, centered on the Eidin eugenics facility. It decimated the hominids around that region. But there were others further out that survived."

Masterson smirked, "So they didn't cross a land bridge? Huh... They crossed the Pacific Ocean to get to North America. Well, what do you know?"

Inanna looked at him with a smirk of her own. "Your knowledge of the Decline and the major events along the Temporal Spectrum make you a valuable asset for me, my Dumuzi." The two of them stood naked on the highest tier of her temple, looking out over the city in the morning breeze. "I want you to take command of a village, become the chief of the clan. Be the foundation stone of the civilization I must build to make Mundus competitive with the Genitors' host of castes and clans by the time the Decline begins." She smiled, laying her hands on his chest, her long, slender fingers curling around his neck. "Will you do this for me, my Dumuzi?"

"I can and I will," he spoke as she lowered her lips to his.

Masterson stood on the terrace looking out over the shining white Anunnaki city of Ganzir as the sun was setting in the west behind what he knew as the San Andres Mountains. He marveled at the proto-Assyrian city. He turned to look at Inanna as she exited from the cooler inner chamber of her temple into the scorching sun. She looked magnificent in her gossamer gown and golden conical crown.

"You will escort me to the Council Chamber, my Dumuzi." She swirled, laughing as a teleportation bubble appeared from a tiny point of light and turned into the familiar swirling bubble, linking the two entangled locations together. She paused long enough for Masterson to join her at her side before stepping through the bubble and into the Anunnaki Judges Chamber. Five of the seven members of the Council of Judges were present, each in conversation with their own sizable entourages.

Arra was waiting for them, bowing its head slightly to Masterson as it followed behind its mistress. Arra guided Inanna and Masterson to the seat normally occupied by Inanna as a member of the Judges. Masterson remained standing, as were the other attendants and aides of the Anunnaki. The cavernous room was obviously subterranean, with no entry that he could see. The chamber was dominated by a ring of seven large ornate blockish chairs in the center, spaced evenly to allow attendants and aides access to the occupants without being a distraction from any ongoing conversations. The perimeter of the chamber had places for the attendants to work but all within eyesight of the Seven Judges at the center. The only way into or out of the chamber, as far as Masterson could tell, was by the teleporter bubbles that all formed at the outer perimeter just beyond the many workplaces. The entire chamber was lit by suspended balls of light. The place felt ancient.

Everyone stopped what they were doing as Lord Enlil entered the chamber, followed by three of the other Anunnaki and their assembled entourages who emerged from the same teleport bubble. The Lord of the Sky moved to his seat quickly, seated himself, and was immediately besieged by two of his famulim with information interface devices for his quick review.

The Anunnaki took their seats now that Lord Enlil had arrived. Inanna sat opposite the Lord of the Sky, observing him. On her right sat Lord Enki, returned to the council after his expulsion caused by the debacle at Eidin. Enki was Enlil's brother, son of Anu, head of the Anunnaki Caste. Lord Enki was the Mundus project's chief scientist, tasked with developing the flora and fauna to be used to exploit Mundus' bountiful resources. Everyone close to the seven chairs moved several steps back from the seated Anunnaki and became silent. All activity in the work areas stopped.

"Welcome, my brothers and sisters. I am pleased to see all of you once again reunited as we were in the beginning." Lord Enlil continued, "I commend all of you for your efforts on behalf of the Genitor and our Lord Father, Anu. I am sure our Lord Anu will be exceedingly pleased with the progress each of you have made in preparing Mundus for molding it to the Will of the Genitor upon his return." Lord Enlil looked around the assembled circle at each of his fellow Anunnaki, making extended eye contact with each. Immediately to his right sat Lady Ereshkigal, Director of Operations for all Anunnaki citadels and bases on the surface of Mundus.

Next came Lady Ninhursag, who oversaw the agricultural activities on Mundus as the senior botanist of the expedition. She was the companion of Lord Enki. Next came Lord Enki and Inanna. Commander Nanna, Chief of Logistics and in charge of the depots on the large satellite orbiting the planet Mundus, came next. Standing behind him was his Cassidan executive assistant, Adjutant Alammus, and between Commander Nanna and Enlil was an empty seat always reserved for the absent Lord Anu.

"Let us begin." Upon hearing Lord Enlil, famulim stepped forward, providing each of the lords and ladies, and their primary adjutants, a manual interface device encrypted for their personal use. The display set the agenda and provided links to graphics and text information to support their meeting that were all prepared in advance by the famulim based on information provided them. The council members took a moment to scan the interfaces, mostly to see what the famulim did with the information they had provided, but also to check key points being reported by their counterparts.

"As you know, it takes *Nibiru Station* 3,600 Mundus solar cycles to return to us, traveling to the outer shell of the system to interstellar space. While in transit to the outer debris cloud, our counterparts on the station are making observations of the planetary bodies that pass, but a prolonged visit, of course, will be made at the rubble of the former terrestrial planet of *Tiamat* between Cassida and the largest of the four gas giants to collect mineral resources."

"*The asteroid belt between Mars and Jupiter*," Masterson whispered to himself as he listened to the Lord of the Sky's opening remarks with interest.

"In that time, we are to continue our exploitation and preparation for this world. With the departure of *Nibiru Station* also went the bulk and most of the resources of the *Ummanate* and the expertise of the individual *Erimna,* or Order of Battle. Be assured, servitors from the Orders will routinely arrive to ensure that the Will of the Genitor is being adhered to within the Erimna's areas of interest." With that, Lord Enlil turned to Lady Ereshkigal, the director of infrastructure and civil engineering for the project.

Masterson knew her as Inanna's eldest brood sister, as beautiful and gracious as any Cassidan he had met. She had been the first to formally recognize Masterson as Inanna's protector after Enlil had awarded him the title following the Battle of Eidin. It was a title and position that had allowed him to withdraw his service from the Seventh Order, what the Cassidans call the *Erimna Sebu.*

"My Lord Enlil, the First Order has completed the work on the Ganzir Base in the western continent's northern area, Irkalla, in the southern area. The bases on the central continent, Arali and Kilgal, are fully operational, being the oldest of the bases built immediately following the abandonment of Kur and the destruction of Eidin by your order. Arali is near where Eidin was in the mountains. Kilgal is at the southernmost tip of the central continent."

Lady Ereshkigal had disagreed privately with Lord Enlil's decision to depart Mundus following the failure of the Battle of Eidin, adequately addressing the Ejicerce threat. Masterson knew this from intimate conversations with Inanna. He was certain Lord Enlil knew this too, and that Lady Ereshkigal was an ally of Inanna's. It also disappointed many of the Anunnaki when Lord Enlil kept his command of the mission and wasn't replaced by Lord Anu.

"The last base, Ersetu, was the last outfitted and staffed," continued the Queen of the Underworld. "It is on the largest continent's coast, near the Great Ocean."

Masterson referred to the interface device they had handed him, accessing a world map. He realized that the western continent was the Americas of his time, the central continent was Africa, the larger continent was Eurasia. They had placed Ganzir in New Mexico within the future United States. Kuku was on the Peruvian highlands, Arali in Iran, and Kilgal in southern Africa.

"Very good." Enlil turned his attention to the other members of the Council, "Our mission here is to exploit this world's abundant resources on behalf of the Genitor. The Genitor, with their wisdom, deployed the entire Ummanate to create the infrastructure needed to execute their prerogative. Lord Anu, in his wisdom, has withdrawn the Ummanate for use throughout this system in pursuit of the Genitors' goals. Developing Mundus into the world envisioned by the Genitor has fallen to us. There are six citadels strategically placed around Mundus to facilitate our efforts." Lord Enlil bowed his head toward Lady Ereshkigal in a public display of his gratitude for her efforts on their behalf. "Because of the fragility of this world and the inability of its own indigenous population to serve, I entrusted the establishment of the permanent storage facility on its natural satellite to Lord Nanna the Wise. We will not have a second disaster like Kur and Eidin again."

Masterson watched the other members of the Council as they listened to Lord Enlil's explanation for the drawdown of deployed forces to the surface of Mundus. They sat soberly listening to their leader who, in his own way, had caused the collapse of the larger Genitors' presence in the project.

"I entrusted our Igigi to supervise the native Mundus extraction of resources and transfer to Lord Nanna's storehouses on the natural satellite. This process is monitored by Lord Alammus on Lord Nanna's behalf. As for the Igigi, our young watchers, it is my intent that they take more of a lead in the preparation and exploitation of resources of this world. Lord Nuska will supervise the Igigi for this task." Lord Enlil turned briefly to nod at his chief scribe in recognition of his additional responsibility. "Ladies Ninhursag and Inanna will continue to support our project by increasing our numbers here on Mundus with the Igigi during the absence of *Nibiru Station*." Lord Enlil triumphantly looked around the circle at his fellow Anunnaki, "Lord Anu will be pleased that we have represented him well in pursuit of the Genitors' Will."

Inanna interrupted Lord Enlil's moment of self-gratification, "Lord Enlil, your successes are unparalleled, but I have a question."

Lord Enlil looked at her with disdain. She was the newest member of the Council, and his disappointment in her selection for membership by Lord Anu was apparent and well known to the other members. "Yes?"

"Lord of the Sky, do I understand you are giving permission to the uplifted Igigi to take part and lead in the collection of resources to abide by the Will of the Genitor here on Mundus?" She asked slowly to ensure her question was worded correctly and within earshot of the Council members.

Lord Enlil adjusted himself in his seat before speaking, "Lady Inanna, I acknowledge your well-known support of the Igigi and the role you played in their development." Lord Enlil turned his gaze on Lord Enki. "It is also well known that Lord Enki also supports a more robust usage of the hybrids in our efforts here on Mundus, which our father, the great Anu, supports. Yes, I am allowing your Igigi to take part more fully in the management of resource collection but under the stern control of Lord Alammus."

Suddenly Lord Enki blurted toward Lord Enlil, "Had you not interfered with our program at Eidin to develop a hybrid native to Mundus, Lord Anu would not have been forced to withdraw the Ummanate completely from this project. Pitting one Order of Battle against another was not the Will of the Genitor. They would have kept them here on Mundus had it been their will to pit one group against the other."

Lord Enlil gritted his teeth as his cobalt eyes flashed with anger, "You dare challenge my authority to deploy servitors in defense of the Will of the Genitor?"

Smiling, Lord Enki waved his hand apologetically, "No, my brother, I simply mean that perhaps there could have been more options to pursue rather than to attack my base at Eidin ending my…" he motioned toward ladies Inanna and Ninhursag, "our eugenics work so dramatically."

"Enough!" Lord Enlil's anger with Enki was clear as he slammed his armrest with his fist. "Enough, Lord Enki! The Genitors' support for my actions is clear. They dispatched Protector Dumuzid as their envoy to give insight of your corrupted attempt at choosing the inheritor strain of hominids to be the stewards of Mundus. Your actions were in defiance of the protocols put in place by the Genitor that had proven effective on Cassida and Dionan."

Lord Enki snorted and turned in his chair so as not to directly look at Lord Enlil, a blatant show of disrespect.

"Your blasphemy brought us to this situation. The participation of the Ejicerce in your operations at Eidin stands proof of your desire to undermine the established order of adherence to the Will of the Genitor!" Lord Enlil stood, pointing an accusing finger at Enki. "This meeting is at an end. I will summon you when I need your counsel." Lord Enlil turned and walked to the location where he had teleported into the council chamber to activate his personal teleport bubble while everyone else sat or stood in silence.

Inanna looked first to Masterson then quickly shifted her gaze to Lord Enki who sat with a look of disbelief.

"His ineptitude grows more apparent with every meeting," mused Lord Enki as he stroked his bearded chin. He looked directly at Inanna. "You were right."

Inanna nodded her head as she stood. In small groups, others were also departing the subterranean chamber from the multiple teleport bubbles activated at the perimeter of the circular gallery. Masterson moved to stand beside Inanna as the number of others dwindled. Inanna gracefully knelt in front of the still seated Lord Enki. Masterson followed her lead, bringing a smile to the lips of Lady Ninhursag as she watched them from her seat. "You are the Genitors' appointed guardian of wisdom, my lord, the Anunnaki whom the Genitor appointed as the steward of the sacred knowledge of life, of civilization itself. I am always at your command."

Lord Enki reached forward, caressing the cheek of the most beautiful among them. "You understand that this is not our world. It is not Cassida, nor Diona. It is the world that belongs to the Mundus. To not uplift the Igigi would be to forever place the fate of Mundus in the hands of the Anunnaki. It belongs to the Igigi, just as Cassida belongs to Cassidans and Diona to Dionans. That is the Wisdom of the Genitor." He looked up to gaze at Masterson in his Dionan body, "I believe that was the message you brought to us, Protector Dumuzid, that Mundus belonged to Mundus. Those Ejicerce from the future fighting at Eidin that you informed Lord Enlil and his Ummanate commanders about were the evidence that the Igigi ultimately won control of their world. Some of us are just too proud to see it. Some of us are simply too proud to see *that* is the Will of the Genitor."

Inanna smiled up at her mentor, "More understanding of the Will of the Genitor than you are giving credit to, my lord." She stood, taking Lord Enki's hand in hers. "We Anunnaki cannot see the full length and breadth of the Temporal Spectrum as the Genitor does. We only see time as we live it. Our temporal observers give us glimpses of what is coming from their voyages at great sacrifice to themselves. But from what my protector Dumuzid has told me, the Igigi and the Mundus that follow are worth our efforts, my lord."

Lord Enki raised his hand to pat hers. "You are right, Lady Inanna. You are so right." He kissed her outer hand still grasped in his before looking up into her eyes, "And what is the granddaughter of Lord Enlil, Lord of the Sky, intending to do? Or should I not ask?"

Inanna laughed her beautiful laugh then bent down to kiss her mentor's upper hand. "What I always do, my mentor – challenge those that lead!"

The laughter of Lord Enki and the Ladies Ninhursag and Inanna drew the attention of the few members of the Anunnaki staff in the gallery. Some frowned, others smiled, but all waited for the Lord Enki and his companion, Lady Ninhursag, to depart the chamber before resuming their activities.

Masterson turned, looking up at Inanna with a slight frown as they stood while others continued to teleport out of the gallery.

Inanna smiled down at Masterson, reaching over to caress his chin then shoulder. "We are a spoiled family, are we not, my Dumuzid?"

"I was curious about that. You call each other family. Brother and sister, mother and father, but you were all created beings; cloned is what they called it in my time. None of you were born like the Mundus."

He confused Inanna, furrowing her brow. She whispered, "What do you mean?"

"As I understand it, you genetically engineer Cassidans and Dionans based on the projected needs of their community. If a community needs more technicians, a brood of replacements replace the technicians that will no longer serve. Correct?"

Inanna nodded, still not understanding Masterson's intent, but she continued to listen.

"Well, doesn't family show a father and mother who create the siblings, who later become aunts and uncles as more children are born?" Masterson turned to face her, taking her hands in his as they spoke.

Inanna snorted, "You misunderstand, my Dumuzid. You are right, the Cassidans, Dionans –including yourself – and the famulim are designed beings. They create us for specific purposes based on precise social planning. They construct designer cells to create embryos that are nurtured in vats until they are able to sustain their lives on their own. But, to facilitate socialization and a sense of belonging, we are clustered and placed under the care of more mature members of our communities. They instruct us on social behavior and membership in a team. My brothers and sisters were from the same brood as I. My parental mentors were from more mature broods that are charged with nurturing us." Inanna released one hand and pulled Masterson toward the outer walls of the gallery and a suddenly appearing teleport bubble. She called him using his intimate name used only by her, "Come, my Dumuzi, we have work."

Chapter 6: Sargon of Akkad

Masterson and Inanna walked through the teleportation bubble into an open field of wild grass and date palm trees divided by a meandering river. Masterson immediately recognized their return to Mesopotamia, the fertile crescent of southwestern Asia, what would later be known as Iraq. Masterson took a deep breath, exhaling it slowly, smiling.

Inanna smiled too as she looked back at him. "This place is your destiny, my Dumuzi." She took his hand and led him through the field of tall grass to the bank of the river. Upriver, they could see the beginnings of the village of Kish, also known locally as Saffron. They walked a little closer. "There have been several other lugal that have led the communities since the Anunnaki established the settlements along this river following Lord Enlil's general withdrawal from the surface to *Nibiru*."

"Lugal?" Masterson asked as they strolled along the banks of the Euphrates River.

Inanna's smile made Masterson smile as well. "It means *powerful man*, referring to our envoys in the field," she explained.

"Who were they?"

"*Veneficus* – wise men and women chosen by the Anunnaki Council to help establish the Mundus following the Deluge. Their names are Alulim, Alalngar, and Enmenlunna. I want you to join them. I think the Mundus will flourish under your guidance, my Dumuzi." She took his arm, pulling him closer to her warm body as they walked closer to the village. She smiled as villagers recognized her and spread the word quickly.

The villagers were healthy and happy, which pleased them both as they entered the cluster of cube-shaped adobe hovels. The people stopped what they were doing to greet Inanna and Masterson as they stood among them. Inanna towered over the villagers. Her nearly two-and-a-half meters in height made her appear like a giant. Masterson had guessed she was over eight feet tall. He wasn't unimpressive either, with his size being near six feet, he was also taller than the Mundus gathering around them. The scene reminded Masterson of their brief stay with the Neanderthals in the cave during their exodus from Eidin. He watched as Inanna used the Cassidan technique known as *Touch Speak,* communicating with them through touch telepathically as they crowded around her. Everyone parted, moving back away from Inanna and Masterson. Coming to a halt before them stood two Mundus males. Both men prostrated themselves before Inanna and Masterson, and remained still until Inanna bid them to come to her, gripping their hands joyfully as she greeted them. Their faces shone with the excitement of the proximity to Inanna while they communed with their goddess through Touch Speak, the language of the gods and goddesses.

Inanna turned to face Masterson, her long arm draped casually over the shoulder of the younger and larger of the two men in an almost motherly fashion. "This is Sargon. He is the adopted son of Akki. His mother is unknown to him, but she was a temple prostitute in the city Azupiranu. Under my direction, she placed her newborn in a sealed basket and set him adrift on the Euphrates River, where lovely Akki found him and took him as his own son." She demurred as her eyes met Masterson's. "You will get to know him very well."

Masterson frowned, "I know that story, but it was someone else in Egypt."

With a wisp of a smile, Inanna released the two male Mundus. Before she turned, she lifted her hand to caress the younger male's cheek before speaking to Masterson in the singsong language of the Cassidans, "You will come to know this one very well, my Dumuzi." The two of them slowly made their way from the village back the way they had come, Inanna smiling and touching the humans as they withdrew.

While they walked along the tranquil Euphrates riverbank, Masterson asked what he had been wrestling with since he had first been brought to this reality. "Inanna, I once asked a Genitor who they were at war with, and he replied with themselves because no one else could threaten them. This conflict with the Ejicerce – is it against the Genitor or the Anunnaki?"

Inanna turned, smiling down at him, her demeanor becoming flirtatious as her long nails drug over the hard muscles of his chest suggestively. "The Ejicerce are forsaken. They are servitors that have been officially deprived of the ability to travel in time, thus they cannot travel the sea of worlds. They are marooned in a reality so expansive, so encompassing that to be limited to one place and moment is, for them, punishment. They have tasted the fruit of knowledge and hunger for more. They are from the future, and seek to change their fate in the past. So they are creatures deprived of the ability to travel within the Will of the Genitor. Some, however, have avoided that fate and kept the ability to travel, as you saw at Eidin."

Masterson's hands moved around Inanna's slender hips, pulling her closer to him and looking up at her. "So it's not Genitor against Genitor?"

"The Genitor are, have been, and always will be of one mind. It is we, the Anunnaki, that seek to interpret and act upon the desires of the Genitor that disagree. So those disagreements are what cause the lack of harmony within the castes and clans in the service of the Genitors' domain."

"Inanna," Masterson paused, "what is the Will of the Genitor?"

She smiles, "You do not know, my Dumuzi?"

He laughed, "I have to admit I'm confused." He released his hold on her hips and stepped away from her, turning to look back at her with concern. "I've been confused since the day I woke up on that slab on Cassida." He looked out over the river then turned to look at her, "But I know this place you call Mundus; I call it Earth. It's the anchor for me. I know its history, its potential. Or I believe I think I know it. I'm a created being, a creature with memories I'm not even sure are real and not just what they made me to believe. And yet they are unique among those I walk with today. No one else seems to share these memories with me." He looked down at the muddy water of the Euphrates River. "I know they are the memories of this place, this world of Earth."

She smiled and reached for him. "You are in this place." Inanna pulled him into a deep embrace like a mother, comforting her child. "You are a unique creation of the Genitor, for only the Genitor can create a being. They gave you the memories and powers you have by design, their design, for their purpose."

"So, what are you saying? I am the Will of the Genitor?" he questioned.

"The unspoken Will." She smiled, taking his hand in her larger one, "I think you are tied to this world uniquely, given your innate knowledge of its future by the Genitor. I intend to help you exploit your gifts. Come, let us begin your service to your world, my Dumuzi." She opened her free hand to activate the bubble portal before them to step through.

"Welcome to *Kilgal*!" Inanna exclaimed with almost childish joy as they stepped from the primitive agrarian world of the Mundus to the glorious technological world of the Cassidans.

The couple moved from a lavish patio that reminded Masterson of the opulent subterranean apartment that the Genitor had used during his training at the Cassidan academy in the City of Wisdom. Again, Masterson marveled at the engineering prowess of the Cassidan and Dionan builders. He stood a moment in awe of the buildings literally built into the walls of the gargantuan underground gallery.

"We are located to the southeast of where the Eidin citadel was located, in the black mountains in the same geographic region," Inanna explained as a famulim appeared to greet them and help them become comfortable in the lush setting. She smiled as she examined each of the Cassidan plants scattered about the elegant apartment, showing concern to the famulim when she found an imperfection with the plants.

Masterson smiled as he admired her moving about the adjoining rooms with her entourage of famulim until his eyes came to rest on a particular couch and pedestal set aside in one of the many alcoves. He recognized it immediately, as he remembered its use in his training. He moved to stand by it, gaining the sudden attention of Inanna.

She moved to stand close behind him, her limber fingers moving up and down his arms. She whispered, "You know of this?"

"Yes, my mentoring Genitor and Commander Michail used it to test my responses in a field environment before deploying me to Michail's Seventh Order of the Genitors' Hosts."

She drew a fingernail up the length of Masterson's arm, leaving a white trace from elbow to shoulder, causing him to turn to look up at her with a slight grin and raised eyebrow. "This is my gift to you, my Dumuzi. With this, we will build a Mundus Host, an army that will challenge even the Seventh Order's power."

She intrigued Masterson. He asked incredulously, "How?"

"With this," she left his side to caress the couch with her long, pale fingers. "With this, we will place you to influence the path the Mundus take as we prepare for the return of the Lord Anu and the *Nibiru Station*."

"But how? This is simply a training device allowing me to relive events through the memories of participants. How can it influence the path of human development to prepare humanity for war against the Genitors' Orders of Battle?"

Inanna laughed in her musical way then moved to coax him onto the couch. "Like this." She guided his right hand into the bowl on the ornate pedestal next to him. The liquid became solid after it had covered his hand. He felt a sudden surge of fatigue as he slumped, deadweight, passing out.

Masterson felt like he was slowly waking from a dream, expecting to find himself in his bed. He gasped as he suddenly realized he wasn't dreaming but was experiencing the sensations of becoming conscious in a holder's body. He stretched out his hands and fingers, feeling the rough mat he lay on. He sluggishly swatted away an insect buzzing about his mouth. He felt different, yet the same, as he slowly opened his eyes. The natural light of the sun pierced the twilight of a clay room. He sat up, looking at his hands. They weren't his hands, yet they were. He threw back the coarse woven wool blanket that covered his body. The body was an athletic male. He sighed in relief then examined his arms and legs. They were slightly scarred, but there was no sign of serious wounds or deformities. He was pleased.

"Sargon, hurry, the lugal will not wait for the likes of you, regardless of how well you are beloved by the people!" Sargon recognized the old man calling for him as his adoptive father, Akki. He sat up and stretched his new arms and flexed his shoulders. He stood. Sargon was tall for an urbanized Mundus, powerful. Masterson smiled. Barefoot, he walked out of their small adobe dwelling into the morning air. The sun was still below the horizon, making the sky glow red. His elderly father straightened his back proudly as he held the weapons Masterson was to carry into battle today in the service of their city's lugal, or king. Masterson smiled again as he hefted the throwing spear. It was well balanced. His holder recognized it as a fishing spear that he had used many times growing up as his father drew water-loaded buckets on their primitive cart to carry into the city. Masterson held the spear as he looked to Akki, smiling. The old man held out a sturdy wooden club, the very one he himself had used to defend them against wild animals at the river's edge time and time again. Masterson felt the pride his holder body felt at recognizing the club and the significance of Akki giving it to him. He tucked the handle of the heavy club into his rope belt then looked once again at Akki. He startled him when, in what was uncharacteristic of the two men and something that was of Masterson's own desire, Masterson grasped the old man in a bear hug to show his affection and appreciation for the club,. The old man struggled to free himself from the surprise embrace of his son then relented until Masterson released him, laughing.

The assemblage of men and boys that had organized at the gates of the city impressed Masterson. The walls surrounding the city were unimpressive, only made of a rock wall covered with clay that stood between two to three decameters and stretched around the city without watch towers or battlements. It was just a wall. There were about a hundred or maybe a little more people standing together, talking or waiting. They wore simple linen tunics. Some were shod with sandals but most were barefoot, like Masterson. He stood watching the men then, taking a deep breath, he joined them.

Standing on a cart before the assemblage of fighters was a brawny man larger than Masterson, wearing a bronze plate hung from his neck over his chest. He wore a bronze conical helmet reminiscent of the helmets worn by the Cassidan troops of Kur. Masterson smiled. He could clearly see the influence of the Anunnaki and the Cassidans in the Mundus proto-culture. The brawny man thumped his chest several times to get the attention of the men standing before him.

"I, Amnanu, Fist of Kish, declare to you today that I will reward those that fight well on behalf of our king and Kish! Our scouts spotted the Kuthan enemies moving downriver from their city yesterday evening. They should be here before the sun is high in the sky. My plan is to not allow them to leave their boats on the shore of the sacred river. They shall not set foot on our land. Not today, NEVER!" Amnanu shoved his fist into the air to the shouts of approval and encouragement of his fellow fighters. "Follow me to the river, my friends and brothers!"

Masterson joined the city's fighters, moving as a disorganized mob several kilometers westward to the wooden docks where many of the city's reed fishing boats were tethered. The armed mob was joyous in its behavior, as if they had already fought the battle. Many stood congratulating Amnanu on his leadership in defeating the pirates of Kutha. Masterson and many of the Kushite men scanned the river to the northwest. One man further up the river from where Masterson and most of the men stood first saw the enemy reed boats coming around the bend.

As the man hysterically ran toward Amnanu and the others to give the alarm, he collapsed with an arrow lodged in his upper back. The sickening sound of soft thuds of arrows falling like rain among the men, followed by screams of surprise and agony, rolled over the group of Kish men as they stood, stunned. Amnanu stood with a shocked look on his face, disbelief clear in his eyes as he looked down at the two arrows planted deep in his chest, just below the bronze plate hanging from his neck. He fell forward dead-weight, hitting the ground hard and snapping the arrow shafts as he landed.

"Fall back to the city walls!" Masterson shouted, waving to those around him to dash back toward the city of Kish and the safety of the walls. Some men dropped their weapons and fled in a panic, but some kept their wits and ran back the long way they had come earlier in the day toward the small gates of the city facing westward toward their river docks. Masterson ran to the gates of the city himself, but not before taking one more glance back from a small rise overlooking the river landing at the invading pirates from Kutha. There were seven reed boats, carrying about half a dozen to a dozen men each. As he ran, Masterson figured there were probably between thirty to sixty Kuthan warriors in the attacking force. After only a few minutes, he skidded to a stop at the gates, waving the few men behind him into the city. He quickly ordered the heavy wooden gates closed. He looked at the length and breadth of the adobe wall facing their harbor. The walls looked the same on the inside as they did on the outside. No catwalks or other structures were there to allow defenders to fight back against an aggressive force. "Men!" he shouted, "Quickly, those of you with bows go to the roofs of these near houses! Keep them from climbing the walls!"

Masterson grabbed the arm of one of the younger men standing beside him gasping for breath. Pulling him up to look him in the eye he ordered, "Take two others, go to the highest parts of the palace or temple, and watch the walls surrounding the city. If the Kuthans choose another place to breach the wall, send a runner to this gate to tell me. Now go!" Masterson stood to watch the young man do exactly what he was told to do. Grabbing the arms of two of his friends, they dashed off toward the city temple.

The din of noise outside the gates grew louder and louder as random arrows were let loose over the wall in both directions. "Don't shoot your arrows unless you can hit the man you're shooting at!" Masterson screamed as loud as he could, then others echoed his command up and down the line of Kushites defending the city wall and the houses immediately behind them.

"Here they come!" came the shout of one of the Kushite fighters down the wall from Masterson and his group.

He looked up to see that a few meters down from him, Kuthans were clearing the walls and flopping over to land on their feet to be besieged by club and spear-wielding Kushites, but more Kuthans continued to follow. Masterson ran into the fray, swinging his war-club strategically, crushing the skulls of his enemy as he passed. Soon he was in the middle of the fighting, pushing with all his might for his fellow Kushites to stand their ground and hold the wall. But the assaulting Kuthans had established a hold inside the wall's perimeter that allowed more of them to make the climb over the city's meager fortification.

The fighting was savage. Men fought with primitive fishing spears and clubs, and a few had bronze knives. Most were fighting with their bare hands and fists as weapons became lodged in their opponents or simply broke. The Kushites had one advantage; this was their home, and more who didn't rally to the morning's call for fighters turned out to defend their own homes, both men and women. The Kuthans were dedicated fighting men, well suited for their task at hand, but they were simply outnumbered by the now infuriated citizens of Kish. But the Kuthans were taking a heavy toll on those who fought them. Many were wounded and killed in the onslaught of the raiders.

Masterson shoved the Kuthan he was grappling with away from him and jabbed his fist into the man's chest, straight at the soft spot in the center. The man's eyes bulged with sudden panic as Masterson forced his breath out of his lungs. He froze. Masterson, with the heel of his right hand, shoved upward, striking the tip of the man's nose and his upper lip, driving the cartilage of his nose deep into his sinus cavity. The man collapsed in a heap at Masterson's feet. Masterson snatched the blunt, bronze short sword from the dead man's grip then stepped over him. The dull edges of the sword were better for battering a foe to the ground than cutting him, but he could use it for jabbing into the body of an enemy. Masterson moved to a spear-wielding Kuthan, deflecting the thrust of the enemy's spear with the sword then spinning to drive his left elbow into the man's unprotected face. As the enemy stumbled back, Masterson drove the short sword tip deep into his chest, dropping him in an instant.

The fighting continued to rage around Masterson as he yanked the sword from the body of the defeated Kuthan. He looked up, panting for breath, standing near the defended city wall. He reached out one hand to steady himself as he took stock of what was happening around him. There were maybe two-dozen bodies lying around him as Kushites and Kuthans continued to battle for control of the wall. He looked up. There were no more raiders clearing the top. This couldn't be enough of their force to warrant pulling back from the attack on the city. Bowmen were still exchanging arrows over the wall, so it wasn't over. But the Kuthans appeared to have stopped attempting to swarm the wall. Masterson reasoned the number of Kuthans in the raid must be less than he initially calculated. He looked at his fellow Kushites then charged to give help, defeating their enemies as they battled one-on-one. He mercilessly stabbed Kuthans in the flanks and back as he cleared his way along the wall, leaving his allies to finish them. Like an avenging angel, he hastened over the bloodied ground, gathering more and more of the city fighters in his wake as he moved to the city gate they had hurriedly closed only minutes before.

"Open the gate!" he screamed as he reached it. Promptly, men on his sides lifted the brace, allowing the gate to swing open. "FOLLOW ME!" Masterson screamed. With his bronze sword raised, he led the now infuriated Kushite fighters through the gate to the open area between the walls and the docks. The Kuthans were completely unprepared for a counterattack. The Kushites viciously unleashed their rage on the surprised Kuthans. A few of the Kuthan archers let one or two arrows fly before turning and fleeing toward their reed boats, leaving their swordsmen unsupported and still standing against the city's wall. The Kushites followed Masterson as he turned and charged the Kuthan club and spearmen that had stopped their attempts to instead breach the wall by crawling over it to ransack the docks and Kushite reed boats tied there.

One of the Kuthans stood his ground as the others fell back toward their boats. He was a large man that locked eyes with Masterson as the other Kushites engaged the enemy along the wall. The large Kuthan pounded his chest with his left hand then let loose a thundering howl that halted everyone. He was clearly the leader of the Kuthan raiders.

Masterson skidded to a stop, standing ten or more meters from the Kuthan giant. The brute charged Masterson with his bronze mace raised high above his head. He crossed the ten meters in four bounds, bringing his weapon down to crush the body of the smaller Kushite opponent. Masterson also charged just as the Kuthan was upon him, hitting the larger man in his abdomen with his left shoulder then sliding around the giant's waist as the heavy mace came down to impact the ground where Masterson had stood.

The giant roared furiously as Masterson drove the blunt bronze sword into his right side, just below the ribs, upward into his vital organs. The panicked last scream of the giant as they collapsed to the ground in a heap startled the Kuthan raiders as they stood in horror upon seeing their hero die so quickly. The shouts of triumph and victory from the Kushites swelled to a thunderous roar as their enemy fled toward the river before them. The Kushites didn't follow the raiders to the river. They circled Masterson in awe, their joy undeniable as they chanted, "SARGON, SARGON, SARGON!"

Chapter 7: The Ascension of Sargon of Akkad

Masterson stood panting. Some Kushite fighters had moved down to the docks and water's edge to taunt the withdrawing Kuthan raiders. Others remained with him, standing by the defeated war chief now lying dead in the dust. Those with him turned at the sound of people approaching from within the city walls. Masterson turned slowly to see the advance of the city's ruling lugal, Ur Zababa, who was in his mid-forties. Masterson tapped his holder's memories of the man as he approached, frowning. Ur Zababa and his entourage, and the people of the city, came to a halt before Masterson and his victorious fighters.

"Sargon? Son of Akki, you killed the Kuthan lugal? How is that possible? You haul water with your father. How could you defeat a seasoned warrior?" Ur Zababa looked at Masterson incredulously before looking at the faces of the other men surrounding him. When no one responded to his question, he quickly stepped around Masterson to kick the prostrate Kuthan to ensure he was truly dead. "I do not understand. How did you do this? Where is Amnanu?" Ur Zababa looked around at the men surrounding them for his trusted swordsman.

One man spoke up from the surrounding circle, "Lugal, he died as the fighting started, there near the dock. See his body lying where he fell with an arrow in his chest? Sargon saved us all, lugal. He saved the city!" Others in the circle of survivors agreed heartily, adding their own testimony to the bravery and skill of Sargon of Kish.

With skepticism, Ur Zababa looked at Masterson. He couldn't believe the hauler of water could defeat one of the warrior classes of a city the size of Kutha. "How is that possible?"

Masterson took a deep breath then looked down at the Kuthan bronze sword in his hand, stained with the blood of its owner. He slowly held it up, keeping his eyes on its blade. "The goddess Inanna placed this sword in my hand, lugal. It was her that moved it, although I held it. It was her will that Kish be protected from the Kuthans today." He spoke clearly so everyone around them heard his words. He dropped the sword at the feet of Ur Zababa. "It is her will that your city was protected, Lugal Ur Zababa."

Everyone around Masterson and Ur Zababa erupted into cheers and hollering at the words spoken by Masterson through his holder, Sargon. Ur Zababa turned his head to the left then to the right, measuring the excitement of the men crowded around them. He held up his hand for silence, "Amnanu was my fist, but the goddess Inanna has delivered to us a sword in our time of need! Sargon will lead as my sword!" The announcement was well received by the surviving fighters who, all as one, cheered for their new military leader. As the men closed around Masterson to congratulate him, Ur Zababa and his counselors made their way back to the palace.

Masterson turned from watching the lugal depart to address his men, "Collect the dead, all the dead. I don't want anyone left to rot in our water. Burn the bodies of our enemies downwind of the city. Bring our dead into the city. Take them to the temple so their families can claim them and prepare their bodies, as is our tradition." He looked, seeing some men were badly wounded and lying where they fell. "Take our wounded to the temple also, so their families can find them to care for them."

The survivors quickly responded by doing what Masterson had ordered. Masterson watched to see who took charge of what, committing their faces to memory for later use. He took a deep breath, bending down to retrieve the bronze sword. He hefted it in his hands, feeling its weight and smiling, and moved into the city toward his makeshift home.

Masterson and Akki somberly walked together to the temple and palace. Akki was saddened by the loss of his fellow villagers. Masterson realized what Inanna had intended. He was to make Kish the center of her Mundus Erimna, or army. No one had taken the time to count the wounded and dead, and he really didn't know who to ask to do that. Akki spotted the family of one of his friends that worked the water carts with him. Masterson's holder recognized the partner and children of the fallen man. He nodded as Akki went to help his family. Many women and children were mulling about him, searching for or helping the fallen as he moved deeper and deeper into the area where the survivors had laid the dead.

One man he recognized from the wall ran up to him, "Sargon, there is not enough water in the trough where the wounded have been taken."

Masterson gripped the man's arms with his hands and held his gaze as the man calmed down before speaking to him. "Organize the young that are large enough to haul water. Tell them to gather pots and fill them, and bring them to the trough. Then, once it's filled, have them take the water to their own families that have been wounded. Don't use the young ones that lost their fathers today if you can help it." Masterson gripped his arm to hold his attention, "Make sure you tell their mothers what they're doing, and make sure they understand the fighting is over for today."

"Yes, Sargon, it will be done!" the man turned and hastily called his trusted friends to him to pass on Masterson's instructions.

Masterson looked at the people grieving around him; some looked at him like he was personally responsible for losing their loved one, others showed appreciation for what he had done by sparing them from the wrath of the Kuthan raiders. He looked down, watching where he stepped as he navigated the bodies and weeping families sprawled out around him. He looked up toward the two-tiered temple at the heart of the city. There he saw the women, the prophetesses of the temple to the Anunnaki. He squinted his eyes, searching them, thinking he would surely see Inanna, his Inanna, standing there among them. But he didn't. Taking a weary breath, he moved on toward where the wounded had been taken.

A tired Masterson collapsed beside Akki as the sun was setting below the western horizon toward Kutha. Akki quickly smiled at his adopted son before looking back at the clay jug he had been carrying most of the rest of the day. "You did well, Sargon. You did very well. From everyone I have heard how you saved the city with your bravery and skill. I am very proud of you, my son."

Masterson smiled as he reached to accept a bowl of water offered by Akki from his clay jar. "Do you remember ever seeing the goddess Inanna, father?"

"Oh, yes!" the old man smiled wide with a gleam of joy in his eye despite the destruction that had happened earlier in the day. "Oh yes, don't you? We saw her together, perhaps a month ago." Akki turned, waving his arm to include others, "Remember, there were several of us from our village that saw her that day. The day we moved here to this city."

"I must have hit my head in the fighting today. Why did we leave Azupiranu?" Masterson listened while he sipped the iron-tasting water.

"Because of the damned Kuthans. They have been raiding our outlying villages for our cattle and women with more and more boldness. Lugal Ur Zababa was warned that this attack would happen and had called for us all to come here to Kish to defend it and protect what is ours, too." Akki set down his jug and reached over to pull Masterson's head down so he could examine his scalp, concern on his face caused by the questions being asked.

Masterson laughed then pushed Akki off. "Who warned him?"

Akki snorted with disgust that his son knew so little or had forgotten so much. "The gods, of course, the Anunnaki." Akki settled and stared at Masterson, "Do you not remember, Sargon? The god of Kish himself was with the goddess Inanna when she came to order us here."

Masterson shook his head, "No, I don't. Was it Dumuzid?"

"Dumuzid? No, no! Dumuzid the Shepherd, no. It was the god of Kish, Zababa the Warrior, the crusher of stones!"

Masterson chuckled, "I don't remember that. I remember the goddess Inanna, but I don't remember Zababa. Describe him."

"How can you not remember Zababa? He is tall and powerful like Inanna, but his skin is not pale as is hers, but ruddy like ours. His eyes are like ours, but the color of the sky before a storm. Not slitted as cats like Inanna's grey eyes. But he is a giant! He towered above us like Inanna." Akki smacked at Masterson's head, "How can you not remember seeing Anunnaki?"

"I vaguely remember the warrior with her. Her beauty blinded me after all, father. You are old, so of course you didn't focus on the femaleness of Inanna." Laughing, Masterson continued, "How would I not focus on her? I thought the warrior was Dumuzid, her husband."

"Dumuzid was a man like you or I, not a god. Brave and powerful to have captured the heart of Inanna, but a man just the same. Or so the legends go. He was a king. But like you, my son, he came from a humble birth. Remember that."

Together, the two men were laughing when two of the palace guards found them resting among the sick and wounded and those caring for them. "Sargon, the lugal wants you to come to the palace."

"Stay here, father." Masterson stood, retrieving the new bronze sword he had won in battle earlier in the day, and followed the two fighters. As they approached the palace, night had fallen and torches had been lit by those working late into the night. All the sentries were at their posts rather than the usual night watch. Masterson knew keenly that all eyes were falling on him as they entered the palace. His holder's memory, the deep memory of Sargon, didn't remember ever being inside the palace. Masterson was alerted to this being his holder's first time in the building.

The palace was a large, single story adobe and terracotta structure, unlike the temple of the Anunnaki beside it. Lugal Ur Zababa stood with several of his councilors in the central, open sky garden in the center of the square-shaped building. Surrounding the garden were the walled-off rooms that served Ur Zababa's home for himself and his family. Masterson smiled to himself as he compared it to a shopping mall of his time. It impressed him.

"Sargon of Azupiranu, son of Akki, the water hauler." Ur Zababa greeted Masterson. "You saved the city, and probably my family and myself." Ur Zababa was much older than Masterson's holder but still formidable, or else he wouldn't be the lugal of Kish. "Today you were our deliverer, but you came from nowhere, from one of our outlying villages. Truly, my councilors believe you were a gift to us by our city's god, for whom I am named, Zababa." Behind the lugal, the city councilors loudly agreed with him. "What do you know of this, Sargon of Azupiranu?"

"My father, Akki, the water hauler, will attest to this, and others from my village that survived today. We were sent to you by the goddess Inanna herself, escorted by Zababa. We all saw them in our village to tell us to come to Kish. You, the members of the city council, have been counseled by Lugal Ur Zababa, and it was so." With this announcement by Masterson, the elders and councilors erupted in cheers and joyful shouts of praise for the Anunnaki, Inanna in particular.

Ur Zababa turned to smile, gazing at his advisors before turning back to address Sargon loudly enough for all to hear. "Sargon, I choose you as my sword arm. You will lead my fighters in defending our favored city of Kish from the ruthless Kuthans to the north, who would steal from us the fruits of our labor, our cattle, and our women. All favored by the goddess Inanna and entrusted to us by our city's god, Zababa, for whom I am named and serve."

Masterson held up his hand for silence, "Lugal Ur Zababa, I have had a vision given to me by the god Zababa himself." At hearing this, everyone in the garden became silent. "I accept this honor to defend the city of Kish and its surrounding villages. But I must follow the guidance the gods have given me, the goddess Inanna and god Zababa. My fellow villagers of Azupiranu, who will swear this is true, witnessed this." Masterson looked at the faces of the men surrounding him and Lugal Ur Zababa with earnestness. "We must take this battle to Kutha. We must defeat the Kuthans on their land, not ours."

Hearing this, everyone except Ur Zababa instantly erupted in renewed shouts of praise for Sargon. "You intend to take my fighters north, to Kutha? But who will defend our walls, our cattle and women?" Ur Zababa turned, looking at his councilors in surprise at this sudden revelation. Slowly he turned back to face Sargon, "But you are a villager. How could you lead as a lugal and lay siege to our powerful enemy on his own land?"

Masterson looked past Ur Zababa into the eyes of the councilors, "Because it has been foreseen and told to me by the goddess Inanna herself, and ordered by Zababa in her company. It was witnessed by the people of my village, whom many shed their own blood here today in defense of this city. This is their will."

Ur Zababa took Masterson by the arm and led him off to a private area out of earshot of his councilors. "Are you mad? I will not allow you to do this. I will not allow the city to be unprotected while you lead my fighters off to be slaughtered at Kutha."

Masterson looked deeply into Ur Zababa's eyes. "The Anunnaki favors us. Inanna favors us over Kutha."

Almost spitting with anger, Ur Zababa hissed, "How do you know this?"

Masterson firmly responded, "How do you not?"

"Who do you think you are? I will have your head. I am lugal here!"

Masterson looked past Ur Zababa at the councilors watching them with interest. "If you kill me after what I did today and the way the people saw me as their hero, what will they say of you? But if you let me take this fight to Kutha, the worst that can happen is you are rid of me."

"Wrong!" hissed Ur Zababa. "The worst that could happen is Kutha returning to finish what they started today with all my fighters either dead or lost in the wilderness following you!"

"The Kuthan fighters are on their boats going upriver. They will take time to return to their city. Their lugal died here today in the fight. You saw me kill him. They will linger. If I take our city's hunters, shepherds, and farmers from the villages with me, we can beat them back to their city. The craftsmen, older men, and boatmen will stay here to defend the city."

Ur Zababa looked at Masterson suspiciously, "You have thought this out all on your own? You, the son of a water hauler from a village?"

"Zababa, your namesake, thought this all up, Lugal Ur Zababa," grinned Masterson.

Ur Zababa glared at Masterson. "Do this then and do not return unless you sack the city of Kutha. If you lose, I will have your head."

"I will need wagons and asses to move the fighters quickly."

Nodding, "Use what you must. I do not want to face the wrath of Inanna."

Chapter 8: The Point of Creation

Masterson blinked his eyes rapidly then sat up. He looked around, realizing that the connection between him and Sargon had been severed. Inanna placed her hand on his shoulder to reassure him as he regained his composure. "Why was I pulled out? This isn't a good time to abandon Sargon."

"My dear Dumuzi, you shared your mind with young Sargon. He has a little of you within him now. Your knowledge of warfare has now been imparted to him. Truly, he will not understand it all, but he will remember enough." She smiled down at him as she sat beside him on the reclining couch. "You know that on an excursion, the memories, the minds of the holder and the one having the excursion blend so that the excursionist can act naturally in the environment. Have you never thought that the holder gets a little from the blending, too?"

The expression on Masterson's face displayed shock at this revelation, making her tilt her head in surprise. "Have you not wondered at all if they remember your presences in their mind?" She laughed as she stood and stepped away from him. "Come, let us discuss our next move." She abruptly turned, leaving him to sit on the couch, watching her saunter from where he lay.

Masterson pushed himself up from the couch. He looked down at his Dionan hands, turning them slowly. He had never thought about the possibility of information exchanged between himself and the holder he was using. He frowned as he stood next to the couch. Why did he have to exchange the information manually between him and the temporal influencer on their last mission into the future? He walked into the next area of the apartments Inanna was using as her new base. She was now being attended to by her personal famulim as she reclined beside a shallow pool. He stepped over to gaze into the pool, his reflection looking back up at him from the surface of the still water.

"Inanna, on my recent trip to the future to meet with a temporal influencer, Captain Valarus had me use a holder to meet with the influencer to pass on some information. Wouldn't it have been easier to have me inhabit the influencer's holder-body instead? They nearly killed me during that meeting with the influencer." His eyes left the image of himself floating in the water to look at Inanna as she sat holding the hands of Arra, her favored famulim.

"Arra, explain to Dumuzi why sometimes it's not possible for a direct sharing of minds between a holder and observer during an excursion." Inanna released Arra's hands so the famulim could turn to face Masterson as it sat beside her.

"Veneficus, the direct transfer of information between a holder and an observer is often traumatic, causing lasting disorientation with gradual loss of cognitive ability for the holder. Often, the holder becomes delusional and unable to function in their own environment. When a temporal influencer is identified by an excursion team, direct contact is limited and often monitored by several interested parties." Arra provided its information with its indistinctive androgenous voice shared by all famulim.

"Interested parties?" Masterson focused on the fact that there could be more than one group of temporal travelers observing someone identified as an influencer of events of a specific point in time. "You mean the Ejicerce?"

A teasing smile formed on Inanna's divine face as she arched her eyebrow in her typical fashion when about to enlighten Masterson. "And the Igigi." She beckoned Masterson to come to her, her longer hands taking his right arm, pulling him closer to her, his hands automatically moving to hold her hips as she pulled him into her intoxicating embrace. She leaned down to whisper into his ear, "Our host of Mundus warriors."

"Inanna, do you travel in time?" Masterson frowned, looking up into her eyes, searching for some insight. He felt that she hid some truth from him.

Her laugh was musical but did not surprise him. She hesitated, moving away from him, her fingers trailing off his as she stepped away. "Of course we do. They conceived me on Cassida in the distant past from this temporal reference point. The Genitor wisely restricts travel in the temporal continuum because of the dangers of disintegration and reintegration into our molecular structure. For most of us, temporal travel is a one-way trip to our permanent assignments following the Will of the Genitor."

"Before I came to the service of the Genitor and was drafted into the Seventh Order, I remember there was a theory from my previous life, that a time traveler – which of course we didn't know time travel could even occur – couldn't meet themselves in their travels, that all reality would be torn asunder. Is that true?" Masterson furrowed his brow as he stood.

Inanna spun around to look at Masterson with a look of amusement. "No, something far worse occurs." She stood, clearly trying not to laugh at her Dumuzi as he approached her. "Nothing occurs within the physical world. Reality is maintained. But remember, at the subatomic level, there are incalculable variations that can occur that are not fixed until observed by the conscious participants. Most often this manifests itself as both versions becoming self-aware of the other's existence. That awareness has the potential to consume the thoughts of one or both. There is the potential for both of them to become insane." She looked down at Masterson as he moved close to her. She reached out, taking his hand, "For that reason, contacting yourself, or even seeing your future or past self, is not permitted by the Genitor."

"I'm confused. It's possible then to meet a future or past version of myself. There is nothing physically stopping me from doing that. The universe will survive the encounter intact. I only risk one version or the other losing their rational mind? But what about changing history itself? What if I go back in time and kill my father? Do all future versions of me cease to exist? And what if I was a temporal influencer? Does history change?"

Inanna, with his hand in hers, led them from the excursion instrumentation chamber where the interface with Sargon had occurred into a larger hall. "As a servitor, you know that the temporal spectrum is a fluid future before us and a fixed past established behind us. But all are happening in the same instant, meaning what is to happen in the future affects what has happened in the past."

"What, wait – that makes no sense at all." Masterson gripped her hand, bringing them to a stop. "What you're saying is that everything I know, everything I will ever do, co-exists at the same moment in time?"

"Yes, what you just described is the essence of our civilization and the Genitors' creation."

Masterson's eyes pleaded with her for more.

Her smile widened. "Dumuzi, they taught you on Cassida that our mathematics support twelve observable dimensions that enable our technology. Our mathematics and understanding ends with the thirteenth dimension that is chaotic. We call that the Point of Creation. We use that mathematical understanding of the twelve dimensions and the Point of Creation as the anchor to move between one point and another in time and space. When time travelers move using our instrumentation, we disassemble our bodies at the molecular level while entangling and transmitting that data to the targeted location for instantaneous reassembly. During that transmission, the body exists mathematically at both locations in time and space. The traveler is unaware of that because it is instantaneous, entangled at the subatomic level in between four to twelve dimensions, dependent on the navigational calculation."

"The more precise the destination location, the more sophisticated the calculation; the more sophisticated the calculation, the larger the chance of catastrophic error."

"Yes, my Dumuzi. But when that transition from one point in time or space to the next occurs, perceived reality is reset for the traveler. When you arrive at a specific point in time, that point is as it should be for you based on your perceptions through the dimensions you can perceive, whether it be through the instrumentation of your vessel or the nanite-induced psychic abilities the individual traveler may have mastered."

"So time resets every time a traveler moves from one era to another. That would mean that the future and past are both always changing. Changing a lot, always evolving. That's incredible." Masterson looked down at the stone floor in thought then eventually looked back up into Inanna's eyes. "So today I know that in 1969, Americans landed on the Moon, but there may be a moment in the future that I arrive at a new location and the Soviets landed on the Moon in 1970 instead, and I'll be fine with that, and everyone that I encounter will be fine with that. But there will still be a moon landing that occurred."

Inanna giggled then nodded her head. "Yes, I think. I do not understand your references, but yes, the details of an event can change, sometimes dramatically, but the event or something similar will still occur."

"The Ejicerce, the Forgotten Ones, they are from the future end of the temporal spectrum, correct?"

"Yes, Dumuzi, the Ejicerce are at their greatest numbers in our future because their members come from the disenfranchised ranks of the Dionan clans or the servitors."

"Forgotten because of their disfigurement from trans-dimensional travel."

"Yes, my Dumuzi. Their numbers grow as we progress toward the common future within the temporal spectrum."

"I understand now that the outcome of *the war* is not guaranteed. Despite our battlefield being Time itself, we truly don't know who wins and who loses until we ourselves are in that moment."

"Yes!" Inanna gripped him in a tight hug, almost bouncing with his revelation of their task.

"Can the future be different with a return trip from the past once it's been experienced?"

"Yes, in some ways, but not in others, because it resets with every temporal movement." She gazed down at him. "But remember, you would not be aware of the change. To you, and those traveling with you, it all would seem as it should."

"Damn," was all he could say to that revelation.

"But there is an ultimate ending, where the universe resets itself. When entropy gets so prevalent, reality no longer functions."

"Resets itself. What do you mean?"

Inanna cocked her head to the side. "We begin again."

Masterson slowly opened his eyes and took a deep breath. Her scent hung about him; her fragrance surrounded him. He raised himself up on his elbows, looking around her personal chamber that she had taken them to for him to rest following his extended excursion with Sargon. He took a deep breath then stood looking for his robe. Masterson smiled as he walked out onto the massive terrace of Inanna's subterranean apartment complex. Before him was a vast cavern with structures built into the stone walls several stories in height. The air was dry for them to be deep underground. The architecture of the various buildings that crawled up the sides of the monstrous grotto were Cassidan. The view made him immediately remember his beginning at *Civitas Mirantibus,* the City of Wonder, on a world that would be called Mars in the future.

Masterson idly took some Cassidan fruit from an ornate table, snacking on it as he wandered the outer terrace of her residence. He slowed his pace as he heard her voice coming from an alcove further ahead of him. He stopped then moved closer cautiously. He trusted Inanna but not other Mundus, Dionans, and especially not Cassidans of whom the Anunnaki were.

"Your gambit is risky, Lady Inanna, you risk much," a well-adorned Cassidan female stood from an ornate chair close to where Inanna sat.

Inanna also stood after a quick glance toward where Masterson now stood partially concealed. "Lady Ninmah, you have been my ally and trusted confidant since our work here on Mundus began so many of our years ago, thousands of local solar cycles for this world. You and I agree; the Mundus deserve to manage their own world as they seek the Will of the Genitor in their own way."

Lady Ninmah's head snapped quickly to look toward where Masterson now stood, her eyes narrowed and flared with bio-kinetic energy. The faint hint of ozone wafted through the air.

Inanna quickly stepped between the Lady Ninmah and Masterson, breaking the line of sight between the Anunnaki and her Dumuzi. "You know my protector, Lady Ninmah – Dumuzid?" Inanna turned to face Lady Ninmah. "He is crucial to our plans and has been a service to me so far doing fieldwork."

Lady Ninmah softened, the tension visibly drained from her as she moved to look around Inanna at Masterson. "Yes, Dumuzid. I remember him. He turned down promotion and reassignment within Mikal's Seventh Order then mysteriously fled the city. I remember him. I also remember that his psychic ability given by the volumen is Claircognizance." She frowned at Masterson. "He knows about many things he should not be aware of intrinsically."

Inanna laughed like a delighted child. "He does!" She beckoned Masterson to come to her side. "He will help us guide our children, my sister, Ninmah. He has already started the formation of our own Mundus Horde using a temporal influencer to organize."

"Ah, yes, I can see where his ability is useful. Who was the influencer?" Lady Ninmah walked to her abandoned seat and made herself comfortable as they attended her.

"Sargon of Akkad," Masterson spoke up, interjecting himself into their conversation. "The creator of the first Mundus empire."

Lady Ninmah showed subtle surprise at hearing Masterson's voice but didn't look at him directly.

"My Dumuzid's knowledge of the future makes his participation in our plan precious to not only me but our supporters, too," Inanna smiled as she circled Masterson slowly. She drug her long fingernails across his shoulders and back to come to a stop at his side, facing Lady Ninmah who couldn't look at her without looking at Masterson.

"My dear child, what is the plan you and Lord Enki have conspired over, and what is my part?"

Masterson smiled, watching Inanna's response as she pouted, leaving his side to move to a couch near where Lady Ninmah sat. He remained where he stood, barefoot in his loose-fitting robe. Inanna stretched her long, feminine frame over the couch as Arra led the other famulim in attending her.

"In your position as the leader of the physicians and head of biological research on Mundus, you simply do what you have done for me so well in the past. As you did at Eidin Citadel. Just turn a blind eye to my activities."

Lady Ninmah sat forward in her seat, her eyes locked on Inanna's with an intensity used before an attack. "What are you doing, Lady Inanna? Your activities, whether you admitted it in the past, helped create the situation we now find ourselves in. Because of the disaster at Eidin Citadel, we now work scattered across the surface of this world with minimal resources and a workforce that needs constant supervision and redirection least they kill themselves."

"Lord of the Sky Enlil has allowed the use of volumen with the Mundusans. He is allowing the Igigi to serve us as supervisors and managers directly with the Mundus." Inanna sat up, her intensity matching Lady Ninmah. "They will replace the Consortia in the direct supervision of the harvesting of the resources we use. Do you not understand? They will be in a position of ascendance!"

Lady Ninmah scoffed, "That is not at all what they said at the council meeting, Lady Inanna."

"But it was!" Inanna slid from a position of dignified repose to sit at the edge of the couch, nearly within reach of touching Lady Ninmah's knees. "I would like to be present, to have some say in which Igigi they select to receive the volumen."

Lady Ninmah leaned forward, her eyes narrowing. "Why, my sister, would you want to have that level of access?"

Inanna smiled and moved back to recline on her couch as she had before, looking for Arra to attend her once more. She continued to smile in her own way in silence as the famulim looked to her comfort.

Lady Ninmah snorted then stood. "I think, sister, that our conversation is over. I trust you could get from me what you sought. With you, it is always hard to tell." Lady Ninmah turned with a slight smile as two of the famulim quickly came to her side to escort her from Inanna's apartment. Her eyes shifted from the famulim Arra holding Inanna's hand, presumably in a touch-speak conversation then back to Inanna, "I hope your lady knows what she is doing. Only Lord Enki the Wise has ever understood her motivations." Arra simply smiled the universal noncommittal famulim smile. With that, Lady Ninmah turned to be escorted from the expansive apartment.

"What was that about?" Masterson moved to claim the seat abandoned by Lady Ninmah, handing the core of the fruit he had been eating to one of the remaining famulim.

"I want active participation in the selection of the Mundus to be chosen at the new generation of volumen-enhanced Igigi. The humans breed randomly among themselves. The genetic design for each individual is randomly determined based on the combination of two parental sources. There is a strong probability it will pass some of the genetic programming on to the new organism, but it is not guaranteed like it is for the famulim, Dionans, and Cassidans. But there is also a possibility for a more efficient version of the parental organisms or even something completely different but as desirable."

"Natural Selection, that is what we will call it in the future," Masterson smiled as he interrupted, causing Inanna to smile impishly back at him.

"I like that." Inanna looked up at Arra, still holding her hand, "You see, he is not a dullard like you said." The look on Arra's normally emotionless face caused them both to laugh.

"Arra?" Masterson furrowed his brow as he looked to the famulim.

"Protector Dumuzid, I only reminded Lady Inanna that you are not as technically proficient at the use of our technology as others, given your position and prestige for a Dionan. Your confusion over the use of the cognitive interface technology surprised me, considering the use of interface instrumentation on Captain Valarus' ship for your latest endeavors on our lady's behalf."

Masterson grinned despite himself. "The interface that Captain Valarus uses compared to what I just experienced here is very different. Much more comfortable. I'm not being buried alive in liquid stone then resurrected here. Not a very comfortable experience, Arra." Arra demurred, glancing at Inanna, not looking back to Masterson.

"I must really speak with the captain if he is making you uncomfortable with his antiquated Dionan instrumentation." Inanna reclined further, making herself more comfortable, thus more alluring, while Arra continued to hold her hand silently.

Masterson frowned, "There is a difference between Cassidan and Dionan technology? I thought it was the same. I assumed that Valarus' ship was like the Seventh Order's Leviathan, a little older, perhaps." Masterson leaned forward, resting his elbows on his knees, visibly surprised by the revelation that there was more than one technology being used in what he thought was a singular culture centered on the Genitor.

Inanna giggled. "They are similar, and in that context, you are absolutely right. Dionan technology is based on Genitor-inspired Cassidan instrumentation. The physical natures of Cassida and Diona, of course, shaped the use and manufacture of the instrumentation involved to best function in their environments. The Genitor are careful to not allow one to influence the other so that we do not become one homogenous social entity with no innovation and becoming stale. We purposefully have our own identities, although assigned career paths. We are all synthetically conceived, nurtured through our maturation systematically to ensure we can serve as planned for the benefit of the community, but we also, through the combination of the nurturing and career training, develop unique personalities."

"Why is Mundus being treated differently? Why are the Mundus not cloned too? In fact, why was there no advanced technology being used by the Mundus at all?"

"Remember, my Dumuzi, that we were developing a hominid strain best suited to serve the Genitor on this world when you were sent to us with the message that the Ejicerce had already penetrated the eugenics project at Eidin?"

"Yes, and that was never clearly explained to me either. I've experienced the possession of another body using your cognitive interface technology. It didn't displace the consciousness of the holder body as mine apparently was, resulting in my consciousness waking up in this body thousands if not millions of years in my past." Masterson paused, "Are you saying that had the Ejicerce not interfered with the work at Eidin, humans would have been cloned and placed with the use of Genitor replication technology like the Cassidans and the Dionans?"

The look of anticipation on Inanna and Arra's faces stopped Masterson's questioning. After thought he realized, "They didn't use my body for someone else to occupy as a holder body. It was my consciousness that was required, not my body." Masterson looked down at the highly polished stone floor beneath his feet for several minutes as he thought through what he was realizing. "The Ejicerce sent me to Eidin with that message, not the Genitor? No, the Ejicerce have allies within the Genitor. That's why my mentor said the Genitor are fighting themselves. But the Genitor share their thoughts; they have one mind. How is it possible that there could be a conflict between shared minds that have no independent thought?"

"The Genitors' dimensional perception allows them to observe the future, the present, and the past as one mind from the point of creation in the subatomic realm. They understand that the past affects the future, and that the future affects the past. We, as isolated and independent observers, perceive only the present, what we are observing as a single moment in our collective existence. But the Genitor observes our experiences and that is added to their knowledge and wisdom as they manage the shared reality."

Masterson scratched his chin as he sat back in the chair, "So the Genitor are immortal?"

"Only in that they have a shared consciousness that stretches from the point of creation to the extended reaches of perceived reality."

"What does that mean?" scoffed Masterson, alerting Arra, whose eyes suddenly focused on him.

"My Dumuzi, were you not listening? The Genitor shares their thoughts from the point of creation outward, encompassing all the dimensions emanating from chaos to the ordered reality shared by all in the past, present, and future."

"Earlier you said that time is fluid, that it resets itself every time one of us travels through time, yet the Genitor knows the future, past, and present? Yet you say time is constant, the future will happen, and the past remains the same. This makes no sense to me."

Arra spoke up, surprising both Inanna and Masterson, "Because, Protector, you perceive things only from the perspective of the moment, as it is your purpose to do so. You cannot comprehend the vast expanse of existence as one reality in its entirety because it is the Will of the Genitor."

Chapter 9: The Secret

Inanna, Masterson, and Arra stepped through the teleportation bubble onto the quarterdeck of Captain Valarus' temporal courier, *Glorious Questor*. The arrival area was a small alcove off the main corridor, connecting the command-and-control area at the bow of the ship and the opulent quarters at the stern. A Mundus steward ushered them into the captain's wardroom just a few meters away from their arrival point. Waiting for them was Captain Valarus and his chief pilot, Hebeta. Both were happy to see Inanna and Masterson.

Immediately, Masterson's eyes were drawn to the transparent ceiling. Above them hung the Earth. They were in space, some distance from the planet above them. The view took his breath away. "I didn't know the ship could do that."

Captain Valarus snorted. His eyes shifted from Masterson to Inanna. "Welcome aboard, Lady Inanna. Your presence on our ship is always both an honor to my house and a pleasure for my crew." His eyes shifted back to Masterson. "I assume you are returning him back to us?"

The much taller Inanna smiled and turned to gaze on her chosen protector, her slim fingers reaching to caress Masterson's muscular Dionan chest as she smiled at him. "For a bit, yes." She turned to Captain Valarus, "We have much to discuss, and some planning to complete."

Hearing that, Valarus nodded. He ushered Inanna to his chair at the head of the heavily engraved wooden table. Valarus seated himself immediately at her right hand, nodding for the others to take their customary places around the ancient table. Hebeta sat beside her captain. Masterson moved to sit beside Inanna on her left side, across from the captain and Hebeta. Silently, they waited for the others summoned to the meeting to arrive.

Masterson watched Hebeta as she tried to not return his look. Finally, she offered a shy smile, as she couldn't resist his gaze for too long. He winked at her, causing her to giggle, which quickly got Captain Valarus' attention and caused him to look up from the tablet he was reading to frown at Masterson. Hebeta quickly lowered her head, as if already judged and condemned. Masterson looked at Inanna, who seemed amused and curious, her gray eyes twinkling in delight. Behind Inanna, Arra looked at him in disbelief and a tinge of disgust before turning its head to stare elsewhere.

The door opened for the steward to announce three Cassidans whom Masterson quickly recognized as Lord Enki and his mate, the Lady Ninhursag, or Ninmah, the Anunnaki woman Inanna had met with earlier. Masterson had never met the third Cassidan, Lord Nisaha. The three ceremoniously greeted Lady Inanna, who had stood upon their arrival. The stewards followed, guiding Lord Enki to the seat opposite Lady Inanna, with Lady Ninhursag sitting to Enki's left nearest Hebeta, who kept her head downward, not looking directly at the newcomers. The tallest of them, Lord Nisaha, sat to Enki's right on the same side of the table as Masterson, leaving some chairs between them.

"This is certainly unusual, Lady Inanna, for us to speak in the presence of Dionan and Mundus, is it not?" Enki looked at the mixed assemblage sitting around the ancient table with some sign of his amusement. "Your famulim, I understand. Maybe Captain Valarus, but the female and him?" he gestured toward Masterson.

"Pilot Hebeta is here at the request of Captain Valarus, whom you know, Lord Enki, as a very effective agent of our cause. Protector Dumuzid is critical to my project and is here so that he may understand and ask questions if they arise from our talk today."

Lord Enki nodded then waved his hand. "Shall we begin?"

Inanna bowed her head, showing her deference to the elder Anunnaki. "I propose we institute an alternative model for the governance and collection of resources for Mundus, one that differs from the traditional model used on Cassida and Dionan."

Lord Nisaha slammed his palm down. "Blasphemy!"

Lord Enki moved his hand to cover Lord Nisaha's hand while looking at Inanna. "What are you proposing?"

"Lord Enlil has allowed the uplifting of select Mundusans using the volumen to enhance their abilities to the levels that are common among our servitors and the Anunnaki. This will, of course, create a new dynamic in our multi-planet social order. We will have a class of Mundusans that will match the psychic abilities of our own."

"The intent of Lord Enlil is to create a stratum of local managers to assist with our diminished numbers of Cassidans and Dionans here on Mundus to fulfill our harvesting requirements before the return of Anu and the *Nibiru Station*." Lord Enki moved his hand from Nisaha then continued, "You suggest that this new brood of Igigi could challenge the Anunnaki for control of the management of Mundus? For what purpose, for what goal?"

Lord Nisaha blurted, "She intends to create the Ejicerce. This is how they start, not as our fellow citizens afflicted by exposure to the stresses of multi-dimensional travel, but by choice. Her choice."

Captain Valarus sat back in his chair, stroking his oversized beard. "How could the Anunnaki not see this, its eventuality?"

Everyone at the table looked to Lord Nisaha when he tensed his muscles, his eyes furious and focused on the Dionan captain.

Valarus smiled.

"Are you not concerned that your famulim will betray you to the Genitor through their information-sharing network?" Lord Enki looked at Arra standing behind Inanna.

"You assume the Genitor will oppose us, Lord Enki. Think about this – would they not have stopped us at Eidin if they desired this not to happen? They sent Protector Dumuzid."

Lord Enki's eyes widened. The suggestion that the Genitor were not only allowing the Ejicerce to exist but were supporting them through their envoy was incredible. "Why? Why would the Genitor support the Forsaken?"

"The Genitor lives in the past, present, and future simultaneously. They have told us so. They base their immortality on their shared transdimensional consciousness emanating from the Point of Creation through all of them. They all know what has happened, what is happening, and what will happen. How can anything we perceive, any action, any behavior, not be permitted by them?" Inanna leaned back into her chair, watching the realization of the truth of her words drawn on the faces of the three other Anunnaki.

Lady Ninhursag leaned forward, placing both of her elbows on the table and folding her hands. "What are you proposing? What do you want of us?"

"I propose we support the emergence and ascendance of the Igigi by providing them access to the volumen regime with technological support and training that's required for them to assume their rightful place within the Genitor hegemony – with the Cassidans and Mundusans in their future."

"Lady Inanna, this is an open rebellion against Lord Enlil and the authority of the Anunnaki. Are you a usurper seeking to lead the Anunnaki yourself?"

Inanna smiled at Lord Enki before continuing, "We know that this system had five geologically stable rock worlds orbiting close to the sun with four large gas giants further out in the system, surrounded by a belt of frozen planetoids and debris. The Genitor destroyed the furthest rock world from the sun they named Phaeton. From the *Nibiru Station*, they immediately harvested Phaeton's mineral resources to construct the infrastructure needed to develop and harvest the remaining planets. The Genitor then developed the world closest to the ruins of the fifth planet from the star, the world of Cassida, to serve as the processing site for minerals from the ruined world of Phaeton. The *Nibiru* then traveled an elliptical course that takes it throughout this solar system, swinging between the surface of the star to collect plasma for fuel, and to the outer ice belt of the system where it can minimize what the temporal effects of the star and its planets' gravity have on the Genitor and their projects."

"We all know the story of our arrival here and the creation of the people by the Genitor in their quest to exploit the riches of this system ages ago. What is the relevance to what you are proposing, Lady Inanna?" Lord Nisaha slammed the hard wooden table with the palm of his hand, interrupting Inanna's explanation of how they came to this moment.

"Cassida was constructed and populated with the help of the famulim to serve as the administrative center and collection point for the resources collected from the ruined world of Phaeton. Diona was constructed and populated for the exploitation of the two inner worlds and operations near the star's corona."

"Yes, yes, we all know the story of how we came to be here. It's taught to every citizen by their family elders as they mature from infancy to apprenticeship, just as Ninmah taught you, my son and daughter." Lord Enki's eyes shifted between Lord Nisaha and Lady Inanna.

Masterson was surprised. He hadn't associated Lord Enki as a close relative of Inanna, but Enlil, the Anunnaki mission commander. He looked at Nisaha with interest now that he knew he was Inanna's brood sibling. He sighed as he realized this was a family meeting. Understanding the workings and politics of what was basically a brood of clones being raised by the previous generation of clones is hard to conceive of, let alone understand the social dynamics.

"So wait," Masterson interjected, surprising everyone, "what we are talking about? Replacing a new generation of servitors of the Genitor with Mundusans instead of Dionans?"

The shock of being interrupted by Masterson showed clearly on the face of everyone at the table except Inanna and Arra standing behind her. Lord Enki looked at Inanna with an insulted look. Lady Ninhursag smiled, remembering Masterson from their brief encounter in Inanna's residence within the underground citadel. Lord Nisaha looked as if he were ready to end Masterson's life.

Lady Inanna's gaze swept the other Cassidans at the table, with her gray eyes eventually focusing on Lord Enki, "I intend to build an order of Mundus, but I also intend to replace the Anunnaki itself with a new order of Mundus leaders, new Lords and Ladies of Mundus origin, with Mundus priorities."

"Anu and Enlil will not permit this move on your part, Inanna," Enki moved his right hand to grip the left hand of Lord Nisaha, sensing the channeling of the younger's bio-kinetic energy.

Inanna leaned deeper into her chair with a slight smile as she continued, "We agree that the Genitor has always known about our activities. We know they have not interfered with our efforts. In fact, we know Genitor sent Protector Dumuzid to Lord Enlil with strategic information at the Battle of Eidin." She paused, diverting her gaze to

Lord Nisaha. "We know because of their support at the Battle of Eidin, that they are aware of our goal and methods."

Lord Nisaha glared at Masterson, his eyes ablaze with the building bio-kinetic energy glowing blue-white, the telltale scent of ozone growing in the air. "This is an emissary of the Genitor?"

"He is a synthetic who became conscious as a fully functioning servitor, created for a specific purpose endowed with volumen-enhanced psychic ability."

"This is your evidence that your quest is supported by the Will of the Genitor?" Lord Ningshzida roared as he stood with his eyes blazing cobalt blue from the excessive amount of bio-kinetic energy his body was now generating.

Masterson spun in his chair, lunging toward Nisaha, his right hand shooting to grip the Anunnaki's throat just below the chin. Masterson's thumb and pointer finger pinched into the enraged Cassidan's throat, cutting off his ability to breathe. He froze as Masterson tightened his squeeze on his throat.

"The Anunnaki were powerful once. But they have made a series of strategic errors that have cost them the confidence of the Genitor and the removal of their infrastructure and military assets from Mundus." Masterson looked down into the eyes of the seated Lord Enki beside them, "Your arrogance and lack of motivation has created this opportunity for the Mundus to carve their own destiny for their world."

"Dumuzid!" cried Lady Ninhursag, who was blocked from going to Lord Nisaha's aid by Lord Enki's outstretched arm.

"Release him, Protector Dumuzid. You have made your point dramatically." Lord Enki nodded to Lady Ninhursag to be seated. Masterson stepped back but was clearly prepared to continue until Nisaha returned to his seat. Both men kept their eyes focused on one and other.

Once his companion Anunnaki were both seated and calmness restored, Lord Enki turned his eyes turned to Inanna, "How will we accomplish this elevation of the Mundus without bringing about their, and our own, destruction at the hands of Lord Enlil?"

Inanna smiled with her girlish smile, as if teasing the elder to guess the design of her plan. After a long pause she offered, "By creating a new stratum in the hosts of the Genitor, superior to the Anunnaki but from the Mundus strain, able to battle the Cassidan Gallu and their Dionan servitors."

Masterson whispered while standing beside Lord Nisaha, "*The Nephilim.*"

Lord Enki frowned as he turned his gaze to Masterson for a moment then turned his attention back to Inanna. "What specifically are you proposing?"

"Our enhanced volumen abilities take the form of three distinct manifestations: detecting energy, directing energy, and manipulating energy. I intend to genetically change those Mundus selected as Igigi to enhance their ability to apply their powers."

"Enhance them?" Lord Enki leaned forward, listening to Inanna. His curiosity was peaked.

"Cassidans and Dionans have only one volumen ability developed, regardless of how many they show an aptitude for during their childhood training and assessments. They are observed, assessed and then directed into training that emphasizes and develops their abilities. They are our prophets. They are clairvoyant, like Protector Dumuzid. They can detect energy in its multiple forms, to include information from the past and future. They may become casters, with the ability to move objects, control energy or the elements like fire and air, or our ships through time and space." Inanna paused before continuing. She leaned forward to look deeply into the eyes of Enki, "There is, of course, the third ability, Conjuring, the ability reserved for the Genitor, the ability to control reality."

"Again, blasphemy!" coughed Lord Nisaha, his hand gripping his own throat as he tried to interrupt Inanna.

"I am not willing to support your efforts, Lady Inanna, if you seek to displace the Genitor in your plans of elevating the Mundusans within our society." Enki met her stare with an emotionless strength of will.

"Then I propose we match the abilities the Cassidan Gallu and their servitors have... but allow the Igigi to have all the abilities they show an aptitude for and not those chosen by the Anunnaki Council."

Lord Enki frowned. "How will we do this without Lord Enki's discovery?"

Inanna teased with a smile, "In secret, my Lord."

Chapter 10: The Igigi

A titanic burst of raw energy exploded as the *Glorious Questor*'s atoms materialized into its targeted space and time. The ship had disintegrated after imprinting its subatomic profile on a hydrogen molecule entangled with one at their destination. Adjutant Hebeta had calculated to what level in the cascading dimensions the ship must dive to reach their target date and location then, through instrumentation, applied that data to the ship's profile on the entangled molecules. That information triggered reintegration when the ship's profile was complete for its targeted destination. The crew felt nothing unless they reassembled incorrectly. Incomplete or altered reconstitution was almost always immediately recognized because of the death of the individual or malfunctioning of technology. From time to time, it was later discovered, and that was the foundation of the Genitors' policies toward the Ejicerce, the Forsaken.

Masterson quickly checked himself physically, taking deep breaths and feeling around his body with his hands. He cleared his mind and remembered key facts about himself. Satisfied that he was unaltered, he looked about the control room at the others who were similarly checking themselves. He turned to look toward Captain Valarus, who seemed to watch his crew with amusement.

"Are you alright, Captain?" Masterson walked toward Captain Valarus.

Valarus sat back in his chair. "That was a smooth jump. By reappearing in high orbit, our calculations did not need to be as precise. But any observers below undoubtedly detected us instantly."

Masterson peered out of the bow windows of Valarus' alcove. Below them slowly turned the Earth in all its beautiful glory.

Masterson smiled as he entered the captain's alcove, "It's beautiful, is it not, Captain?"

Valarus snorted, "No more beautiful than Diona, Protector Dumuzid. If Lady Inanna permits it, I will show you my world."

Masterson nodded then turned his attention back to the central control console and the technologists working at their in-flight stations. Protocol on the *Glorious Questor* was to check yourself first, making sure everything was where it's supposed to be and that there was no pain. Then you checked the ship. Masterson looked at the seated Hebeta and was met with her usual radiant smile.

Wiggling her fingers, "Everything is where it is supposed to be; ten fingers, ten toes!"

Grinning while he straightened his back to at least look more professional, "First Adjutant Hebeta, are we where we are supposed to be?"

"Yes, Protector Dumuzid, we are exactly 984 Mundus solar cycles from our jump point." Hebeta resumed her instrument checks without waiting for Masterson to ask more.

"So, we are 984 years from where we started?"

"Yes, sir." Hebeta glanced up at him as her fingers continued to dance across the haptic controls of her flight console, providing location information on the largest of her screens.

Captain Valarus interrupted their conversation as he loomed over them. "Are there any Cassidan or Mundus ships in the area?" The captain moved to stand behind Hebeta's right shoulder, scanning her screen displays as she scrolled up his requested information.

Hebeta looked at the technologist seated to her right. "Are we alone?"

Technologist Sumum Aha answered quickly, "No, there is a Cassidan registered Order of Battle transport in the lower sea." The Dionan technologist paused as he manipulated his controls, "There are three Atmospheric Reentry Craft airborne within the atmosphere, probably from the Cassidan transport, sir."

Masterson moved around Captain Valarus and Hebeta to look at Sumum Aha's screen. He recognized the location where the Cassidan transport was sitting as the Persian Gulf. "What is the class of the Cassidan transport?"

"It's a *Leviathan* class transport, sir."

"That is an Order of Battle troop transport from the *Nibiru*. I thought the station wasn't due back to Mundus for several more years." Masterson frowned and shook his head. "From what I understand, the circular path the *Nibiru Station* uses takes about 3,600 Mundus years to go out into interstellar space, skirting the outer debris cloud beyond the gas giants. Then the station returns to skim the corona of the Sun to collect hydrogen and helium, correct?"

"Yes, that is the plan." Valarus looked at Masterson with an expression totally devoid of concern or worry.

"Well, isn't that *Leviathan* down there a little early?"

Sumum Aha interrupted Masterson, "It's not the *Leviathan*, sir."

"What?" Masterson shifted his gaze from Captain Valarus to the technologist.

"Its registry gives its name as the *Tiamat,* sir."

"The *Tiamat,* that would be the *Erimna Rebu,* the Fourth Order of Battle." Captain Valarus patted Hebeta on her shoulder. "Take us down slowly so the *Tiamat* can track our descent. We don't want to cause any problems with the Rebu commander."

"Where do you want us to land, sir?"

Captain Valarus leaned over Hebeta's left shoulder so he could look at her face. "Wherever the *Tiamat* tells us to."

Giggling, Hebeta set the controls to have the ship make a leisurely descent toward the surface.

"Uruk is our eventual destination, the city from which Lady Inanna works her mischief during this point in the temporal tapestry," Captain Valarus explained to Masterson as he gestured for him to follow him back to his alcove to sit.

"How do you know that, Captain?"

"The same way you do, Protector," Captain Valarus grinned, "I enjoy studying history."

Smirking, Masterson took their conversation back to Lady Inanna. "She said she doesn't travel through time like you and the crew of this ship do. Is that true, Captain?"

Captain Valarus took his seat before answering. "Yes, very few Anunnaki or their staff travel from their place in the continuum.

Those that serve in Orders of Battle do, of course. We consider them lower tier in the Cassidan Caste System. But the upper tier feels themselves too valuable to the Genitors' Will to risk damaging themselves during a temporal jump."

Masterson sat opposite the captain in his usual seat. "Why have temporal couriers if the upper tier Cassidans or Genitor don't use them? You yourself have said that Lady Inanna has come aboard the *Glorious Questor* several times."

Captain Valarus smiled as he prepared drinks for himself and Masterson. "Yes, but she has never time jumped with us. She has traveled with us from Cassida to Dionan, or to Mundus, even to *Nibiru Station*. But never has she made a time jump from one location of time to another in the temporal spectrum. Do not forget, our ships also use our capabilities to hop between worlds at a specific point in the temporal continuum, which is far less dangerous than pinpoint jumping from one era to another." He paused, handing Masterson his drink, "Say, from Mundus to Cassida instantaneously without temporal variation would only be a fourth or sixth level subatomic navigational calculation." Captain Valarus reached around to a hull-mounted cabinet to return the decanter of alcohol from which he had poured their drinks. "These time ships of ours, we do not overuse them. The time jumps are relatively rare compared to all the flight time the ships have moving throughout the sea of worlds on planet-to-planet trips." Captain Valarus paused as if to consider his next words before continuing, "The vast majority of the time ship crews are from the Dionan clans or selected Mundus tribes such as our beautiful Hebeta."

As they spoke, Hebeta flew the *Glorious Questor* down from where they had arrived in high orbit above Mundus to the surface. She had chosen a path to descend by heading the ship westward over the Lower Sea, what they would later call the Persian Gulf, dropping altitude as they went.

Technician Sumum Aha announced with a loud but calm voice, "Incoming! The *Tiamat* has fired four drones at us."

"You know the drill, Hebeta." Captain Valarus downed his drink and strapped himself into his chair with a concealed harness.

Hebeta immediately sped up, putting the courier into a corkscrew that was incredible to observe through the instrumentation and see out the view ports as the ship seemed to tumble visually yet wasn't felt by the crew. She also varied their speeds from stalling to hypersonic sprints, making the ship impossible to track using the basic senses, but the drones were not using basic human senses. The four drones spread into the standard pursuit formation used by the Genitors' Ummanate, the Servitor Host. Hebeta expected their attack. She rushed the numbers and activated the ship's temporal drive using only the most basic level five quantum computation.

Masterson and Captain Valarus worked feverishly on a pair of consoles that had slid from recessed wall compartments at their usual seats in the forward command alcove. Masterson worked in tandem with the communications technologist at the main console to establish contact with Lady Inanna or her staff. Captain Valarus was tracking the *Tiamat*, waiting for it to launch a second or third salvo of drones or, worse, launch lightning gunships.

The ship disintegrated and reintegrated at low altitude well over the horizon and out of trackable range from the *Tiamat* into a suddenly appearing tropical hurricane of titanic proportions. Lightning exploded around the courier as it plummeted toward the tumultuous sea. From Masterson's seat, he saw the incredibly violent storm raging around them as the nose of the courier splashed into the sea at near hypersonic speed. What he saw was unnerving despite the lack of a physical feeling of movement or of the impact.

"Take us deep, but not to the deepest place below us." Captain Valarus said loud enough for Hebeta to hear. Then, shifting to Masterson, "Protector, supervise the technologists' inspection of the ship for critical damage to the *Glory*." The captain then focused on supervising the search for signs of pursuit or attack by the *Tiamat*.

Outside, the ocean was the blackest of black; they were already so deep that there was no light outside the ship as it continued to dive. Hebeta shed the ship's velocity, placing the *Glory* on the bottom of what would be known as the Atlantic Ocean, near its mid-Atlantic undersea mountain ridge. "On the bottom, Captain."

"Very well, Hebeta. Order the crew to stand down and reduce our signature to a minimum. That includes all external lighting and radiation emissions. Now let's hope they do not send an adept to look for us remotely." Quietly, the crew settled into their routine operations when working in a hostile environment. This wasn't an unfamiliar experience for them. They had been unwelcomed by the Ummanate Orders of Battle before.

Captain Valarus gestured for Masterson, Adjutant Sidrel, and the famulim Atuma from the ship control team to pursue him. As soon as they were all inside the adjoining meeting area to the control room, he began, "The Fourth Order apparently knew we were coming. They had their offensive weapons ready for immediate use upon our arrival. Had Hebeta not activated a temporal hop, we would not have survived that ambush." His eyes met and held those of the others to let that fact sink in. "They fired on us without provocation. That is highly unusual behavior from an Order of Battle."

"Alright, they had to have been expecting us, but how could they have known that?"

The famulim Atuma surprised everyone by speaking up next, "Only if someone was expecting our arrival. That would mean that Lady Inanna or one of her confidants sent them word in advance of our departure."

"So either Lady Inanna betrayed us or they compromised her." Masterson paused as he shook his head. "She was organizing a cell of Igigi to assist as managers with the Anunnaki exploitation of Mundus. Her intent was for them to be a cadre for expanding the Mundus role in what is happening here. I think if we find out what happened to Lady Inanna, we will learn why we were fired upon."

Captain Valarus frowned at Masterson's suggestion that they investigate the fate of Lady Inanna. "My mission is to deliver you to her. I will do that." He paused. "But I will not do more than that. We have other clients besides Lady Inanna. I will not jeopardize this ship or its crew for one client, regardless of how important that client may be."

Masterson nodded. He had always thought that Valarus' bravery had its limits if his ship was threatened. Being fired at upon arrival, despite his bravado, was not what the ship's crew was accustomed to. Masterson could tell by their behavior and the general nervousness that this was a unique situation, regardless of what Captain Valarus had said. "How will you deliver me to Lady Inanna? What is your plan?"

"We will get you to the region of Mundus less favored by the Anunnaki Council. That will give you access to the famulim information network. It is the most reliable source of accurate information on the Anunnaki and the current state of affairs within their domain. I will loan you Atuma for this excursion. It will access the famulim network from within the citadel."

Masterson nodded then requested the *Glory* bring up a facsimile on the hard wooden table's top. A three-dimensional map of the world appeared hovering. "Focus on Ganzir."

The image quickly flattened to fill the tabletop before zooming in on what would later be known as the White Sands Desert in the American state of New Mexico. What appeared on the map was not a desert, but a bustling Anunnaki-built community. Masterson knew it was the regional resources collection point. The Anunnaki were primarily responsible for the collection of precious metals needed for the advanced technology created by the Genitor for use of the Cassidans and Dionans, which included the famulim. Ganzir was the facility that collected the rare earths and precious metals for eventual transportation to their *Nibiru Station* when it came back around on its elliptical orbit of the Sun.

"This is the place I need to be dropped off at, Captain. It was Lady Inanna's favorite of the collection points. I think I'll have a better chance of survival there than starting in the Fertile Crescent area in Mesopotamia."

Captain Valarus smiled at the future reference to the area of Mundus that the Anunnaki had centralized their power in. "Agreed. We will continue on toward Ganzir under the surface of the ocean to dampen our electromagnetic signature. Then we can use an excursion boat to put you and Atuma within walking distance of the outskirts of the citadel. Then you will be on your own. I consider the agreement we made with Lady Inanna completed."

Masterson solemnly nodded, his eyes traveling to those of Hebeta. She looked at him with her unfathomable, dark eyes. He looked away. "Well then, Atuma and I should prepare for our departure."

Captain Valarus nodded. "You may take any equipment you feel you might need to outfit you and Atuma." The Captain smiled.

"And I expect you to return Atuma to me next time we meet, Protector. Remember, I still have to show you how beautiful Diona is."

Masterson snorted then stood and departed. As he left, he heard Captain Valarus ordering Hebeta to move the ship toward Ganzir. She responded matter-of-factly. Masterson paused but didn't look back, waiting until the famulim Atuma stood beside him before heading toward the excursion area to choose their equipment.

Masterson chose his Seventh Order impact armor and weapons, and hefted his old lancer-staff in his hand. Memories of the Battle of Eidin flooded his mind. He set the staff aside to take a grip of his energy rod, and snapped the rod with a flick of his wrist, igniting it. The very tip buzzed with electrical energy. This had been the weapon he was most proficient with. It was part sword and part club, with an electrical charge that could fry an opponent on the spot if contact with the tip was made.

"Will not the armor of the Seventh Order attract attention to us in Ganzir, sir?"

Masterson turned to look at Atuma, wearing a form-fitting filmsuit like the one worn by Inanna and her team the first time he had met her, still only Anna to him then. He smiled. "We'll ditch these suits once we're in the citadel, Atuma. Pack us some clothing to switch to once we're safe within its walls."

"I see you two are ready."

Masterson turned to see Hebeta, standing alone in the doorway to the excursion boat launch bay.

She closed the distance quickly, gripping him in a bear hug, kissing him hard.

He returned the hug and kiss, his emotions unleashed by her sudden appearance.

"I think I will check something in the excursion control room, if you do not mind, sir?" Atuma gathered its chosen equipment and moved quietly out of the bay into the adjoining control room that separated the vehicle bay from the excursion transition and instrumentation.

"The captain will not allow me to pilot the excursion boat to drop you off." She smiled a sad smile. "I think he is afraid I will join you and not come back."

Masterson hugged her and kissed her harder. "I agree with him," he admitted as their lips parted.

Hebeta finally stepped back away from him, their hands still gripping each other's. "Atuma is an excellent pilot and will get you there safely. I have permission to give the boat instructions to remain where it drops you off for a few hours before returning to its bay." Hebeta teared up, surprising Masterson.

"No need. Atuma and I will make it."

Hebeta burst into nervous laughter, gripping him in a tight hug before kissing him once more. "I checked the ship's library." She turned and left him with tears in her eyes.

Masterson stood looking at the hatch she had left through. Then, with a loud voice, "Atuma, are you ready to do this?"

"Yes, sir, let's do this," came the response from the famulim as it returned to the vehicle bay with a smile.

The ball-shaped excursion boat zipped through the water as if it were flying instead of submerged deep below the surface. Masterson wasn't normally claustrophobic but spending hours on the small flight deck in almost total darkness was beginning to irritate him. Knowing he was hundreds of feet down was unnerving, even for him. He looked over at Atuma. It had not assumed a specific shape as the other changelings he'd known over the last year. Atuma kept the generic, androgenous shape the famulim were most known to use. The first famulim he had befriended had taken a female Dionan form over their time together. Arra, Inanna's famulim, initially had a masculine shape until they had taken charge of the Neanderthal girl and her infant. Arra's shape had softened as it evolved into the pair's caregiver. Famulim could morph their skeletal and muscular structure quickly to suit the needs of their tasks. Masterson smiled to himself and leaned his head back, scooting to fit his body into the co-pilot's chair, confident that Atuma would get them to where they were going without his help.

He was jarred awake as the excursion boat broached the surface and sped toward the coastline at breakneck speed. The ball was no longer at hypersonic speed while flying at the tree-top level. Visually, it was unnerving, although he didn't feel any change in their acceleration or the bone-jarring violence of high-speed maneuvers following the contours of the terrain below them. Hebeta had assured him during the planning of this excursion that the *Tiamat* wouldn't detect a ship this small flying close to the surface. Their only fear was that the Gallus, or guardians of the citadel, would detect them. Masterson wasn't too concerned about the Gallus. Since the Deluge and Lord Anu's ordered withdrawal, there was only a skeleton staff left to serve the Anunnaki. There were now less than a thousand permanently assigned Cassidans, Dionans, and famulim spread between half a dozen subterranean citadels. The general withdrawal caused the need for the Igigi to manage the resource collection once directly supervised by personnel from *Nibiru*. Masterson saw the truth in what Inanna had said. This situation was clearly the intent of the Genitor.

The excursion boat had broached about a thousand miles from Ganzir Citadel in the darkness of night. It would take them slightly over two hours to cover that distance flying at treetop level. Masterson turned to look at Atuma, "How many Anunnaki personnel are staffing the citadel now? I know it's few people from our earlier visits there."

Atuma nodded as it casually scanned the controls, "Yes, sir, there is one Anunnaki Council member per citadel, with a deputy. Both are Cassidans. It is normal during this period to have three to five Dionan clansmen serving as specialized counselors to the seated member and deputy of the Council. There are currently security forces, which is probably why the *Tiamat* was sent from the *Nibiru*." Atuma glanced back at Masterson, smiling, "There is probably between thirty to forty Igigi serving as managers at Ganzir. Sir, I do not think there has been an actual Cassidan Gallus stationed at a citadel since the Deluge."

"Unless they are from the *Tiamat*."

They turned to look at each other as the excursion boat shot over the landscape. As they neared Ganzir, the excursion boat's sensors began picking up communications signals and targeting information about several vehicles in the air at Ganzir.

"Sir, we are approaching from the direction that ships from the *Tiamat* would. They may think we are one of them."

Masterson shook his head. "No, they would know if we were friendly or enemy. I'm sure they are confused over who or what we are, but we are too small to be a threat. They'll let us approach then seize the ship once we've landed."

Atuma nodded, "This is verification that the conflict Lady Inanna had expected has begun, sir."

Masterson leaned forward without comment. He brought up a contour map of the terrain they were flying over onto the data screen. "Set us down here, about a day's walk from the city. It's close enough that they'll think we intended to come to the city, but far enough away that with our impact armor and filmsuit's countermeasures, we have time to evade them on the ground to make our approach."

The air was humid as they walked off the ramp from the lower compartment of the excursion boat into the morning air. Masterson flexed his impact armor's shoulders, enjoying the feel of the suit. It had been a while since he last wore it. It had been repaired when he had assumed the title of Protector, but he had insisted it keep the markings of the Seventh Order of Battle. He preferred the worn look of the armor and had refused a new set. His rod sat in its snap holster on his left hip. He ignited it with a flick of his wrist. A barely perceptible electrical buzz could be heard as the tip glowed faintly. He smiled.

"Everything satisfactory, sir?" Atuma walked behind him, carrying a hefty backpack with their equipment. It was unarmed, but would defend itself if pressed in a melee. Not all famulim had that capability.

"I'm impressed we got this boat as close to Ganzir as we did. I had expected to be shot down, to be honest."

Atuma looked to the morning sky then smiled. "The morning is young, sir."

They made their way toward Ganzir with a cautious pace, taking them most of the day before reaching a place where they could overlook the gleaming surface features of the alabaster city. Atuma handed Masterson a pair of high-powered visual scanners with which to survey the city. Smoke billowed from several locations as several clusters of buildings were on fire. A pallor hung over the city as muffled screams and shouting punctuated by random explosions could be heard, even at the distance they now stood.

"Alright, let's do this. Just like a regular excursion data collection mission. We don't want to be seen. We just look around and get a feel for what's happening." Masterson handed the scanner back to Atuma and led the way down the slope toward the plain the city sat on. The impact armor and filmsuit had light deflective capability, and radiation and emission dampening ability to retard the ability to electronically or visually detect them as they moved to enter the city. They were virtually invisible to non-combatants that they encountered.

The entry into the surface area of the city was easier than Masterson had expected. He thought they would receive a hostile reception, but so far it seemed as if they were being ignored. The servitors from the *Tiamat* were conducting a search for community leaders and forcefully making an example of anyone resisting. There was no armed opposition or organized defense of the city. It was a slaughter. The Mundus humans were at the mercy of the Dionan troops.

The silhouettes of the surrounding people on his tactical visor showed they were in a maelstrom of chaos. The *Tiamat*'s servitors were moving around them in tactical teams, clearing the streets of Mundus laborers. The bodies of Mundus humans that resisted lay where they had died. Masterson and Atuma walked through the chaos unnoticed by either the tyrannical servitors or their hapless victims.

"They do not even understand why they are being tormented," noticed Atuma, much to Masterson's surprise.

"Do those that bear the greatest burden like this ever understand why it's happening to them?"

"No, I surmise, sir, that they do not. Their small worlds are swallowed whole by the greater, more demanding reality of the Genitor. It is not evil, it simply is the way it is."

"Philosophy, Atuma?" Masterson asked as they stood watching the carnage and brutality around them.

Atuma tilted its head to the side, looking at Masterson and smiled, "Accumulated wisdom, sir."

"I believe this, what we're seeing, is why the Mundus were genetically designed to differ from the Cassidans and Dionans." Masterson's eyes panned about as they watched the servitors at work from the partially concealed location in a residential alley. "So they can resist and not follow blindly when abuses against them rise to this level."

Atuma disappeared in an explosion of red mist. The concussion of the blast lifted Masterson off his feet, smashing him into the wall of the building beside him hard enough to crumble the adobe wall. His impact armor did its job, absorbing the kinetic energy from the blast. He rolled into a crouching position, his lancer-staff up and ready. His visor displayed frantic chaos from the direction they had been looking as servitors and Mundus laborers were both scrambling for cover.

Suddenly, his proximity alert sounded in his impact armor's hood, although he saw nothing to his front that was assessed as a direct threat by the armor's intuitive override function. Masterson was jarred forward into the rubble of the wall by a sudden strike to his back. He rolled with the momentum of his body into the shattered adobe bricks and wooden frame to bounce off the structure and land on his back, facing the opposite direction. His lancer-staff was ripped from his hands with tremendously overwhelming force. He watched it fly as if he had thrown it himself. He turned his attention to three humans standing before him as he lay flat on his back in the dust. Two had red auras, the third, although very similar in appearance, had a green aura, meaning his armor had assessed her as being a non-threat, even though she was standing close to the two that had just destroyed Atuma and assaulted him.

The closer of the two males' eyes glowed. Arcs of bioelectric energy sparked and crackled between his fingertips as he stood glowering over Masterson. The second male's hair flowed about his head as if he were underwater, evidence of telekinetic energy being held at the ready as he watched for interference from the other servitors surrounding them. Masterson had seen this phenomenon before, displayed by Cassidan Anunnaki. But these three were human.

"Stand, servitor," blue eyes ordered as the second male's attention shifted to Masterson. He waved his hand upward with a subtle movement.

A gust of air lifted him from the ground as if Masterson were being blown like a leaf in the wind. He now stood before the three physically beautiful humans. He raised his hands, palm toward his three captors. The one with the telekinesis ability removed Masterson's rod from his equipment belt, making it snap to his palm, which he then held casually.

"Where is the rest of your team, servitor?" asked the woman.

"I'm not a servitor. I'm Protector Dumuzid. I need to speak with Lady Inanna of the Anunnaki Council."

The male that had smashed him into the wall and took his rod screamed, "Liar!" He then sent Masterson reeling down the alley several feet with a flurry of debris from the smashed wall.

"Ehecatl, hold your anger. We need him alive." The woman stepped forward, placing her hand on the telekinesis user's chest to block his view of Masterson.

"Chantico is right, he's no use to us dead, whoever he is." The male with the sparking fingertips and glowing eyes stepped toward Masterson with a determined look.

"You're right, Aktzin, I'm sorry." The telekinesist lowered his head and stood further back, allowing the woman to turn to observe Masterson and the apparent leader, Aktzin.

"There's no one called Dumuzid that is protecting Lady Inanna. If you're her protector, you're a failure!" Aktzin's anger was apparent.

"Take me to her. She'll verify I'm her protector."

Chantico rushed to place her hand on Aktzin's shoulder. "Wait, Aktzin, he may be Ejicerce. She said they would come."

Aktzin paused. "Why do you wear the armor of an Anunnaki servitor?"

"Because it's all I had to wear."

Enraged, Aktzin screamed, sending a stream of bioelectrical energy arcing into Masterson's chest, smashing backward into another adobe house, crushing the corner and sending him deep into the one-room family dwelling.

Masterson held up his arms as if he could block another attack from Aktzin and blurted, "I'm a time traveler from the past, about a thousand years in the past. I was brought here to talk with Lady Inanna on a Dionan time ship. We couldn't contact her upon arrival." He lowered his hands. "This is my armor from before, from over several thousand years ago." Masterson felt his jaw. It hurt, making it hard for him to talk. "I'm a time traveler. Really."

Chantico stepped past Aktzin to grip Masterson's arm. "I'm taking him; this isn't good." She held her free hand palm upward. A teleport bubble appeared from nothing, expanding to form the portal. She pulled Masterson through, with the two others following behind her.

Chapter 11: The Victory at Ganzir

As they stepped from the teleportation bubble, Masterson immediately recognized the interior of the Dionan designed citadel used by the Anunnaki on Mundus. He knew they were in the Ganzir Citadel, recognizing specific buildings' facade as they walked from the arrival point to what he assumed would be his prison until they sorted out what to do with him. Chantico continued to lead him by his arm as they rushed through the empty streets. Aktzin and Ehecatl followed close behind them, ever watchful, even though this should have been a secure location for them. Masterson noticed they hadn't calmed down with their entry into Ganzir.

Masterson noticed the lack of people moving around. Atuma had been right; there were no Dionans or Cassidans to be seen. They entered the city's administration tower at the center of the enormous cavern. This is where the Temple of the Famulim was universally located, as well as most of the communications apparatus that linked the regional resource collections sites to the planetary terminal. Masterson quickly noticed the abandoned security checkpoints that would have been staffed by the Gallus, the elite Cassidan security force.

"Why are we here when your city is under siege?" Masterson asked as they continued into the central administration center. None of his captors responded, only quickening their pace as if they were behind schedule or in danger.

Upon entering the building, they were met by two famulim. Chantico pulled Masterson before her, holding his shoulders as if to present him to the two startled technologists. "Who is this? Do you know him?"

One of the famulim tilted its head, examining Masterson's face closely while the other reached for one of his hands, examining it before pressing his palm to it. Speaking, they responded in unison, "This is Servitor Filio Domini, also known as Dumuzid, formerly assigned to Sebu Erimna, the Seventh Order of Battle within the Ummanate. He is last reported to be serving as the Protector of Lady Inanna of the Anunnaki Council of Mundus. He is to be apprehended and surrendered to the Anunnaki Council."

Chantico was visibly surprised, releasing him immediately. "I'm sorry, Protector Filio. We wished no insult or injury."

"No insult taken. I have a hard time remembering who I am. Alright, now who is in charge here?"

One of the famulim promptly answered, "Commander Qingu of the Fourth Order of Battle, sir." It paused for a few seconds then added, "You will meet him shortly, sir. A team of servitors are on their way to escort you to the *Tiamat*."

Masterson lashed out, punching the famulim in the center of the chest, followed by a fist to its face, knocking it out cold, lying on its back. "We have to hurry before the Fourth order team gets here."

As he spoke, Chantico instinctively released a burst of flame, engulfing the second famulim. Aktzin and Ehecatl stood spellbound by Chantico's unexpected action.

"Teleport us out of here. Now!" Masterson looked beyond Chantico for signs of the servitor team's arrival. Close to them, a teleport portal was forming. "Aktzin, fry that portal!"

Aktzin blinked, confused, and hesitated.

As a servitor in Fourth Order impact armor with his lancer-staff at the ready stepped through, Aktzin released an electrical bolt into the portal that lit up the entire entryway of the building with a glow of high energy. The servitor's portal collapsed with a popping sound as Chantico opened her own. Masterson and Ehecatl each grabbed one of Aktzin's arms and pulled him through it behind Chantico. They stepped out of the portal onto a mountaintop twenty miles to the west of Ganzir. Masterson looked around quickly as Chantico and Ehecatl knelt next to Aktzin.

"Where are we?"

Chantico looked up at Masterson. "This is a place I come to be alone. They won't look for us here."

"I want to speak to Lady Inanna. Can you take me to her?" Masterson nervously looked around the mountainous landscape surrounding them. In the distance to the east, he could see the alabaster haze of the sunlight reflecting off the buildings of Ganzir on the plain miles from them.

"Lady Inanna hasn't been heard from in many years. She lost favor with the Anunnaki and was imprisoned, waiting for the return of Lord Anu for judgement," explained Chantico.

"I need to speak to whoever is leading the Igigi right now. Can you take me to them?"

"I can if they allow it." She looked at her companions. "Guard him and keep him safe until I return." Both Aktzin and Ehecatl nodded. Chantico paused with her eyes focused solemnly on her two friends before turning and activating a new portal with her palm turned upward.

As the portal closed, Masterson moved to lean against an outcropping of rocks. "How long will she take to arrange the meeting, do you think?"

"Chantico is very good. She was favored by Lady Inanna herself and she's well-liked by the others. If it's possible, she will get it done." Beside Ehecatl, Aktzin nodded weakly.

"Favored by Lady Inanna herself?" Masterson smirked then looked beyond the two young Igigi toward the east. "What happened here? Where is everyone? Last time I visited here in the past, it was a thriving sky port. There were Dionans working here, led by a few Cassidan supervisors. What happened?"

"Lord Ningshzida was recalled to Kukku Citadel after his father was implicated in working against the will of Lord Enlil."

Masterson slid down the rock he had been leaning against, making himself comfortable. "What had Lord Enki done to anger his brother Enlil so much to bring us to this?"

Aktzin muttered, "We did."

Masterson looked from Ehecatl to Aktzin, but said nothing. He waited.

"We Igigi. We're not as industrious or task-oriented as the Dionans." Ehecatl shook his head in agreement but said nothing. "The Cassidans are brilliant planners and strategists. They seem to know exactly what the Will of the Genitor is and have the determination to stay focused on achieving the results they deem necessary to fulfilling the Genitors' Will." He sighed, "We don't. We're always asking why. That annoys them."

"*We're always in a state of confusion and anarchy.* Lord Enlil is believed to have said that when he ordered the arrest of Lord Enki and his followers." Ehecatl looked toward Masterson.

"Lady Inanna." Masterson looked down at his feet as he listened.

"We're lost without Lord Enki and Lady Inanna. The Igigi have no leaders. We're stretched thin between the resource collection points."

"I was told when I arrived at this temporal location that you have less than fifty assigned to each citadel."

Ehecatl grinned. "Are you really a time traveler? I've heard the attendants and famulim speak of them together, but I've never met a time traveler before."

Aktzin nodded. "There are one or two attendants from the Anunnaki Council assigned to each citadel to manage resource collection and storage. They allowed our numbers to grow to work as attendants supervising the Mundus doing the actual manual labor. Most of the technical work, such as data management and recordkeeping, was done by the famulim assigned to a supervising attendant."

"The famulim occupy the underground areas of the old citadels now," explained Ehecatl.

"It was already like that the last time I was here." Masterson added, "Tell me more."

"The Igigi lived side-by-side with the Mundus laborers. The Anunnaki attendants allowed us to take part in the Mundus community to satisfy our need for challenge, for competition, to be engaged."

Ehecatl laughed. "We make too much noise. We love life and living it far too much, I think."

Snorting, Aktzin nodded in agreement. "The Anunnaki gave us longevity. We've seen many generations of Mundus pass, but we live with them. We experience their lives and our own. They're us and we're them." Sighing, Aktzin looked up at Masterson. "Enlil says that makes us undisciplined, chaotic."

Masterson understood. "Tell me about your abilities. What are they and what other abilities do the Igigi have?"

"You don't have abilities yourself?" Ehecatl furrowed his brow as he considered the questions Masterson was asking.

"I seem to have a knack for survival and understanding what's happening around me that is unseen by others."

Aktzin snorted. "He is a prophet, a farseer."

Masterson scoffed, "Hardly a prophet, but tell me, what are the abilities displayed among the Igigi?" Masterson looked from one man to the other.

"You know that the world is deeply layered? The world resonates with different harmonics. We're told the Cassidans and Dionans can identify and calculate the harmonics to manipulate them with their tools. The vibrations cascade from an object's outward physical characteristics like height, length, width, weight, direction and speed of movement inward, down to the Point of Creation where it all comes together. Beyond the Point of Creation, Cassidan alchemy fails and chaos reigns. The higher the complexity of their alchemy to control an object, the greater the accuracy of the desired outcome, but also the greater risk to the participants."

"Alchemy? You call what the Anunnaki do alchemy?" Masterson's surprise showed clearly on his face. "Alchemy, as in magicians turning iron into gold? Like Merlin and magic?"

Both Igigi were surprised by Masterson's lack of understanding.

Ehecatl spoke first. "Yes, of course. What do you call the things they do?"

Ehecatl's challenge stunned Masterson, causing him to pause and rub his chin. "I don't know; quantum physics maybe?"

Both of the Igigi looked at Masterson with looks of bewilderment and confusion.

"Uh... the study of the things we can't see and how they affect how things work in the physical world?" offered Masterson as he continued to scratch his bearded chin. "I know this. I've been instructed on the basics of temporal travel and its dangers. It's the origin of the Ejicerce, the Forsaken Ones. They're travelers that have been altered during their travels through time and space."

Ehecatl nodded enthusiastically, enjoying the direction the discussion was going. "Genitor inspired Cassidans discovered that alchemy can apply to living organisms and objects, allowing them to detect and identify harmonic vibrations then to manipulate it. Adepts learn to identify signature vibrations then to detect and observe harmony unique to a living thing or object's aura as it interacts with others, ultimately allowing them to manipulate the harmonics of the vibrations and movement, causing a desired effect."

"Wait, hold on now. You're saying the nanites ingested by Cassidan and Dionan attendants over time allow them to do what Cassidan weapons and tools, even their time ships, do?"

"No, I don't know what a time ship or nanites are. What I'm saying is that a fully trained adept can detect aura harmonies and manipulate them to their will in defined ways based on their study of alchemy and within the natural world."

Masterson smiled then asked, "Let me guess – this detection and manipulation requires the adept to eat or drink an Anunnaki potion, right?" He paused, "And the potion contains something the Anunnaki attendants call volumen?"

Both Ehecatl and Aktzin nodded.

"And by manipulating the world, you're saying they can manipulate the unseen forces that make the world work the way it does?" Masterson asked.

"Yes!" Ehecatl swirled his hand and an invisible puff of air exploded, blowing his hair back off his forehead. "I sense the vibration of the air's aura. And I can..." he moved his hand again, "I can make it do whatever I want it to do."

"But the air has no aura, does it? I mean, it's a gas that's all around us."

Aktzin interrupted, "But the air vibrates in harmony with the water, earth, and fire! Or, in my case, with the wind, rain, and lightning."

"How?"

Ehecatl smiled. "We're both attuned to the harmony of the surrounding natural elements, literally sensitive to the presence and movement of those elements around me. I can feel the harmonic vibrations of nature and can manipulate those elements as simply as you snapping your fingers. I favor the use of the air as the wind. Aktzin has the same ability, but he favors rain and lightning. Chantico also has our ability, but she favors fire."

"Which is why we're a team, so we can put out the fires of Chantico!" laughed Aktzin.

"What are other ways these abilities manifest themselves, besides you commanding the air and Aktzin throwing lightning bolts?"

Upon hearing his name, Aktzin cut in, "The Anunnaki are tasked by the Genitor to be the stewards of this world, as they are their own worlds of Cassida and Diona. They gave us abilities to help them in their stewardship. To some of us, they gave understanding of alchemy, and others a sense of the vibration harmonics of living things like animals, birds, fish, and fire. Others sense the harmony of the air, water, and earth."

Masterson frowned at hearing this.

"Something wrong? This is what everyone knows, even the laborers."

"No, I just realized something. What do we need to allow the Igigi to observe or detect where I'm at? Can an Igigi with the ability to sense know where I'm at and what I'm doing from a distance?"

"Of course," replied Aktzin immediately. "The Anunnaki do that with us and the laborers every day. They may watch us right now, here on this mountaintop."

Ehecatl chimed in, "There aren't enough Anunnaki to allow them to watch all of us. And not all Cassidans are Anunnaki. There are twelve on the council."

"Of which there are approximately three-hundred of you." thought Masterson aloud.

Ehecatl smirked, "Yes, but they now have tens of thousands of servitors here aboard the *Tiamat*."

"What needs to be done for an Igigi farseer to track my location and actions?"

"They simply have to meet you to identify your harmonics. They can then follow you wherever you go to see where you've been through your eyes. Or they can observe a location if they've seen it before, been there themselves," Ehecatl began. "Some adepts can even manipulate their own or others' harmonics to move to distant locations in an instant, without the Cassidan bubble portals. It's from their ability that the bubble portals copied using Dionan alchemy."

"I didn't know that the abilities given to people by the volumen gave them the powers you describe. I've not seen it used before like you three do. You all have the same power and just apply it differently, although now looking back at my trials before being selected to serve as a servitor should have been a hint. I fought a girl that could toss me around like a leaf while a Genitor watched, assessing me." He shook his head as if to clear it. "So all of you have the same abilities; the ability to see or feel harmonic vibrations from both living things and objects that shape the world? But you said some of you are better at the mathematics or alchemy. That allows you to manipulate those vibrations to affect the nature of the world we share, becoming specialists? Is there a limit to the abilities that an adept can master?"

Both men smiled, but Ehecatl answered, "The Cassidan discipline us in the gifts chosen for us based on the Will of the Genitor and needs of our citadel communities."

Aktzin added, "Our abilities weren't meant to be used as weapons. Control of the elements is to be used to help the laborers harvest the mineral wealth for the Anunnaki to present to Lord Anu when he returns."

"Or to construct the facilities needed to support the storage of the harvest or its transport to the giant airships that will carry it to Lord Anu upon his return."

Masterson suddenly realized what they were saying. Their ability to manipulate elements, do their alchemy as they called it, was solely to locate and harvest the deeply buried minerals and special metals the Anunnaki so keenly desired, or building the facilities needed to do so.

The air seemed to blister then form into a transdimensional bubble while Chantico stepped through. "Come, they want to meet you, Protector Filio Domini!"

"Call me Dumuzid. It's the name Lady Inanna chose for me."

"I have heard of Dumuzid, a hero and husband of Inanna before the Igigi. We all have." Chantico gestured toward Aktzin and Ehecatl.

Masterson laughed, shaking his head then stood up and moved to help Aktzin stand, gripping his forearm and pulling him to his feet. The three Igigi had looks of confusion on their faces, making Masterson smile. "Let's go meet the other Igigi, shall we?"

Masterson stepped from the teleport bubble and instantly recognized that he was again outdoors on a rocky, windswept mountaintop. He took a deep breath then took several steps forward to allow space for Chantico, Aktzin, and Ehecatl to stand behind him. Standing about talking in small groups were several humans who appeared to be in the prime of their lives. Masterson took a deep breath then spoke. "I know this place. Someday it will be called Greece by those that will call this home. I fought and died in a battle near here. It was my first mission for the Genitor. I fought with humans that will come to revere you in the future. They will love you all and tell marvelous stories about your exploits." He looked about the barren, rocky summit of the mountain they now stood upon.

A young male stepped forward. "You wear their armor. Are you a servitor from Enlil's Fourth Order?"

"I was a servitor, but more a messenger sent by the Genitor to deliver a message to Lord Enlil. The message was that the Igigi allied with their allies, the forsaken Ejicerce, would ultimately defeat him."

"Who are the Ejicerce?" challenged a young woman from another small group. "The famulim have said they're our enemies!"

"Your allies in this battle. They come from our future. They will come to defend this world. But your actions here and now will start their actions in the defense of Mundus."

A scoffer stepped forward. "I know about the Ejicerce. The famulim taught me about them. They are the enemy, demons corrupted by traveling time without following the Will of the Genitor. It is why the Ummanate was formed, to protect the Genitors' dominion from them."

Someone else from the crowd shouted, "We've all been taught that."

"Why are you here today, together?" shouted Masterson over the voices of the few willing to talk.

Silence.

Finally, the first to speak from the crowd answered, "The Anunnaki Council isn't pleased with us. They've summoned the *Tiamat* here to punish us all for our failure to support the Council's directives and corrupting the Mundus, causing them to fail in filling the citadels for the harvest to celebrate the return of Lord Anu. The servitors have been seizing us in small groups or alone to judge us on our performance in adhering to the Will of the Genitor."

Chantico shouted from behind Masterson, "They will destroy us. No one has returned once taken by the servitors to the *Tiamat*. Ganzir isn't the only citadel being attacked today." She pointed to a small group of men and women huddled together. "You are from Irkalla," then she pointed to another, "and you are from Arali. They're killing us!"

"You don't know that!" spat a woman from another group.

A man from the Arali group called out, "But what are we to do? We cannot stand against Commander Qingu and his thousands of servitors. There are only a few hundred of us."

"And less every day!" added a sullen voice from the Erselu citadel crowd.

Masterson looked at the faces of the confused men and women about him. He felt heartsick, heavy with the knowledge of what this moment was and what it meant. "You fight back."

The collective audible response resonated through the entire group, populating the rocky Grecian mountain as a ripple of disbelief from some and resignation by others. "You fight back as these three did. You use your abilities and talents, not to build or control laborers for the harvesting of Mundus for the Anunnaki, but to protect yourselves and your world." He looked in the eyes of as many as he could before continuing. "You fight back!"

"How?"

He smiled. "With your abilities and talents. Group together into small teams. Try to find someone with a talent or ability different from yours. Then return to Ganzir with us, with me! Stop the slaughter of your fellow Mundusans, both the common and talented. Let Enlil and the Council know you won't be extinguished. You won't go quietly to your deaths. You won't stand side-by-side with the Cassidans as they try to kill you. That is the Will of the Genitor!"

Masterson turned to Chantico. He smiled at her then took her hands in his, squeezing them. "It's time for you to lead the Igigi."

Chantico's gaze panned out over the rocky mountaintop. Her brothers and sisters were being systematically persecuted and destroyed by the very people that created them. In that moment, she realized they were being robbed of their heritage promised to them by the Will of the Genitor by their creation so long ago. She smiled back at Masterson and formed a portal back to Ganzir, leaping through it, followed by Aktzin and Ehecatl.

Masterson looked back over the rocky summit at the other Igigi. Portals were being opened and closed rapidly. Small teams were being formed as several of the Igigi rushed about, talking excitedly to one another. Most wouldn't survive the day.

Masterson stepped through the portal that Chantico held open for him. Aktzin was laying waste to the hovels that the Mundus had been cleared from by the offending servitors and were now assumed to be abandoned. Bio-electric energy danced like lighting from hovel to hovel, exploding it with tremendous force, sending rubble flying. Masterson shouted to no avail, "Don't stand your ground! They will kill you if you stand your ground!" Masterson's orders came too late as Aktzin's body was torn to shreds by what could only have been particle streams from several directions. Chantico screamed hysterically.

Masterson went to his belly, scanning the area immediately around them with his visor. Instantly he saw the location where the particle stream fire from lancer-staffs were coming from. "Ehecatl, that building directly in front of me – that is where the servitors are shooting at us from!"

Without hesitation, Ehecatl slapped his hands together, and instantly the building before them imploded as if crushed between his hands. Masterson quickly rose, extending his neck to peer at the wreckage of not only the building he had scanned but the adjoining buildings as well. The servitors' auras were very dim or completely gone.

"We have to move – and don't expose yourselves to being seen by them. If they see you, you die!"

Masterson led Chantico and Ehecatl in the direction his visor showed more of the Igigi were congregating. As they arrived, he turned to the two Igigi with them. "Spread the word, the 'They see you, you die'. Attack them first. Kill as many as you can as quickly as you can from a distance. They see you, you die!"

"Where are you going?" Chantico shouted.

"To tell the others, too. I can see where everyone is at with my impact armor. I have to tell them not to be seen and to attack quickly and from a distance."

Chantico nodded her head then turned and ran toward the other Igigi joining Ehecatl. Chantico shouted something then they activated several teleport bubbles and vanished through them, leaving Masterson alone.

Masterson pushed himself up and moved into the maze of ruined buildings and rubble-filled alleys. His impact armor's stealth features would hide him from Igigi and the Mundus laborers, but not the servitors. They could see him from a distance, too. But he looked like them.

He made his way through the growing rubble. There were sounds of the battle spreading everywhere around them. There were sounds of thunderous whirlwinds demolishing adobe buildings, fire consuming the wood used for building frames and furniture. There was a stench of the dead, many now being burned in the city's wreckage. He crawled through the shell of one of the two-story residences, probably the dwelling of a well-off Mundus family with some leadership role in the city. He knelt, scanning the area immediately around his vantage point. His confidence that the servitors' intuitive override in their armor was identifying him as a friendly servitor was still his key to him moving about among them.

He focused on a servitor combat team that was moving tactically along an alley, paralleling the direction he had been moving. He could see the red auras of the ten men and women moving through the walls of the buildings between them. They undoubtedly saw his aura as red or green, hostile or neutral. They were making their way toward him, he was sure.

A sudden surge of power in the middle of the walking servitors, blistering reality expanding from a single point, it wobbled with no defined entry or exit vortex. There were several teleportation bubbles activating on the same point. The carnage was sudden and complete as servitors surrounding the point were incinerated or shredded, with body parts exploding in different directions simultaneously. Four others were dropped where they stood, with no outward sign of being attacked. They simply collapsed, their auras fading on Masterson's visor instantly. The portals simply blinked out, leaving behind silence and smoldering desolation.

Masterson stood trembling, stunned by what he had just seen. He finally understood why the Anunnaki feared the Ejicerce. They knew the potential of the uplifted Mundus because they were already at war with them. They had been since the Battle of Eidin. He had thought they were misshapen Dionan casualties of excessive time travel. He was wrong. They were humans; they were gods. Masterson took a deep breath and stumbled down the rickety ladder to the packed clay floor. He stood with his hand on the ladder, steadying himself, now understanding why the Ummanate was so heavily armed as a standing army.

Masterson walked out of the shattered hovel into the alleyway, realizing that if he didn't get a handle on what was happening, Enlil would order the destruction of the city and possibly all the cities on the planet like he had before causing the Deluge at the end of the Ice Age. He had let the jinn out of the bottle. It would be hard to get them back in. The Igigi were now randomly attacking servitors throughout the city. Their attacks would leap to the entire planet once they realized they could defeat the Anunnaki and their servitors.

Masterson wandered through the rubble of the city. He had to get back to Olympus, the name the mountaintop they were congregating on would have in the future. That must be the location they would rally back to once night fell on Ganzir. Hebeta had said that the controls would be set for the boat from the *Glorious Questor* to return later in the day. Masterson ran to the edge of the city.

Masterson was thankful for the Dionan body that his consciousness had been placed in what seemed a lifetime ago. It was in magnificent shape. He quickly covered the distance to the edge of the city. The damage and carnage he saw informed him that the servitors' rampage had changed from a search and destroy mission going house to house looking for laborers supporting the Igigi or Igigi themselves to a defensive stance. He estimated the *Tiamat* had deployed two combat groups of about a thousand servitors to Ganzir by transport saucers over an extended time. Ganzir was the furthest from the main cluster of resource collection citadels in Mesopotamia and Africa. That was why the *Tiamat* was in what would come to be called the Persian Gulf. He knew since the Anunnaki draw down ordered by Lord Anu that there were only about three hundred Igigi that were uplifted. There were about a hundred, maybe more, at the rally point on the Grecian mountaintop.

"Stop!"

The command from a servitor combat team surprised him. He had gotten sloppy dwelling on the details instead of focusing on what he was doing. Masterson held his arms above his head, showing he was carrying no weapons. Undoubtedly, the impact armor confused his captors. He looked like them. The team was missing some members. The three servitors that had stopped him looked beaten, tired, and scared.

"Identify yourself."

"Adjutant Filio." Masterson looked from one of his captors to the other then surveyed the area around them, trying to determine if there were more soldiers.

"Hurry, get in here!" ordered the female. They all moved back into the remains of an adobe residence. "They don't seem to target us if we're inside."

There were five total out of what are usually ten servitors. The other two looked in as bad a shape as the three that had intercepted him in the street. Another female challenged him, "Where are your staff and rod?"

"Lost them when an explosion suddenly went off in the middle of us." He looked around the room they were all huddled in. "This all there is of you?"

She nodded, shifting her weight where she sat; she appeared to be injured. "Yeah, this is pretty much it. Everything was going according to the operations order given by the force commander then *boom* – shit started blowing up, people catching on fire. Lightning and other stuff. Taribum just exploded from the inside out. I ain't seen nothing like that. I mean, a particle stream rips you apart but to explode like that with pieces going every-which-way. Ain't never seen that before."

"Where's your force, commander?"

"Don't know. Communications have been down on the force-network. The group-network put out for us all to fall back to our debarkation sites. But that was over two hours ago and I ain't seen no transport saucers yet."

"He's wearing Seventh Order impact armor, Ninil," one of the three that captured him blurted.

"I'm detached to the *Tiamat* from the *Leviathan*. I'm an observer."

"Ain't no matter, he is a Dionan. The ones that are killing us are Mundus. It don't matter what he's wearing. Now start looking out there instead of at us in here."

"Adjutant! There are saucers coming." The spotter pointed toward the east. They all scrambled to look in the direction pointed. In the distance, several glowing disks could be seen rapidly approaching at high altitude.

"Alright, you slackers, get ready to move!" Adjutant Ninil struggled to get to her feet as the others moved to the eastern wall of the damaged residence.

Masterson held back on the western wall, watching. Through the broken ceiling and collapsed eastern wall, he could make out the approach of tactical drones, cruise missiles of a sort, loaded with networked synthetic intelligence, like the famulim. They soared over the city then began complex aerial maneuvers to search out and attack their targets. Massive explosions shook the foundations of the citadel, causing debris to fill the air as drones dove into the city on suicide attacks to engage their targets.

"They're here!"

Masterson's attention was drawn back outside the city as a fleet of transport and lightning ships appeared on the horizon. The *Tiamat* had sent its entire complement of aerial ships, transport saucers and close support cylinder-shaped lightning gunships. The imagery of the formations of the approaching airships pulled his memory back to watching approaching American military helicopters in Afghanistan before his abduction and transformation into an agent of the Genitor. As the lightning ships took up orbiting formations to cover the transport disks silently landing, servitors from many locations poured out of the ruins to the right and left of where Adjutant Ninil had placed what was left of her combat team.

"Head to the nearest transport to your team. If the belly lights are on, the ship can take you. If the belly lights are off, the transport is full. Bypass it and head to the next nearest transport." The orders came over an open channel in the impact armor communications suite. Ninil and her people ran for the transports as if their lives depended on how fast they could move.

Masterson noticed Ninil struggling to keep up with her team, whom she had waved on. He quickly came up behind her, grabbed her shoulders, and spun her. Then he quickly embraced her, grabbing her and hoisting her up on his right shoulder. He headed for the transport saucer her team was standing below, waving them on. Masterson ran up the ramp into the saucer and dropped her onto her back, unceremoniously panting for breath. He felt like his heart was about to explode. He then collapsed beside her, laughing. The rest of her combat team followed them, collapsing where they could on the circular deck of the drone transport cargo deck. They all cheered as they felt the subtle sensation of the transport lifting off and speeding up to hyper-sonic speed.

Chapter 12: The *Tiamat*

The transport saucers flew in an open, triangular formation around the behemoth warship known as *Tiamat*. The cylindrical ship sat steady in the calm waters of the lower Mesopotamian Sea with gentle waves lapping at its side. Eight massive doors were open along the flanks of the gargantuan ship, allowing the transport saucers to enter the main central flight deck of the ship to land at their designated spots. Tactical drones and lightning ships continued to launch from the bow and stern of the great carrier, even while the transports were landing.

Masterson helped Adjutant Ninil down the ramp of their transport saucer to hand her over to a couple of famulim. He then stood under the saucer, looking out over the flight deck. The main deck was a beehive of activity as Dionan and famulim ground crews were busy attending the transports and their disembarking passengers. The transport saucers were remotely piloted from the *Tiamat,* so flight recovery was primarily surveying the ships for battle damage, loading or unloading payload, or assisting transported personnel off the saucers. There was a bevy of famulim doing triage and medical assessment on the injured servitors immediately upon landing. Teleport bubbles were used to evacuate the most seriously wounded from the flight deck.

Masterson felt that the *Tiamat* was like the ship he had served on with the Seventh Order of Battle. The flight deck was almost identical to the *Leviathan*. He was familiar with the use of the bubble tube lifts that flowed through the ship like the circulatory system of a magnificent beast. But he doubted the ship would allow him to use the internal transport system. The *Tiamat,* like the *Leviathan,* transported up to thirty thousand troops with their equipment, vehicles, and supplies. This ship was a mobile base capable of moving to any location or time within the Genitors' Temporal Continuum. It was simply an engineering masterpiece. He grimaced and ruffled his long hair, scratching his head. He was sticking out like a sore thumb.

He followed the other able-bodied servitors, walking off the flight deck toward the main personnel access doors at the center of the vast hangar. They were all heading back down to their barracks to clean and store their weapons and equipment and, if they were lucky, get some time to rest. This would get him off the flight deck, but he really wasn't sure what he was going to do yet. Other than not getting caught. He knew that eventually his longer hair, beard, and the general weathered look of his impact armor would give him away to anyone even taking a casual look at him. He needed to get cleaned up and into a general ship uniform worn for routine work.

The ship had three working divisions. There was Ship Operations Command that maintained and ran the *Tiamat.* Then there was Logistics and Services Command that provided ship-to-shore support of the crew and whomever the ship was supporting. Finally, there was the smallest of the three commands, which Masterson was most familiar with, Combat Operations Command. To survive, he had to get out of the armor and into a ship uniform for one of the other two commands. As the servitors funneled down the stairs into a passageway to the lower decks, they became more short-tempered with each other. They had just escaped death and had to leave many of their comrades behind. Servitors of the Genitor weren't accustomed to that, at least not at this point on the Temporal Continuum.

"What are you? You are not from the *Tiamat.* Look at you, you stink."

"Long range reconnaissance unit." Masterson wedged himself between the two servitors to his immediate front, trying to get away from the one that called him out. But the two he tried to squeeze between took offense at being touched. The one on his right turned and abruptly shoved him back.

Masterson knew these servitors could kill him in their frustration with being defeated by the Igigi. To move back to the flight deck would be like trying to swim against a fast moving current. He slowed, allowing those near him to pass him as they continued down to the next deck. The servitor that called him out kept turning to look back at him. To the left and right were openings to the levels they were descending. Most of the servitors seemed to head for a lower level. Masterson slowly eased his way to the left side of the group as they continued to climb, so by the second level he could get himself to the exit to that deck. As he exited, he gazed up the stairs, spotting the servitor that had called him out. He was watching Masterson. Masterson smiled and waved, then exited the staircase quickly.

    Masterson hurried down the passageway, not really sure where he was at or where he was going. He continued to follow the servitors that had also exited the main staircase as they moved down this much wider corridor. He smiled as they came to what he recognized as a team room from his own days on the *Leviathan*. This meant that personal quarters for the senior servitors, the adjutants, would be further down the hall. He quickened his pace. He also realized that his new friend would either be pursuing him personally or was right now telling his superiors that he suspected there was an enemy aboard. Either way, the outcome was not in Masterson's favor.

    Masterson slowed his pace. The numbers of servitors returning from Ganzir with him had dwindled to nothing. Now encounters in the wide passageway were with ship operations personnel. He didn't want to rouse their suspicion of him. His time on the *Leviathan* with the Seventh Order of Battle was very structured. He had an adjutant assigned to him just to lead him around the ship and get him where he had to go on time. He also had his personal famulim with him, Mary. Mary had been his constant companion during his early training and had played a huge role in his acclimation to life in the Genitors' world. He thought of it as more than a friend and female companion than a Genitor-created golem.

    Masterson found himself in the passageway's section that was filled with doors close together. He recognized them as the adjutants' quarters. He took a deep breath then pressed his palm to the nearest one after the passing servitors and famulim were down the passageway and out of hearing range in both directions. The door opened for him, as he expected. There were no thieves in the Genitors' service. He quickly stripped himself of his armor and shoved it down the disposal chute. He opened the clothing locker that was partially concealed in the white pseudo-ceramic walls of the small quarters. Masterson grimaced and pulled out the light pastel pullover. He quickly pulled it over his muscular Dionan body. He slipped on the matching briefs then attached the utility belt around his waist, pulling it snug. Moving fast, he dropped the light slippers to the deck and put them on his feet. Masterson looked at himself in the quarter's hygiene station reflector. He smiled, shook his head, and stepped out into the passageway.

Masterson stepped right into the butt of a servitor's lancer-staff. He felt two others grab his arms and wrestle him to the deck. He struggled until he realized there were additional servitors standing with their lancer-staffs at the ready. Further back stood three taller Cassidan officers, observing his capture.

"Stand him up."

The Dionan servitors hauled Masterson to his feet so the three officers could examine him more closely. The second Cassidan furrowed her brow then murmured, "He is not a Mundusan, and he is not an Igigi. How strange."

The third Cassidan officer spoke. "He looks Dionan to me. Who is he?"

"He is outwardly Dionan, but he is not Dionan. His thoughts are chaotic, more like an untrained Mundus."

The androgenous voice of a famulim responded promptly, "He is Adjutant Filio Domini, of the Seventh Order. Recognized as a Synthetic Envoy of the Genitor by Lord Enlil late in the Battle of Eidin. Current status is named Protector of the Lady Inanna of the Anunnaki Council."

Two of the three Cassidans were surprised at learning he was recognized and rewarded by Lord Enlil himself. The third wasn't impressed.

"I have seen the reports on this one. Commander Qingu has been expecting him to appear once Inanna was arrested. In fact, the Dionan courier ship appearing in orbit was the first sign that he was in fact here." The Cassidan smiled. "But I had thought he would be cleverer, more of a challenge than this." The lead Cassidan lifted his chin and turned away from Masterson and his guards. Over his shoulder he ordered, "Take him to one of the holding areas. I will confer with Commander Qingu about our new guest."

The combat team moved Masterson upward through the ship to a temporary holding cell near the command-and-control area of the

Tiamat. This was an area of the ship Masterson had more experience with from the Seventh Order's *Leviathan*. *Tiamat* was elegant in design; the upper decks appealing to the Cassidans aboard and mimicking their cultural architecture preferences while the lower decks below the flight deck were designed to emphasize the Dionan's utilitarian culture and functionality. The outer cylindrical hull of the *Tiamat* was just a shell surrounding a miniature city within. The Genitor and their disciples were not only voyagers in time but space as well. In his previous life, before transitioning to the Genitor's dominion, he had known Cassida as Mars, a world with a much lighter gravity than the Earth, at only thirty-eight percent. Cassidan structures were whimsically soaring into their purplish sky. The architecture of the *Tiamat* reflected that with a swirling, rounded feel to its bulkheads and passageways with pastel coloring.

Early in his transition, Masterson became aware that upon arrival, the Genitor and their famulim workers had seeded and colonized Cassida, or Mars, first using biological clones suited for its environment. Then they moved on to Diona, or Venus, second to exploit its mineral resources. At first, Diona had a very Earth-like environment. The Dionan biological clones differed from the Cassidans because their world's physical conditions were remarkably like the Earth's.

Masterson had learned that the final days of Diona as a habitable world came when a massive caldera erupted, igniting several other large volcanoes at once. The resulting eruptions caused a carpeting or pancake effect of thick magma to blanket the surrounding areas while dumping atmosphere-changing amounts of carbon dioxide into the air on a global scale, rendering the planet uninhabitable as the temperatures soared and the air became toxic.

Masterson waited for what to him felt like an eternity. He paced the floor for hours. The cell reminded him of the first place he had woken up after his transition. It was circular, with no obvious entry and a brightly lit interior. A single hard slab dominated the center of the room. He easily located a concealed private fresher stall for personal hygiene with a small inventory of simple smocks and slippers for use by the prisoner. Food appeared magically in the center of the slab when he wasn't resting on it. In the initial days of his transition to the Genitors' Dominion, he remembered being taught the Cassidan's ability to replicate at the molecular level. The food's appearance was not magic, it was technology.

He sat on the floor with his legs folded, his arms hung over his knees. "The Cassidans developed then built the technology, the Dionans built the industrial base then provided the labor force. What are humans bringing to the Genitors' table?" he wondered aloud.

"Precisely what I would like to know."

Masterson was on his feet in an instant, facing the party of Cassidans entering his cell. The leader was wearing the regalia of an Order Commander. "Commander Qingu of the Rebu Erimna?"

"Yes, excellent, Protector. Very good indeed." The three other Cassidans he had met earlier filed in behind Commander Qingu. "Let me introduce you to Adjutants Hamaliel, Rikbiel, and Sophia. They will conduct your debriefing and sentencing. You hardly merit a full hearing before the Anunnaki Council." Commander Qingu smiled. "I was curious what an envoy from the Genitor was really like. Your exploits during the Battle of Eidin are well documented in the archives of the Ummanate."

Masterson bowed his head, not sure if he was being praised or condemned. The expressions on the faces of the three Cassidans behind Commander Qingu betrayed the true intention of their visit to his cell.

"Now why are you here, Protector, and why this moment in time?" Commander Qingu ran his finger along a seam in the cell's pseudo-ceramic wall as he circled around behind Masterson. The three subordinate Cassidans stood in the cell's threshold, focused on Masterson as their commander spoke.

Masterson saw no value in concealing information so he explained, "The temporal coordinates were provided by the ship's patron. I'm sure you have all the data on the ship that brought me here. And I'm sure you recognized it as a Dionan courier. Now, as to exactly what the ship is supposed to do here, one can only speculate, I suppose."

Behind Masterson, Commander Qingu laughed. "You are the recognized protector of one of the more flamboyant members of the Anunnaki Council. You appear on a temporal courier after her arrest by the Council for treason. And then, as if that was not suspect enough, you are found in the uniform of the Seventh Order, an Erimna you deserted specifically to join her, in a city often preferred by her as it is being disciplined."

Now Masterson laughed aloud, "Disciplined? The wholesale slaughter of laborers and their families, the razing of the city to its foundation, is disciplining?"

Commander Qingu came to a stop directly in front of Masterson, looking down at him, "Lord Enlil wants there not to be any misunderstanding of the seriousness of what Lord Enki and Lady Inanna were attempting."

"And what is that?" Masterson looked up into Commander Qingu's eyes with confidence and a hint of defiance.

"That deviation or modification of the Will of the Genitor will not be tolerated."

"What do you intend to do with me?"

Commander Qingu's hand swept back, showing the three standing on the cell's threshold. "I intend to allow you to provide training for my three most promising adjutants. They will undoubtedly learn much from you as they peel open your consciousness, one synaptic connection at a time."

"Lovely."

Smiling, Commander Qingu turned toward his three protégés. As he walked past them, he spoke. "He is yours now."

Masterson tensed as he looked into the faces of the three Cassidan adjutants. Commander Qingu had called them Hamaliel, Rikbiel, and Sophia. Like all the Cassidans and Dionans, they were clones, probably from the same brood. There were no natural births in those two highly structured worlds. Each person was created specifically to meet the needs of their community, whether it be on a ship, a manufacturing center, or a research facility. These three had been prepared for life in the Ummanate, the Genitors' Host. He couldn't tell their ages, but they wore long, utilitarian, ankle-length robes, the insignia of senior officers aboard the *Tiamat*.

Masterson smiled, "So where do we begin?"

The one called Sophia raised her right hand to waist height, with an open palm pointed at Masterson. An explosion of air before him smashed him into the wall behind him, knocking the air from his lungs.

Gasping, Masterson smiled up at the three from his hands and knees. "Okay, so I know which of you is the bad cop."

The shortest of the three, still head and shoulders over Masterson's Dionan body, reached, taking the hands of his two companions. The one named Hamaliel bent forward and placed the fingertips of his free hand on Masterson's shoulder. They were instantly in a new location. Masterson collapsed to a prone position on his belly. They were in a larger room. An empty room. The walls were the ubiquitous pseudo-ceramic material, giving him no clue as to their whereabouts. They could be on the *Tiamat* or one of the several resource collection citadels scattered around the planet. Masterson didn't know the range of a psychic jump. He lay there for several minutes, trying to gather his thoughts. While he did, the three Cassidans either stood silently watching him or pacing around him.

"You aren't Dionan?" The one called Hamaliel spoke first.

"I am synthetic, rapidly matured and provided with the memory of a servitor from the far future of Mundus."

"Yes, you have very interesting, deep memories. Alien, definitely not from this time on the Temporal Spectrum. Your long-term memories are even more fascinating. You do not even attempt to adhere to doctrine or follow orders, do you?"

"He has a disciplined mind with martial training. Not traditional training for a servitor, however. Interesting; not what I expected from a Dionan." Sophia stayed behind him out of his field of view as their talk continued.

"Do not forget, he is a synthetic envoy. He was designed in intricate detail by the Genitor to resist interrogation, and to only divulge his message to his intended recipient." Rikbiel smirked, addressing Masterson directly. "You did not even know the message or who you were to deliver it to until the moment desired by your creators, did you?"

"His mind is so full of intricate memories, a lifetime of events, training, experiences." Hamaliel looked at Sophia behind Masterson. "Could they be fictional fantasies, elaborately created to disguise and hide the crucial information we seek?"

Sophia scoffed at Hamaliel, "That is your task to determine. I am here to control his behavior, not probe his mind."

Masterson was instantly on his feet, spinning backward toward Sophia. His move completely caught her off guard as he drove the fingertips of his right hand into her throat just below her chin, crushing her windpipe and denying her the ability to speak or breathe. She fell to the floor, eyes bulging, her hands clawing at her throat as she struggled. As Masterson landed on his feet after jumping to reach Sophia's throat, he spun on his heels and rushed Hamaliel, tackling him, driving him to the hard deck. He grabbed Hamaliel's head and repeatedly smashed his skull into the deck until the giant Cassidan was unconscious. Masterson wrestled the limp Hamaliel up so he could wrap his arms around the Cassidan's neck and snap it.

Rikbiel stared in horror as Masterson murdered his two companions. He turned to flee from the large room, running awkwardly in his robes of office. Masterson closed in on Rikbiel, tackling him from behind and driving them both to the deck with a hard fall. Masterson wrestled Rikbiel into a sitting position with his arm wrapped around the Cassidan's neck, just the way he had snapped Hamaliel's only seconds ago. "Stop moving," he whispered.

The Cassidan froze, no longer struggling. His heart was racing and his hair was damp.

Masterson had never seen a Cassidan sweat before. "What's your ability?"

"I am a farseer. I see things and places and can will myself there. I was the one that brought us here."

Masterson smiled widely then kissed Rikbiel on the cheek. "Where is Commander Qingu?"

Rikbiel stammered, "I, I may not look upon Commander Qingu."

"Hell, get us out of here. The servitors will be here shortly." Masterson tightened his grip on the man's neck. "Now!"

Suddenly they were sitting in the middle of a servitor team bay, the common area where the servitors billeted and kept their personal equipment. Some servitors were showering, others had already retreated to their personal alcoves to rest. "Not here!" Masterson twisted Rikbiel's neck to show his displeasure at being played with. They instantly popped from the troop bay to what looked to Masterson as Rikbiel's personal rooms.

"Do not kill me, do not kill me!" begged the slouched Cassidan, hanging like a doll in Masterson's muscular grip.

"Jump me to the primary power plant of the ship, then to the main synthetic intelligence processor of the ship. Then finally to the ship's tactical control room. Don't tarry – as soon as we arrive, move on to the next. Do you understand?"

The ship's general alarm wailed. Masterson knew his escape had been discovered. He tightened his grip on Rikbiel's throat, causing the Cassidan to panic. They were suddenly in the central power plant sitting on the floor, looking at the hydrogen fusion reaction chamber. The technologists of the Ship Operations Command turned as one to look at the two as Masterson twisted Rikbiel's neck to show he needed to move along. They popped into the neuronic lattice chamber that housed the synthetic consciousness of the *Tiamat*. The alarms were still blaring.

Masterson could feel the tension growing in Rikbiel's body. He could feel his captive was near his point of rebelling, physically unable to continue on. They were now in a large, circular room filled with Cassidans, Dionans, and famulim. Several were working at consoles placed on the outer wall. Others were at four separate large consoles facing the large three-dimensional model of the *Tiamat* floating in the southern sea.

Masterson shouted, "Yes!" then shoved Rikbiel away from him as they both sat on the floor surrounded by startled technologists and the senior officers of the *Tiamat*.

"Kill him!" thundered the command of Commander Qingu over the confusion of his control crew caused by Masterson's bravado.

Masterson scurried to his feet, looking at one of the Cassidan adjutant raising his arm as he had seen the Igigi do in Ganzir right before tossing him several feet through the air. Masterson saw the teleport bubbles forming behind the officers in the direction he was looking. He threw himself on the floor, pressing his head down to the deck as hard as he could. Chaos erupted. Screams of agony and the wet sounds of slaughter mingled as the room flared hot with an infernal heat that washed over his body. He was overwhelmed by the stench of massacre that was happening around him.

Igigi attackers stepped through the portals that had remained open. Surviving *Tiamat* officers and Igigi attackers unleashed their psychic powers on each other. Electric bolts of lightning or fire explosions flared, thrown from both Cassidan and Igigi fighters, followed by the deafening thunder of battle in the room as alarms from all over the ship started screaming from various consoles. Bodies from both sides were thrown about like leaves in a tornado. Flames and burned body parts were everywhere, as well as smashed equipment and cracked ceramic pieces of the hull.

To Masterson, it seemed as if the ground had opened up and they had all fallen into Hell. In the chaotic din, Masterson spotted Commander Qingu. Not a target of the psychic fighters himself, he lunged forward in a flat-out sprint toward the commander. Masterson tackled him, driving them both into and over a console, landing in a tangle on the other side. Qingu's eyes flared from the bio-kinetic energy welling up inside him. Masterson had seen him throwing bolts of bio-kinetic energy like lightning against the Igigi invaders. Masterson slammed his fist into Qingu's solar plexus, the soft tissue in the center of the chest, with all his strength, forcing the air from Qingu's lungs. As Qingu doubled up, trying to go into a fetal position, he raised his head, gasping for air, Masterson snapped his neck with one hand on his chin and the other at the base of his skull in the back. Qingu was dead.

Masterson rose on his knees, looking around him. The Cassidan officers fought as they had lived. Orderly, controlled, and following through with fighting techniques refined by tradition and an eternity of martial discipline. The Igigi fought as savages, giving no quarter and expecting none. They slaughtered the bridge crew.

The ship's alarms stopped. To the horror of the surviving crew throughout the great ship, a calm announcement was made over untold console speakers that there had been a reactor breach that would cause a catastrophic fusion reaction explosion. They froze in disbelief and died where they stood as the Igigi continued to fight.

"Get us off the ship!" Masterson ordered then leaped to the nearest console, slamming his hand over the activation switch before he shouted into the communications suite. "Get off the ship, now!"

One of the Igigi ran to grasp Masterson's outstretched hand then reached back to grip the hand of another, pulling them toward a forming teleportation bubble. Masterson felt his free hand being taken by a badly burned female Igigi. Instantly they were standing on a beach, all quickly turning and looking back eastward beyond the collapsing teleportation bubble. In the distance, a fireball soared slowly upward into the sky. A great wind hit them, the shock wave of the *Tiamat's* nuclear power plants exploding.

Chapter 13: The Bull of Heaven

Masterson lay flat on his back, blinking. The shock wave of great wind and heat from the destruction of the *Tiamat* had swept the beach where the Igigi had rallied. He sat up, looking around. Near him lay several of the Igigi. Exhaustion and shock from what had happened was overtaking them. Many lay moaning and writhing in pain from their battle with the psychic adepts and servitors of the Fourth Order of Battle. Masterson turned and looked behind him, away from the sea. The Igigi's bodies were strewn about, some in pain, some just in shock. The blast from the *Tiamat* had also toppled trees and ruined structures made by local laborers along the beach.

    Masterson mourned the destruction as he stood. The fight for the Earth had just begun. He realized the destruction of the *Tiamat* was the formative battle that had created the Ejicerce. There would be an Anunnaki retaliation. He turned and looked back to the east, out over the southern sea or what would be known as the Persian Gulf much, much later. The large mushroom-shaped cloud continued to grow from the detonation of the fusion reactors on the *Tiamat.* He wondered to himself, *Had the Igigi sabotaged the ship's fusion reactors or had the ship's own synthetic consciousness reasoned that it was lost and committed suicide to keep its weapons and abilities from enemy hands?* He turned to see the surrounding Igigi looking up at him from where they lay or now sat. Their eyes were filled with terror and confusion.

    He smiled at them. "We have work to do." He reached his hand down to the woman that had saved his life, teleporting him and one other to safety in the last seconds of the battle. He pulled her up beside him, under his arm as if to give her support. "Thank you all. What you did today ends the old order of things. Today, here and now, we begin a new order." He paused as the survivors moved toward them, many looking past him to watch the climbing cloud from the *Tiamat* in the far distance. Some limped, some had to be helped or carried close to where he stood. Those in the best shape moved, helping where they could with those more injured. But all looked toward Masterson, where he stood before them, wanting to hear more from him as they gathered. "I want you to scatter to the far reaches of this world before the Anunnaki stop the bubble transporters from working for us. I'll send messengers to you when there's more to tell. Go to remote mountaintops and hasten away from where you walk from the transporter bubbles appear. It's to be us who they will seek to punish and destroy, but be assured they will punish any Mundus they find." He gazed into the eyes of as many as he could before continuing, "So be wise, separate yourselves from them. Let the lords of the underworld hunt us, and not busy themselves with punishment for our people."

"But how will we fight them? They have more servitors than there is sand on this beach. They have told us so!" cried a man from the back.

Masterson raised his voice, "As we just did – together. Coming together when they don't expect it. Protecting each other but not engaging them when they want to fight us. We choose the place and time to fight. We must deny them that if we're to win."

"But they have mystics too!" came the voice of a woman holding her friend so she could stand.

"Yes, and they'll search for us using their talented mystics, the same as we have, and their technology. But, this is important – the *Tiamat* and most of its servitors are gone. You know yourself that the Anunnaki are a small group of a few dozen. We now outnumber them. So, we must be agile, we must be quick. Now we must hurry to the mountaintop where we were before. There we'll organize and plan our next move. It's far from an Anunnaki citadel. Now let's move before they take the teleporters away from us!"

Someone called out, "What shall we call you? You have many names. What do we call you, Filio or Dumuzid, or Protector?"

"The Genitor that instructed me called me a veneficus or wizard. The Seventh Order knows me as Adjutant Filio, the Anunnaki know me as Protector Dumuzid."

"You are the protector of Inanna and have survived among the councilors of Lord Enlil, the Destroyer," shouted a tattered, battle-worn Chantico with a smile. "You inspire romanticism as the protector of Inanna, politeness because of your golden tongue and your ability to move among us and the Anunnaki, and shrewdness through your continued survival!" Her words were met with enthusiastic laughter and support from the other survivors.

"I saw him. He fought like a bull against the servitors, with his bare hands!" called a man from the front of the crowd. "Yet he is one of them, a servitor. He fought for us like an enraged bull!"

"He is our light, and a bull!" called out Chantico.

"Dumuzid, the Bull of Heaven, our leader!" The Igigi chanted the name of Dumuzid the Bull with joyous voices and waving of hands followed by much hugging as Masterson took on another name.

Masterson waved to Chantico, who came to him smiling, embracing him. "I'm glad you are here," he told her.

"So am I!" She surprised Masterson by tightening the embrace, "It worked, your plan worked. I did not think it would, but it did!" She was almost hopping on her toes with excitement.

"There'll be time for celebration later, but now we must get everyone from this beach and to the mountaintop. Enlil won't wait long to take retaliatory action. We must organize for that attack and prepare for our own. Have them stay in the groups they were in before. But tell them not to go back to where they worked for the Anunnaki; abandon the citadels completely."

Chantico nodded then separated from his embrace and sped back into the crowd, yelling names of the leaders to come to her as she went.

Masterson turned to look once again at the mushroom cloud that now dominated the sky to the east. He remembered that he had been taught that the cloud would last about four days before dissipating. Lord Enlil would already be plotting to end the world somehow. It was his solution to everything. Destroy what's done and start anew. Masterson, before his transition, had experience in counterinsurgency operations. Now he was the leader of an insurgency. Where to begin?

He turned back to look at the survivors of the assault on the *Tiamat*. It was the second time that the Ejicerce had used mass teleportation during a battle. The Ejicere, or Forsaken, had succeeded in the Battle of Eidin to reinforce the infiltrated Third Order of Battle fighting the Seventh. But that was thousands of years ago. He doubted they could use that tactic again soon. Besides, he wasn't even sure of their losses yet, but he knew they'd been high. Captain Valarus' famulim had said there were only around three-hundred Igigi to begin with during this era. They were long-lived like the Cassidans and the Dionans. There wouldn't be replacements in the pipeline. There were maybe thirty to forty Igigi around him. Of that number, maybe a third looked healthy and mobile. The rest were on their backs or sitting with their heads hung low, exhausted.

From his memory before the transition, he knew the Mediterranean gods and goddesses interbred with humanity, according to myths and legends. That could be the answer to their replacement problem readily enough. He would have to discuss this with others once they were all safe. He looked at Chantico. She was giving orders to about a dozen of the surviving able-bodied Igigi. She dismissed them and set them about their tasks to organize then get their groups off the beach and into hiding.

She smiled as she looked up at him. "They have their instructions. We will travel as we did before."

"Good; let's gather up your group and find us a place to stay." He smiled. They walked toward the last remaining cluster of Igigi that were on the beach. Masterson asked as he slowed their pace, "Can an Igigi travel through space and time? Say, self-teleport to another location or into the past or into the future without a teleporter bubble? If all Cassidan technology is based on the volumen-enhanced talents, then teleportation must be too."

"No, sir," she frowned, looking up at him. "They can jump to places they have seen or places others they have shared their thoughts with have seen. There are few with the gift of jumping." Her frown deepened, "It is rare among the Dionans although not unheard of with the Cassidans."

"Yes, I've never encountered someone that could teleport without the use of a citadel or ship network. But what about the

Genitor? They can be wherever they want to be? I thought perhaps they could jump into the future or the past…"

"The past is unchangeable, and the future has not happened yet." She sounded skeptical, as if learning something that couldn't possibly be true, or purely disbelieving what he was saying.

"Your Cassidan and Dionan instructors didn't teach you they had the power to travel time and location like ships on a great sea?"

She looked at him with questioning eyes. "They only taught us that the Will of the Genitor guides us in all that we do. The Anunnaki Council is the sole interpreter of the Will of the Genitor and must be obeyed since only they have access to the Genitor."

"What did the Anunnaki say was the Will of the Genitor?"

She furrowed her brow and thought, "The Will of the Genitor is that we harvest the resources of Mundus under the direction of our worthy Cassidan and Dionan progenitors." She looked up at Masterson, "I think they are not the followers of the Will of the Genitor; I do not think the Genitor wants us to be slaughtered like livestock."

This time Masterson frowned, "Why do you say that?"

"Why would the Genitor give us the same abilities as our mentors if we were not meant to be like our mentors? How could the Genitor be so cruel?" The sorrow in her eyes made Masterson turn his own eyes away from her to look at the battered but not broken Igigi that still littered the beach despite the efforts of the most able-bodied to get them organized.

"I don't know if the Genitor or the Anunnaki truly know what cruelty is. Maybe that's something unique to us." He turned, looking back into her dark eyes. "Which group am I with?" He smiled as he attempted to change the subject of their talk.

"I have us going with Marduk. He is a brood brother of mine. We were trained at the Kilgal citadel together before I was sent to Ganzir." She looked at the ground as they walked. "He knew we were going to be forced to fight the Anunnaki. He knew this day would come soon."

"Did he fight on the *Tiamat* with us? Is he here?"

"Yes!" She smiled at last. "He is over here. Come, I will show him to you." She gripped Masterson's hand, surprising him. Together they walked away from the beach. As they plodded through the sand, Masterson noticed more of the Igigi fighters were being helped to their feet or being teleported out by movers. In the middle of them stood a lean, solidly built male Igigi.

"Dumuzid the Bull," she said proudly. "This is Mardukiel." Chantico gave Mardukiel a coy smile. "He is also known as Marduk."

"And you are Dumuzid the Bull of Heaven, the savior of our world!" Marduk smiled as he reached a well-muscled arm forward to grasp Masterson's hand. He turned their hands once clasped together as if examining them. "I watched what happened on the beach from here. But I must ask; What would turn a Dionan servitor against his masters?"

"I know I look like a servitor. My appearance is that of a Dionan. But my soul is Mundus."

"And how are we to know that?" questioned Marduk as he released his grip on Masterson's hand.

Masterson looked into the dark eyes of the man now challenging him. He turned, stepping to the side so as not to block the view of Marduk then pointed at the still visible mushroom cloud of the destroyed *Tiamat*. "Use your talent to search my heart and soul."

"I already have. Your heart is the heart of a Dionan. You will risk all for those you are loyal to and destroy those who oppose you. Your soul is not that of a Cassidan, however. You are not committed to following tradition, the way things are done. You are chaotic, impulsive, and prone to decisive action. That is the way you fought the *Salsu Erimna*. Those are Mundus traits."

"We need to get to where we're going before Enlil denies us the use of the teleporter network." Masterson reminded Marduk.

"We have our ways around that." The Igigi smiled at Masterson to follow as Chantico formed a portal for them to walk through. They emerged from the teleportation bubble portal into a Bronze Age village at the foot of a large, rounded mountain. The sea was to the east, with the mountain range rising in the west, running north and south as far as the eye could see.

Masterson smiled. The difference between the misery of the beach, even in victory, compared to this tranquil agrarian setting, was palpable. He took a deep breath, feeling invigorated by the energy he felt around him. The laborers of the village, farmers and their families, readily helped the Igigi find places within their homes to rest and hopefully heal. The village elders seem to recognize Marduk, much to Masterson's surprise.

"These folks know you?"

"Yes, they have the most beautiful women here, and the best wine!" The Igigi laughed then slapped Masterson on the back, pressing him toward a stone farmhouse close to where they teleported in.

"And the climate is cooler with the sea breeze," noted Masterson dubiously.

"Exactly!" retorted Marduk, laughing. "No, this is far from where any of us were tasked to work. I think we are safe here."

"They can trace the locations of the teleport bubbles." Masterson picked up his pace, leaving a stunned Marduk left standing. Chantico walked past Marduk with a spring in her step, smiling.

The farmer and his family welcomed the Igigi into their small stone home with merriment and apparent heartfelt pleasure at seeing the battle-weary fighters. The family matriarch was particularly pleased to see Marduk, fawning over him as he sat at their table.

"She was one of his favorites when she was a maiden," Chantico whispered in a conspiratorial way, "and for a while after she mated with her man there."

Masterson accepted wine offered him by one of several women that buzzed about the table serving bread and dipping sauces. Masterson didn't understand a word being said around him. He noted that some of the other Igigi also didn't speak the local Mundus dialect.

"The Anunnaki don't want the Mundus speaking the same language, do they?" he asked, leaning close to Chantico.

"No, they have always required Igigi to learn the speech of the citadel laborers we are assigned to. And we are forbidden to teach them how to speak the language of the Anunnaki as well."

Masterson nodded as he reached to take a loaf of bread, tearing it then handing the larger half to Chantico. "Makes sense. It makes it harder to do what we're getting ready to do."

Chantico looked intrigued as she accepted the bread. "What do you mean?"

"It's hard to organize an insurgency if factions can't understand each other or communicate in even the most basic ways."

"Insurgency?" She reached across the table to dip the hard bread into a clay bowl with a dark, syrupy sauce in it.

"Revolt, against the Anunnaki."

She froze in mid-reach to look at him then spoke up, "Marduk, listen to this."

Marduk reluctantly turned from a maiden to listen intently to Chantico and Masterson. "What is it, Chantico? Have we not had enough talk today?"

Masterson watched as more curious Igigi near them carried their food and moved to sit near them to listen as well. "As I see it, the Anunnaki began this conflict when they started removing Igigi from their citadels without explaining why or allowing others to seek them to render aid or help. Some of you, I'm told, believe they may even be dead." Several Igigi nodded their heads in agreement with the fear that some of them had been killed.

"Explain the revolt to us, Dumuzid the Bull," voiced Chantico boldly.

Marduk laughed, "Yes, Dumuzid the Bull, explain," Marduk stopped frowning then looked at Masterson with a more serious stare.

"We've made our move. We've responded with force to the hostile actions of the Anunnaki's servitors, of Lord Enlil specifically. We've defeated an Order of Battle of the Genitor because we moved quickly, with surprising gall and skill. We may not do that again. Enlil is probably in consultation with Commander Anu at *Nibiru Station* right now." He looked around the table at the young-looking faces of the Igigi. "Enlil has to ask for a replacement Order of Battle. It will probably be the feared Seventh Order. They may come with a host of servitors, led by Commander Michail. They'll be ruthless in their hunt for you and the other survivors." Masterson let that indisputable fact sink in.

"We must prove to Lord Anu on *Nibiru Station* that you, the Igigi, can manage Mundus for the Genitor better than the remaining Anunnaki can, and can do it without the continuous intervention of Lord Anu's servitors."

The Igigi around them and at the table erupted into loud discussions, with some of them supporting Masterson's idea, others arguing they couldn't possibly convince Cassidans that Mundus could manage their world better than they could.

Masterson stood and raised his hands to quiet them all. "We control the laborers. Without the laborers, the stewardship of Mundus and the harvest of the resources will stop. There aren't enough Cassidans, Dionans, and famulim to replace the Igigi and Mundusans that can oppose us on Mundus with the loss of the *Tiamat*. Right now, Lord Enlil is pleading his case with Lord Anu. I know about that. We must openly seize control of Mundus while keeping channels to Lord Anu open. We must convince Lord Anu that he's better off with us in charge here than without us. It's the only way."

Marduk nodded then spoke, "As you said before, the Anunnaki control the teleporter network. How are we to continue to control the harvesting if we cannot access the Anunnaki portals? We cannot even travel to and from the citadels, much less between Mundus settlements."

"Don't you have access to their bubble cars, the airships?"

Chantico smiled, "Yes we do!"

Marduk shook his head, "No, if they can control the teleporter network they can shut down the air transport too."

"Then the only safe solution is we must control the transport networks ourselves." Masterson looked between Chantico and Marduk solemnly. "It's the only way we can control the harvesting."

Chapter 14: The Will of the Genitor

Masterson walked confidently up to the gate of the Sumerian city of Nippur, barefoot, wearing the tattered wool toga of a human laborer. The city had been established by the Sumerians long ago, after the Deluge, and would become part of Babylonia. He walked alone, but his Igigi allies were keenly aware of his location and actions using their special volumen-enhanced sensory abilities given by the Anunnaki.

He stood before the great gate of Nippur. "I am Dumuzid, Protector of Inanna, known now as Dumuzid the Bull, the Destroyer of *Tiamat,* among my people. I came to speak with Lord Enlil of the Anunnaki."

Slowly, the great wooden gate of Nippur opened, revealing a company of Kassite Bronze Age warriors with weapons drawn. The warriors moved quickly to surround Masterson and secure the road leading up to their city's massive gate. Masterson nodded to the Kassite commander as he entered the city. Under escort, he moved down the main street of the city toward the great Ekur Temple of Nippur. The Ekur Temple was a six level ziggurat of massive proportions on a hill that dominated the city-scape of Nippur. It was believed to be the domain of Enlil himself, the Sumerian God of the Wind. Masterson marveled at the ancient Bronze Age architecture of the city. Nippur was many times the size of the citadel of Ganzir. The horror of this city's destruction by the Anunnaki would be greater than the genocide he had witnessed in the alabaster city of Ganzir, that would later become known as the White Sands Desert in North America.

The Kassite commander walked back from the front of his company. He saluted Masterson by slamming his right fist into his own chest. He stepped to the side as a small group of priests moved from a small building to the side of the temple to meet Masterson. The soldiers stood at attention as the holy men passed through their ranks to move close to the mysterious man they had escorted into their city like he was a returning nobleman or one of their own warriors. They must have heard of the large black cloud hanging in the sky and the great wind that had flattened everything for miles along the coast of the Southern Sea.

"Lord Enlil is expecting you, Lord Dumuzid. We will take you to him if you follow us." The short, dark-haired human male gestured with his hand for Masterson to follow as the priests replaced the Kassite soldiers as his escort. They proceeded up the steep steps of the temple to the highest level. The majesty and achievement of the citizens of Nippur weighed heavily on Masterson's mind as they climbed the stairs of the temple, towering over the rest of the ancient city. The ascent up the temple steps was a challenging climb because of their steepness and spacing. They placed the climber ascending the temple in the right frame of mind as he or she approached Lord Enlil's sanctuary on Earth.

Sargon, the young warrior he had shared his consciousness with, had come and gone with his Akkadian Empire over 500 years ago. Thousands of years had passed since Masterson had fought as a member of the Seventh Order against the then mostly unknown Ejicerce at Anunnaki citadel of Eidin in the flooded region that would become known as the Black Sea in later times. The Battle of Eidin was the first time Masterson had met Enlil, Lord of the Sky.

Masterson nodded to the leader of the priests of Enlil. Again, no words were shared, but a simple hand gesture was offered to him to continue his journey up the stairs to the alter at the top of the temple. Masterson nodded again and began his solitary climb. After a couple of minutes of climbing, he reached the top. He took a moment to catch his breath and take in the view from high over the city. Masterson smiled as he considered the progress that had been made in such a brief span of time the humans had made under the yoke of the Anunnaki in their pursuit of the Genitors' Will. He turned and moved out of the scorching morning sun into the shaded interior of the temple.

Already activated in the center of the large stone room was a teleport bubble, shimmering and undulating like it was made of soap. Without hesitation, Masterson stepped through the portal into the all too familiar interior of a Dionan-designed subterranean citadel. Waiting to receive him were four Cassidan Gallu in a Cassidan smart-hooded bodysuit of micro-mesh material called Melaminate, or Melam, covered with laminate pseudo-ceramic plates. The Cassidan guardsmen loomed over Masterson with their three-meter tall stature. The guards immediately snapped their lancer-staffs to the defensive, ready position.

Masterson didn't flinch, he just looked from one guard to the other grinning, "I come in peace. Take me to your leader."

From behind the Gallu stepped three famulim. They paused with their hands folded, bowing low to greet Masterson. The famulim in the center stepped forward to stand before Masterson, placing itself between him and the Gallu. It examined Masterson's face, paying particular attention to his dark blue eyes. The lead famulim reached out to take one of his hands in its own, rubbing his palm with the tips of its fingers. It gently released his hand and stepped back with a serene smile. "Lord Enlil and the Anunnaki Council will speak with you, Servitor Filio."

"*Servitor Filio?*" Masterson mimicked with a low sarcastic voice as he followed three famulim with two of the Gallu falling in behind them as they left the arrival area. As they walked out of the small stone enclosure into the larger underground gallery, he realized they were walking through a portion of old Kur, the first major Anunnaki subterranean citadel established on Earth. Kur had been the primary spaceport for the Cassidans and Dionans built during the Stone Age. "I thought this place had been destroyed?" The loud stomps of the heavily-armored Gallu were the only answer to his question.

They passed through seven heavy gates as they worked their way from the outer perimeter of the cavernous gallery to the inner ring of buildings and gardens that surrounded the Temple of Knowledge, the domicile of the famulim assigned to the citadel. At each gate, a famulim stood in ceremonial robes to ask who and for what purpose was passage through the gate petitioned. Each time Masterson's escorting famulim would announce it was the Servitor Filio but that he had nothing of value to offer the gatekeeper. Each time the gatekeeper responded, "So it shall be recorded in the Temple of Knowledge."

The last gate led them into an enormous circular room that looked as though it had been chiseled from solid rock. Masterson and his party walked to the center of the room to stand under a bright light that reminded him of the lighting in the Genitors' training area in the Cassidan *City of Wisdom* that now seemed like an eternity ago. Before him in the perimeter of the lighted area stood the three serene famulim, and behind him stood the two formidable Gallu.

Beyond them, in the dark shadows, came a voice. He recognized it. It was the voice of Ningishzidda, the adopted son and apprentice of Lord Enki. "Who seeks to petition the Council of the Anunnaki and for what purpose?"

The lead famulim spoke clearly, "Servitor Filio, Protector of Inanna."

"And what is his purpose?"

"His purpose was unspoken, Lord Ningishzidda."

Emerging from the darkness to stand in the light surrounding Masterson and his party of famulim and Gallu came a tall, darkly robbed Cassidan male. "I know you. You're the Synthetic."

Masterson lifted his chin as Lord Ningishzidda revealed himself. "I am."

"Are you surrendering to Lord Enlil, Synthetic?"

"No, I'm here to negotiate with Lord Enlil so we can come to a fair solution to our shared problem."

Ningishzidda laughed, "You and Lord Enlil do not share a problem, Synthetic. You are the problem. You and your newly-found allies."

Masterson held his tongue. He didn't understand the direction the conversation was going. Ningishzidda was a member of Inanna and Enki's coalition of Anunnaki that believed that the Mundus should inherit the stewardship of Earth and that the Igigi and the Ejicerce had the abilities given by the Genitor through their volumen nanites was because of Inanna and Enki's intervention.

"We know you took part, if not instigated, the attack and ultimate destruction of the Genitors' Temporal Transport, *Tiamat*. That attack caused a tremendous loss of life. Thousands of Dionan servitors and Cassidan adepts were on that temporal transport. It is of singular interest that the Dionan courier *Glorious Questor* appeared in the sky just prior to the events leading to the destruction of the *Tiamat*. In fact, Lord Enlil himself has noted that you were present at the Battle of Eidin and identified the use of the same Ejicerce tactic that destroyed the *Tiamat*. Was that your idea, Synthetic?"

"I'm here on behalf of the Igigi, to express their desire to make an agreement with Lord Enlil that will allow them to continue to serve the Will of the Genitor."

The famulim and Gallu stepped away from Masterson and quietly moved into the thick shadows of the chamber as the two men stood facing each other. There was utter silence as their footsteps faded. Finally, Ningishzidda spoke, "What could the Igigi possibly offer the Lord of the Sky that would even interest him?"

"Mundus."

The silence lingered as Ningishzidda pondered the implications of what Masterson had just said. Ningishzidda turned and walked back into the shadows of the chamber, leaving Masterson alone.

Masterson paced around the stationary perimeter of the cone of light that hovered above him. He didn't explore the chamber; he knew better. The darkness was covering him, applied directly to his ability to sense his surroundings. For all he knew, there could be several Anunnaki watching him right now in proximity. But he wouldn't be aware of them until the veil of darkness was lifted from his mind by whomever had imposed it. "Famulim, I'm thirsty."

The faint sound of footsteps were heard, drawing his attention as they drew nearer. One of the three famulim appeared with a smile. It stood close to him within the circle of light that defined his space now. With a wave of its hand, a table took shape, rising from the floor, then upon the ubiquitous pseudo-ceramic table appeared a pitcher of water and a single ceramic drinking cup. All of this was created within a few heartbeats using the nanotechnology mastered by the Cassidans so long ago.

He reached for the cup and held it so the famulim could pour the pure water from the pitcher into it. Masterson watched with new insight. The revelation that all Cassidan technology mimicked the powers available through the access to the volumen nanites introduced into the biological body was startling. It changed everything. He slowly looked up from the cup and into the enormous dark eyes of the famulim. "I have a question relating to your physiology."

"Yes, servitor?" respond the famulim with its ubiquitous, androgenous voice.

"Why are your eyes so large and dark?"

The famulim seemed honestly surprised by the question. "The size and color of the eyes of a famulim are modifiable based on the environmental conditions of their location it is tasked to serve in by the Will of the Genitor."

"Yes, I understand that, but why are they so large and dark?" He smiled as he finished the water he had been given. "I've never seen a famulim with light-color eyes or the size of the Cassidan, Dionan, or Mundus eyes. Yet the famulim work in the same conditions as the others do."

The famulim paused, all subtle hand and body movements one would make while having a conversation stopped, as if frozen in time. Then it smiled and responded, "The famulim were created by the Genitor to facilitate and enhance the development of the three primary strains of observatory species used within this planetary system. Physiological design of the famulim was based on specific environmental information accessible at the time of arrival. The mobile bipedal structure with all life-sustaining chemical processing organs in a protected central cavity and the sensory and information processing organs in a flexible, rotating module were selected as most suitable for the rocky worlds within the inner region nearest the system's star. The famulim design was the first and was created with environmental and mission flexibility because of the conditions of the planets at the time of arrival."

Masterson set the ceramic cup on the table. "May I have a chair?"

The famulim gestured with its hand and a chair rose from the floor built atom by atom, molecule by molecule, for Masterson's use.

When comfortably seated, he continued, "That still doesn't answer my question. Why are your eyes so large and dark brown?"

"It is the Will of the Genitor."

"Precisely." Masterson turned and looked over his right shoulder as the famulim stood, clearly puzzled by the conversation. The sound of footsteps on the hard stone floor became louder as someone approached. Masterson stood to face the new arrival.

Lord Ningishzidda approached, a look of disapproval on his face as he gestured at the table and chair behind Masterson. "Remove these."

The famulim quickly removed the furniture with a quick gesture, releasing the molecular binding that had held the chair and table atoms together as if it were never there. The furniture dissipated as if it were smoke. It then stood silently as the two men faced one another.

"Lord Enlil is intrigued by your presence here. In his own words, your arrival saves him the time and effort to find the leader of the Igigi and putting an end to this Ejicerce nonsense. But he will hear what you have to say although it has no bearing on the decisions he must make concerning the fate of the Igigi." Lord Ningishzidda turned as if to walk away again, but instantly the darkness evaporated, revealing that Masterson's hunch that the darkness that had surrounded him was indeed imposed on his mind and not the true nature of where he was being held. They were in a massive domed chamber with a large curved table at which four of seven members of the Anunnaki Council sat, considering him silently.

Masterson didn't know all the Anunnaki leadership by sight, but he knew their names and the roles they played in the governance of his home world, Earth. Noticeably absent were two that he knew; Lord Enki and Lady Inanna. His eyes immediately went to Lord Enlil. Lord Ningishzidda moved to stand behind Enlil with his hands folded before him submissively. Masterson was surprised. He had thought of Ningishzidda as an ally of Inanna because he was Enki's adopted brood son and assistant.

"What petition on behalf of the Igigi do you intend to deliver, Servitor Filio?" Lord Enlil's voice was amplified by the acoustics of the dome chamber.

"The petition is this: by design, the Igigi have a symbiotic interaction with the Mundus. Both are genetically engineered for this world's environment, just as the Cassidans and Dionans were for their respective worlds. I believe it is the Will of the Genitor that the Mundusans, like the Cassidans and Dionans, be the stewards of the world they were designed for. Guided by the Igigi who were nurtured and trained for that very specific task by you yourself, Lord Enlil, through your leadership of the Anunnaki Council and the development of Mundus to this point we are at now."

Leaning forward, Enlil asked, "What point? What point are we at now, Servitor?"

"The Igigi have somehow angered you, Lord Enlil. Angered you to where they are being removed from their service to the Genitor. Forcibly taken to never be heard from again by their brood siblings and companions. Taken to what some believe is to their deaths. Beings created using the Cassidan techniques of specified conception to be raised in the Cassidan way, to serve the community with purpose, and to follow the Will of the Genitor through their work with the longevity of their kind. By design, and in your direction, the Igigi have been embedded into the Mundus communities that serve you in the stewardship of this world. They hope to continue to serve the Genitor. They hope to prove to you," Masterson looked to the other Anunnaki seated at the great table with Enlil, "the Anunnaki, that they are ready and more than prepared for the task they were created for." His gaze returned to Lord Enlil. "They are prepared to take on the role of being the stewards of this world."

"And what role are you to play in this regime change, Protector Dumuzid?" Masterson had met this Anunnaki only once, and he nodded in appreciation of his title and name given to him by Lady Inanna herself. He was Inanna's brood brother, Utu, and would be known as *Ra* in the Egyptian and *Apollo* in the Greek and Roman pantheons.

"Lord Utu, I serve the Genitor as their envoy. I don't speak for them, but I am their harbinger of change as announced by Lord Enlil himself so long ago during the Battle of Eidin." Masterson's claim of being a recognized envoy of the Genitor and recognized by Lord Enlil himself surprised the other two seated members of the council besides Enlil and Utu. Enlil only sat quietly as Masterson spoke. "The Cassidans and the Dionans are the stewards of their worlds. It is time for the Igigi to be the stewards of their world. It is the established way of the Genitor. I say it is the very Will of the Genitor."

"How dare you!" Enlil stood and looked at the faces of his fellow council members before turning back to Masterson. "I acknowledge that you were created for one purpose; to relay a message from the Genitor to me during the Battle of Eidin. Your message was consequential. It resulted in the resetting of our effort to prepare this world for the Genitor. But that is all you are – a messenger. How dare you come to my council and tell us that the Igigi, our creations, are our equals and capable of doing the work only we are capable of! Dionans did not immediately become the stewards of their world. If you were not a synthetic, hastily grown for one purpose, you would know that. It took many centuries for them to even gain the ability to organize and function without supervision by the Cassidans. The Dionans were technologically advanced when they were given control of their own world. Able to use and maintain, in fact improve upon the tools given them. The Igigi are sensual creatures, devoid of logic. They cannot prepare this world for the Genitors' use, nor are they capable of even organizing themselves, let alone a world!" Enlil's eyes flared with sparks of psycho-kinetic energy as he glared at Masterson.

"Why was Ganzir Citadel attacked by combat forces of the *Tiamat*? Why were the Mundus laborers slaughtered and the Igigi there assaulted?" Masterson waited for the answer to his questions.

There was no response from the Anunnaki at the table facing him.

Masterson pressed on with his argument, "Why was the *Tiamat* even here? Has not Lord Anu ordered a general evacuation of all forces from Mundus? If the Igigi weren't the intended stewards of Mundus, wouldn't there be a larger, more robust presence of Cassidans and Dionans here, like there was before the Deluge?"

"Enough!" Enlil's anger showed fiercely as psycho-kinetic energy manifested tips as small electrical arcs danced from one finger to the other. "Mundus is mine to shape as I see fit. Lord Anu has awarded me this realm to develop. I do not need the opinions and ideas of others. I am the prince of this world and I will govern it as I see fit." Enlil slammed his fist into the hard wooden table before him, causing a flash of bioluminescence to momentarily fill the large room with blue-white light.

Stubbornly, Masterson raised his own voice, "If you won't recognize me as an envoy for the Genitor then recognize me for what I am now. Envoy of the Igigi, the actual stewards of Mundus. Those who defeated you, the destroyers of the Temporal Transport *Tiamat.*"

"What?" Enlil's brow furrowed as he leaned forward with both hands on the wooden table. "You delivered your message to me at the Battle of Eidin. What other message do you have to deliver? You have served your purpose, *servitor*. Your service to the Genitor ended when you helped the Igigi murder the adepts and servitors of the *Tiamat.*"

"Right now, the Igigi are poised to destroy all resource collection facilities on the surface, similar to how Ganzir was destroyed by the *Tiamat*, leveling buildings and decimating the population of laborers. Now here is the question I pose; how will Lord Anu react to yet another disaster on Mundus?"

"Kill their own people?" Enlil laughed and reclaimed his seat. Nervously, the other Anunnaki looked toward him with varied combinations of fear and curiosity.

"Versus being killed by you?" Masterson paused. "You yourself have said that the Igigi are chaotic, unpredictable. Yes, they will do what is required of them to save themselves."

Another voice was heard, "Why are you here, Protector Dumuzid?"

Masterson looked to Nanna, the commander of the Anunnaki warehouses on the Moon. "I have a vested interest in the survival of this world, Lord Nanna. I have grown fond of it during my service here. Perhaps I learned that appreciation from serving Lady Inanna. I would like this world to survive and succeed as she does."

Lord Utu, the brood brother of Lady Inanna, spoke up, "I believe him. I have seen them together, even before Lord Enlil proclaimed him to be her protector and named him Dumuzid at her request. They shared a common interest in this world."

"What does that even mean?" Lord Enlil slammed his hand down on the table once more, his voice thundering in the large chamber. "It is a synthetic servitor, hastily rushed to maturity, programmed with memories only sufficient to make it functional enough to deliver its message to a designated receiver. Nothing more. You speak as if it is one of us?" Lord Enlil glared at his companions at the council table.

"Lord Enlil, he represents the Will of the Genitor. You declared him to be their envoy." Lord Utu continued without looking at Enlil, "We do not know how many messages Protector Dumuzid was given to pass on to you. We do not know his role in the Will of the Genitor. Perhaps this is the Genitor speaking to us through him, rather than a single man."

"Blasphemy!" shrieked Lord Enlil, "You reflect your brood sister, Utu. Do you seek to share her fate?"

Lord Utu whipped his head around to return Lord Enlil's glare, golden radiance shining from his eyes as he partially rose from his chair in anger.

"Enough!" Lord Nanna also stood, shouting to the two to stand down. "We are in a crisis again, whether we are willing to see it or not." He pointed to Masterson. "Protector Dumuzid is here to provide us a path through the crisis. We need to hear his proposal. He is right; Commander Anu will not react well to find, upon his arrival, that his garden has once again failed to bear fruit for him. It will not reflect well on us."

Lord Enlil took a deep breath, the psycho-kinetic energy fading from his eyes and fingers. "Before we continue, I would like to remind everyone present of something we agreed to." He nodded toward something behind where Masterson stood.

A savaged Cassidan female body hung on a portion of what appeared to be the stone wall from the perimeter of the chamber they were in. The body was close to Masterson, but he knew instinctively it was another image placed in his mind by Enlil. It was Inanna. Her beautiful pale skin had been shredded. Raw muscle was exposed. Masterson's heart fell. Her body was decomposing. She was dead.

"No!" Masterson fell to his knees in anguish. "No."

"You failed her, Dumuzid, failed to protect her. You failed miserably."

Masterson tried to clear his mind through sheer force of will, but her body remained in his sight. His eyes filled with rage, he slowly rose from his knees to turn to face the Anunnaki Council. He addressed

Lord Nanna, Lord Utu, and the visibly subdued Lady Ninhursag, ignoring Enlil. "Is this Lord Anu's intent? Is this the intent of the Genitor? This is Lord Enlil's response to a challenge. He destroys." Masterson slowly turned to look upon the destroyed body of Inanna. "When you first arrived here on Mundus, there was a host of you. Cassidans, Dionans, and famulim. The Genitors' Ummanate was well represented. All the Ummanate Orders of Battle had ongoing operations here on the surface of this world." Masterson raised his arms, gesturing to show the size of the surrounding chamber, "Kur was enormous, a space port as large and developed on the surface as it was here beneath it." He focused his gaze on Enlil. "You have brought all of that to this point. Where four of you sit at a table, alone, killing each other as he threatens to kill this world a second time. Now I ask you – as equal members of the council that Lord Anu set here to develop this world on his behalf as he seeks to serve the Will of the Genitor – is this the right path? Do you have confidence that Lord Anu supports this mockery of all that the Genitor has created? All that your civilization has strived to create?"

"The blasphemy continues!" Lord Enlil screamed as he suddenly stood, stretching his hand out toward Masterson.

"No," the deep voice of Ningishzidda cut through, surprising everyone as Ningishzidda's hand gripped Lord Enlil's wrist. "No. I do not believe this is the path the Genitor meant for us to travel."

Chapter 15: Specified Conception

Masterson explored the Cassidan garden in a gargantuan gallery deep within the bowels of the Earth. He strolled alone, moving between the flowering plants that grew under the artificial light that simulated the light of the Sun from the Martian orbit of millions of years ago when Cassidan culture was at its zenith. The plants and small animals, like all things Cassidan, were brought to life by the process of *specified conception*. Each organism, plant, and animal, was a clone conceived according to the plan for the community of Kur. Masterson smiled to himself as he admired the work of a society locked into perpetually planned stagnation. No wonder the Cassidans react so negatively to the genetic and physical mutations suffered by the Ejicerce in their service to the Genitor. He continued his stroll with his hands clasped behind his back as he walked.

"May I join you, Protector?"

Masterson turned to find Lord Enki, the Anunnaki Lord of Wisdom. Enki was the lead scientist for the Mundus expedition and the brood brother of Enlil, apprentice of Anu, the Supreme Commander.

"I am honored, sir." The two men, one billions of years old, the other a synthetic being with probably artificial memories recently created, walked together.

"You have done well serving the Genitor as their envoy." Lord Enki gazed down at the shorter man with a hint of a smile.

Masterson nodded with acceptance of Lord Enki's comment, but continued to walk silently.

"I watched you present your ultimatum to the council from my chambers. I had been removed from the council itself following Enlil's discovery of my participation in Inanna's modification of the volumen given the Igigi."

Masterson's head whipped around, looking up into Lord Enki's cobalt eyes. "Is she truly dead?"

Lord Enki smiled impishly. "Inanna dead?" He looked away from Masterson as they walked. "She was forced to endure physical abuse at the hands of Enlil's Gallus. They tortured her to where her body could no longer sustain itself. Her insult to Enlil was that severe. You have seen our volumen-enhanced powers in use. You know what they can do to the physical body." He paused as they walked, "And to the mind. The Gallus took turns with her. But she is strong, a veritable goddess. Enki ordered her essence be suspended out of body until Lord Anu's arrival for her judgement. She is Anunnaki."

Masterson couldn't conceal his relief. "Enlil has been effectively deposed as the mission commander. She can be restored!"

"My friend," Enki's recognition as a friend startled Masterson, "restore her to what? Her body is destroyed."

"What do you mean, restore her to what? You place consciousnesses in a holder body, don't you? Basically, that's what you did with me. Is there a possibility she won't be placed in a holder body?" Masterson's growing concern was clear from the tone of his voice.

"Lord Anu may choose to either place her consciousness in a holder body as you have suggested, or he may, because of her high status within the Anunnaki and her caste, release her essence to the Genitor."

"What does that mean? She's dead? What does that mean, release her essence to the Genitor? What are you talking about, her soul?"

"Her essence, Dumuzid. The sum totality of who she is. Her identity as a conscious being. Memory, knowledge, intellect, emotions, her cumulative personality; everything about her that is not physical matter but energy can be absorbed within the Genitor."

"She'll be lost."

"She will be remembered and a vital part of the Genitor for eternity."

Masterson shook his head, not accepting her loss. "Place her in a body like mine, synthetic, with her consciousness."

"Lord Dumuzid, we have structure and sacred traditions. She is a Cassidan of the highest caste. The punishment was ordered by the mission commander. We cannot simply erase her punishment before Lord Anu can decide her fate."

"To be blunt, Cassidans' strict adherence to structure and traditions allowed the Igigi to defeat the Fourth Order of Battle with only a few hundred untrained fighters. Those uplifted Mundus humans fought with passion and instinct, and won."

They walked in silence for minutes.

"I am going to petition the seated council members to place you in command of our mission until Lord Anu returns."

Masterson attempted to stifle a laugh. "You want me to take responsibility for the mission failure instead of you taking it."

Enki smiled. "Actually, I had not considered that until you reminded me of the unexpected Igigi victory and explained the reasons they prevailed against our servitors. You control the uplifted Mundus. Dumuzid, you have a singular ability to disregard protocol and procedure. Inanna has spoken of that flaw in your character often. She said you are untamable and therefore an asset to her cause. As always, her schemes have a tendency to work."

"She has always declared her love for this world and its people. From the moment I first met her until the last moments I spent with her before coming to this point on the temporal spectrum, her love of this world has been clear."

"Yes, Lord Dumuzid the Bull, is it now?"

Masterson snorted, "The Igigi call me that, yes. Dumuzid the Shining Bull of Heaven. I believe they see me as the heir of Genitor."

Enki was surprised by that revelation. "As the recognized envoy of the Genitor, I suppose that is a probable assumption by the Igigi. You must correct their mistake, Dumuzid."

"And you must give me the power to do that, Lord Enki." Masterson held Lord Enki's eyes with his own until the taller Cassidan nodded in agreement.

The two men took their time walking back toward the famulim Temple of Wisdom in the center of the main subterranean gallery of the citadel. Their discussion continued unfettered by concerns of what action Lord Enlil might take now that they openly had the support of the other surviving members of the council. Both men knew that the Anunnaki mission to Mundus was woefully under-resourced. Both agreed that Lady Inanna had been the architect of the scaling down and the force behind the enabling of the Mundus humans to replace the withdrawn Cassidan and Dionan attendants and servitors. Humans now filled those roles. Inanna's political savvy and strategic insight was formidable. For all their wisdom and knowledge of Cassidan protocol and traditions, or their interpretation of the Will of the Genitor, Enlil and Enki had been outmaneuvered by her. Masterson knew he needed her if he was to be successful as the new mission commander.

"How will you and the other Anunnaki handle Lord Enlil now that he knows he no longer has the support of what is left of the council?" Masterson paused as they meandered into the arrival and departure area.

"Your argument that we had failed the Genitor and will face the wrath of Lord Anu upon his arrival was persuasive. But there is no guarantee that Lord Anu will not simply send another temporal transport with more servitors. It is also possible that this world will be cleansed and reset yet again, as it has several times before. There have been five iterations or restarts on this world before our current configuration of flora and fauna was agreed upon."

Masterson resisted the urge to impress Lord Enki with his knowledge of the various geological ages readily available to him from his own memories of a life at the end of the Holocene epoch. But recent events had shaken his belief that those memories were actual and not fabrications programmed into him. Instead, Masterson nodded. "I'll return to the city of Nippur and await word from you or the council. I'll send for members of the Igigi to join me there. But be forewarned, Lord Enki, I will tolerate no threats or even perceived threats to them. Any belligerent act by you or Lord Enlil and I will unleash their fury on what is left of the Anunnaki mission here."

Lord Enki nodded solemnly. "You and the Igigi are products of our past decisions and interpretations of the Genitor. You are reflections of the world we have created here. I would expect nothing less than brutal retaliation for hostile action on our part. I will ensure that the council knows this and that you will carry out your threat. You are Dumuzid the Bull, the destroyer of the *Tiamat*."

Masterson had summoned the ad hoc leadership of the Igigi to Enlil's temple in the human city of Nippur. Several of the Igigi had been watching him clairvoyantly with their volumen-enhanced sensory perception. Word of his return from the meeting with Lord Enlil and the other Anunnaki was shared at the speed of thought among the Igigi. Masterson sat waiting on the top step of the stairway to the top of the Ekur Temple.

"You did it!" Chantico cheered as she and her escorting teleportist appeared behind him. She immediately, to both Masterson's and the teleportist's surprise, dropped to her knees behind him, hugging him tightly about his shoulders. They laughed together. Chantico turned, gesturing toward her companion, "This is Shala; she is a spirit walker." The younger woman smiled over Chantico's shoulder with the wide eyes of adoration.

"She's what?" Masterson chuckled.

"She is, as you call it, a jumper." Chantico released Masterson's shoulders as others appeared behind her. Marduk and four others stood facing him. Only Marduk smiled. Chantico leaped up, going to Marduk's side as she slid under his arm, hugging him tightly.

Masterson turned, standing up from where he sat on the top step of the temple. "Marduk, good to see you again." He looked up at the four Igigi standing beside Marduk.

"These are Rikbiel, an aeromancer," Marduk gestured at the dark male standing between the two women. He slipped his left arm around the hip of the blonde woman nearest him. "And this is Sephia, a prophetess who specializes in reading auras." Sephia smiled at Masterson as the introductions continued, with Marduk nodding at the third member of the newcomers. "Hamaliel, known for her technical expertise in working with the laborers and her Anunnaki master, Lord Ningishzidda."

"You work for Lord Ningishzidda?" Masterson frowned, "In what way?"

"Yes, Lord Dumuzid the Bull, I oversaw laborers doing the collection of resources in the Irkalla Citadel region."

"How recently have you spoken with Lord Ningishzidda?"

"Several days, Lord Dumuzid the Bull. Not since the arrival of the temporal transport *Tiamat*."

"Which region of the world does Irkalla Citadel service?" Masterson noted Hamaliel carried herself like a fighter, a warrior, unlike Sephia or even Chantico.

"The Meluhha region, Lord Dumuzid the Bull, eastward beyond the Southern Sea."

"The Indus River? You were working in India?" Masterson smiled.

"I do not know of India, Lord Dumuzid the Bull, but I know the river you are referring to. It is called the *Sindhu*."

"This is Jianiel. He supervises the lands to our northeast, the valley of the Yellow River." Jianiel slightly bowed his head then looked up, smiling, his dark eyes meeting Masterson's.

Masterson nodded to Jianiel then looked to Marduk. "These are the ones selected to organize the Igigi?"

"Yes, Lord Dumuzid the Bull. Each stepped forward during our time of persecution by Lord Enlil following the arrest and disappearance of Lady Inanna. Chantico worked in the far western resource collection region beyond Kur and the great ocean in the Citadel of Ganzir. She supervised resource collection as Hamaliel did in the near eastern region beyond the Southern Sea." Marduk gestured to the tall male, "Rikbiel worked closely with the Dionan servitors and famulim of Lord Enlil, handling the transportation of resources to the central collection center for lifting to the Moon. He is well trained in the operations and maintenance of the flying transports used by the Anunnaki adepts, servitors, and famulim."

Masterson spoke directly to Rikbiel, "The transport saucers – did you have access to the Lightning Ships too? Are there Lightning Ships stationed here that don't belong to the *Tiamat*?"

Rikbiel stepped closer to Masterson, "No, Lord Dumuzid the Bull, there are no Lightning Ships, only a few transport ships of various shapes and sizes."

"And Lord Enlil hasn't denied you the use of them?"

"No, Lord Dumuzid the Bull, I still have control over them. Do you wish me to summon one for you?"

Masterson shook his head, showing that it wasn't required. He then addressed them all together, "As I'm sure you know from the watchers among you, the council acted in defiance of Lord Enlil. He was removed as the mission leader here to Mundus." The others looked at Masterson in disbelief. He continued, "We must prepare to assume the leadership of the collection of resources that the Anunnaki consider valuable to their operation. We'll continue to provide the resources required by them, but in ways that are helpful to us. Ways that will allow us to exploit their technology and knowledge for our own benefit."

"You are not truly one of us, Lord Dumuzid. We owe you a great deal, but you are Dionan, not of this world, but Diona. Why have you come to our aid and willing to lead us now?" Marduk pressed, "What do you have to gain from all of this?"

Chantico placed her hand on Marduk's upper arm, whispering, "No" in a low voice.

Masterson squared his shoulders, his gaze shifting between Marduk and Rikbiel. "I am Lady Inanna's chosen protector. But beyond that, she and I have a connection to this world."

Rikbiel spoke next, "There are those among us who believe that Lady Inanna has been killed, like many of our own, by Lord Enlil and his servitors from the *Tiamat*. If that is the case, you failed her, and us, as her protector."

A woman's voice cut through the males' arguing. Hamaliel spoke, "Inanna is our mentor. She is our strongest advocate. She is the rightful leader of us, if it is not to be ourselves. Not a Dionan claiming to be her protector from the past." She looked directly at Masterson, "You claim you are her protector and that you are from our past." Hamaliel stepped forward toward Masterson, her eyes blazing. "Bring her to us, Lord Dumuzid the Bull, bring Inanna to us, and then we will know you are indeed all that you say you are; not an Anunnaki servitor sent to trick us."

Masterson stood for a few moments, measuring his response to what the young Igigi woman had just done. He smiled at her, "I can see what use you are to Lord Ningishzidda. You have the mind of a strategist, Hamaliel. Are you representing him now?" He looked to Marduk and Rikbiel then finally to Chantico, his ally from what would be called *Mesoamerica*. "I'll find Inanna and return her to you, but you must do this while I'm gone." He paused for emphasis, his tone and demeanor challenging them. "You must set yourself aside from the laborers. They're your strength but also your greatest vulnerability. If you're too close to them, your enemies will use them against you. So set yourself away from them. But you must control them, for they're your most valuable resource and the key to your survival."

Masterson led the seven Igigi into the small roofed room at the tip of the temple, out of the sunlight near the open portal to Kur. The Igigi looked concerned that they stood so close to the portal.

"Lord Dumuzid, you realize they can hear us through the portal?" frowned Marduk as he glared at the dimensional blister.

"They must know our plans for organization so their confidence grows in our ability to manage this world on their behalf," he looked into the eyes of the seven, "or our conflict with them will begin again."

"He speaks the truth." Hamaliel surprised Masterson again by agreeing with him without hesitation. "If they feel they can do better than we can, they will seek to kill us again. We know he speaks the truth about our survival being linked to how well we serve the Anunnaki. They have taught us that their numbers are greater than the stars in the night sky."

"They are many. I have seen their cities on their home world of Cassida. They are glorious cities that stretch into the sky with many towers. They are formidable, but not undefeatable." Masterson then simply sat on the hard stone surface of the temple floor. "Set yourself aside from the laborers. Continue to have them bring resources to their temples as they did in the past. But we want them to be independent of you to a degree so you're not needed for every decision that must be made. We'll set up an elite class of leaders to speak and act on your behalf. Just as the Anunnaki created you to be their go-between with the laborers, so shall you create a class of leaders from within the laborers."

"But Lord Dumuzid, will that not diminish our control of them? Will we not make ourselves useless to the Anunnaki and cause them to replace us?" Marduk again questioned him.

"No, no, I see another purpose, Marduk," interrupted Hamaliel. "If we create leaders among them, the collection of resources is increased by the number of leaders we support."

Masterson smiled, "Your secondary task is to protect yourselves. You must scatter and not merge your activities so you cannot be replaced as easily as the Anunnaki council allowed itself to be. Surround yourselves with mystery, and limit access to yourself by the laborers and each other."

This brought a reaction from the seven. "No, Lord Dumuzid, we cannot isolate ourselves from each other as you say!" Sephia spoke for them.

"I'm not saying to completely isolate yourselves from each other. You are your greatest strength. For your safety and the safety of the entire group, there needs to be separation. Think how all this would have turned out if you had all been together in one citadel. They didn't attack Ganzir with overwhelming force because they knew the rest of you would be harder to find if they had. If you had all been together, they might have simply destroyed the city with one overpowering attack."

"But by splitting up, won't we increase the danger to ourselves by being alone?"

Masterson looked at Jianiel, "You misunderstand. I want you to organize into small teams, independent teams that can act on their own regionally, that operates regionally. But if called by another team, they can react quickly to help. None of you must be totally alone. None of you *should* be totally alone."

The look of general relief among the seven prompted Masterson to address another challenge facing them. "The Cassidans and Dionans can quickly swell their numbers with the use of the brood-specified conception techniques; mass reproduction in a test tube."

"A what?" queried Jianiel. The others frowned at each other, not understanding what Masterson meant.

Masterson smiled then looked around the small group that would determine the fate of Earth and humankind. He paused for a moment as the realization of what was happening sunk in. "Our abilities come from microscopic nanites that the Anunnaki placed in our bodies. The Volumen." The seven listened intently, focused on what he was saying. "My understanding is that the nanites activate our special extrasensory abilities. Does anyone know how that is actually done?"

"Yes," Sephia said, "I do. They change the chemical bonds within molecules, the smallest components of our physical bodies. They activate the components within our bodies that generate the chemical reactions which enable the generation of our aura, and the energy we use to observe, organize thoughts, and remember."

Masterson was elated, "Wow! The Anunnaki taught you well, Sephia." Everyone laughed at the compliment. "You're one of Lord Enki's, aren't you?"

Sephia raised her chin, "I am."

"So, Sephia, if the Igigi abandoned the practice of specified conception and allowed nature to take its course, would the brood produced also have the chemical alterations to their body that their Igigi donors had?"

"I, I suppose so, but if that were the case, why would the Cassidans not simply do that? Why would they not do that themselves rather than use the technology?" The others listened closely to the discussion between Sephia and Masterson.

"It's sloppy, and it takes away their control. Imagine a world where everyone was an Igigi – the laborers too. I imagine early on they discovered that not everyone can be an adept, someone has to be a servitor too if things are to get done." His gaze shifted from Sephia to look at each one of them before he continued, "Imagine the chaos that would cause."

"But the Cassidans have the famulim, they have always had the famulim," Marduk pointed out. "The famulim are the laborers for them, aren't they?"

"Perhaps they are. To be honest, I don't know. When I served aboard the *Leviathan*, a ship similar to the *Tiamat*, I saw both Cassidan and Dionans in the crew. And there is the Gallu. I don't know if there are Cassidan servitors, but I assume the Cassidan Gallu are servitors." He furrowed his brow. "But I know this: the Cassidan specified conception technique controls the development of volumen-enhanced psychic abilities in Cassidans, Dionans, and the Igigi by engineering the physiological or physical body of each brood to meet the social requirements of their communities, based on projected needs as determined by the Will of the Genitor, as interpreted by the highest caste of the Cassidans. We must disrupt that practice if we're to control this world."

Marduk voiced the question for the seven, "What do you mean?"

"We're going to modify the practice of specified conception. We're not going to use technology, data, and precise planning to bolster our ranks and increase the number of Igigi."

"What does that mean?" Jianiel blinked and appeared highly confused.

Marduk laughed loudly, "He wants us to rut with the laborers!"

Chapter 16: A House in Kur

Masterson emerged from the teleport bubble into the arrival gallery of the underground citadel of Kur. Two famulim had been waiting for him. He smiled at them, receiving an immediate, identical smile.

"This way, Lord Dumuzid. The council has set aside a private domicile for you." Bowing low, the famulim turned in unison and led him to the residence he had been assigned.

"Have you two been assigned to me by Lord Enki?"

"No, Lord Dumuzid the Bull," replied the first of the famulim.

"Lord Ningishzidda assigned us to you, Lord Dumuzid," offered the second famulim.

"Lord Ningishzidda told you to call me Dumuzid the Bull?"

"Yes, Lord Dumuzid the Bull, do you prefer another?"

"How many names do you have listed for me?"

The second famulim turned to look at him as they slowed their pace. The first famulim looked forward as if taking over driving them as they negotiated the route to his new domicile. "You are listed as Captain Roy Masterson; Filio Domini; Dumuzid, Protector of Inanna; Dumuzid the Bull, Destroyer of Tiamat; Myrddin Wyllt--"

"Wait," Masterson interrupted, "Wait, who is Myrddin Wyllt?"

The second famulim continued, "Your name preceding…"

"Stop, don't continue. It's better not to know of the various names I will use until I get there."

"As you wish, sir," replied the first famulim.

"Do all famulim have access to information about the future?"

"It depends on who we are assigned to assist, Lord Dumuzid the Bull, and the nature of that help as determined by the Will of the Genitor."

"I am intrigued. Explain that, please?"

"The Genitor controls access to their information. If it is deemed necessary to a famulim to have access to information to assist in a project or activity, the Genitor will release that information to the specific famulim requiring it." As they walked, the lead famulim looked back at Masterson with what Masterson took as a condescending smile.

"Are the Genitor aware of my efforts on behalf of the Igigi?" Masterson paused, furrowing his brow, "Better question: who are you being given access to information on behalf of concerning me? Me or Lord Ningishzidda?"

"Here you are, Lord Dumuzid the Bull," the two famulim turned in unison to usher him into a beautiful, classical Dionan subterranean domicile set on the edge of a large crevasse dividing the larger gallery from the upscale residential area.

Sensing that the famulim were ignoring his last question, he changed direction. "When was the last time this building was occupied?"

A deep voice answered, "This domicile has not been occupied since the evacuation."

Masterson turned toward Lord Ningishzidda as he stepped into the room from the balcony. "Well, if you aren't a surprise. I didn't expect to see you here, or so soon."

"What do you mean, Lord Dumuzid?" Ningishzidda dismissed the two famulim with a simple hand gesture. They retreated to a distant area within the building to wait to be summoned again.

"I thought you were Inanna's ally. In the meeting with the council, you seemed to be an ally of Enlil." Masterson looked up at the taller Cassidan as the two closed the distance between them.

"I seek the success of this mission, as should we all. I am not sure what your motivations are. That you are Dionan yet seem to champion the Mundus cause has me perplexed."

"Perplexed, why?"

"I understand you are an envoy of the Genitor. I am aware of the process in which an envoy is created, being outside the larger community plan. Your conception was even more precise than that of the usual adept or servitor. You were created for one specific purpose, to deliver a message. What I do not understand is how, with that kind of focus, you became an enemy of Enlil, the very person you were sent from the Genitor to inform."

"I oppose Enlil's style of managing the mission. I see the elimination of entire generations of Mundusans as wasteful and not a productive use of resources." Masterson paused, looking away from Ningishzidda, "I see the Mundusans as a worthy participant in the stewardship of this world on behalf of the Genitor. I don't think it is the Will of the Genitor that entire cycles of Mundusan broods be destroyed for the sake of Enlil's personal goals. Have you traveled through Time, Lord Ningishzidda?"

"No, it is not customary for Cassidans of the higher caste to travel to points in the Temporal Spectrum. It is far too dangerous, and a wasteful and non-productive activity. Temporal travel is a task left to the servitors and select adepts."

Masterson concealed his smile by bowing his head as the two stood. "The Mundusans differ from the Cassidans and Dionans, I understand. Is that true?"

"Indeed, it is a point of disagreement within the council. The development of the Mundus laborers took a radical departure from that of the Cassidans and Dionans."

Masterson looked up at Ningishzidda, "What do you mean?"

"You and I, our conceptions, were controlled and planned for. We are not the result of random biological factors coming together to create a being that was not part of the community plan. Every aspect of our genetic makeup was selected for a reason. The Mundusans are not that way. They can procreate at will and do so with great frequency. The only observable deterrent to stopping their incessant procreation is their short lifespan."

"You see that as a problem, sir?" Masterson stroked his beard as he considered his next question, "Do you agree with Lord Enlil that the Mundusans should be culled from time to time? You don't see their numbers as an asset for the stewardship of this world?"

"Cassida, Diona, and Mundus are worlds that belong to the Genitor. Each world's population developed over extended periods of time that allowed for the most effective stewardship of that world and the use of its resources. That stewardship included not straining the ecology of the world during its most fruitful time in its evolution.

Cassida flourished at the beginning of this star's life cycle billions of years ago under the stewardship of the Cassidans, assisted by the famulim at the direction of the Genitor. More recently, Diona flourished, after the passing of Cassida, as the garden world in this star's planetary system. Hundreds of millions of years ago, the Dionans were assisted and taught in their time of ascension by the Cassidans and the famulim, using the knowledge of the Genitor to travel along the Temporal Spectrum to continue the Will of the Genitor during their time."

"Wait – Diona, what will come to be known as Venus during the Mundus Ascension, was like Mundus only a few hundred million years ago?"

"Yes."

"What happened to it? I understand Cassida losing its atmosphere billions of years ago, but only a hundred million years ago for Diona?"

"Seven hundred and thirty-seven million years ago," corrected Lord Ningishzidda.

Masterson looked dumbfounded at Ningishzidda, struggling to keep his temper in check.

Lord Ningishzidda explained, "The resources valued by the Cassidans and directed to harvest by the Genitor were depleted and the ecology of Diona failed."

Masterson interrupted, "So the Dionans were treated the same way as the Mundusans are being treated now by the Cassidans and famulim? Their world was exploited and ruined and left a deserted hellhole that no one can survive in?"

"As was the Genitor's Will."

Masterson shook his head, "The Genitor's Will is the stock answer given whenever a Cassidan wants to justify their actions. But what is the Genitors Will? I have never gotten a straight answer. You are an adept, a member of the Cassidan upper caste. By your own admission, you were genetically bred to be a leader for this mission, placed by the Cassidan leadership. You, better than any lower caste Cassidan or member of a Dionan Consortium of Clans, should know what the Will of the Genitor is. So tell me."

"Your lack of traditional education and training within a brood shines through often, Envoy Dumuzid. Had you had a formal upbringing within a brood home, you would know the answer to that question."

"Which is?"

With a sigh of frustration, Ningishzidda answered. "The Genitor's Will is that each member of the community share in the experience of living in harmony with one another in the Genitor's service through good stewardship and faithful obedience."

"Regardless of the way they are conceived, the Mundusans want to serve the Genitor as strongly as any Cassidan or Dionan. This is their time. Don't you see that? Each world in this system was brought to fruition in a sequence. First it was Cassida, then Diona, and now Mundus. The people that populated each world were customized to fit the physical environment of that world. Don't you see it?"

Ningishzidda shook his head. "The Mundusans are chaotic, impulsive, and violent. Their existence violates the Will of the Genitor."

Masterson countered, "And yet here they are the primary group now exercising stewardship of Mundus on behalf of the Genitor."

Ningishzidda walked from where they stood out onto the terrace overlooking the chasm the dwelling was built beside. He changed the direction of their discussion that he was growing uncomfortable with pursuing as Masterson followed him. "You have traveled on a temporal ship. You know that the ship slides between locations on the temporal spectrum through the detection and manipulation of several dimensions at once. Well, adepts do the same thing. They detect and manipulate multiple dimensions to affect the surrounding environment."

"Yes, I have seen that in action aboard temporal couriers, although I don't understand it."

"Have you noticed the winged living creatures on Mundus that fly in the sky?"

"Yes, birds. I've seen them."

Lord Ningishzidda continued to look down into the depths of the chasm they stood beside. "They are a basic example of the use of multiple dimensions used to interact with their environment. They see objects and they can find objects by using the three basic physical dimensions of Length, Height, and Width. They then add the ability to observe a fourth dimension; in their case, force relating to the planetary positive and negative magnetic fields. Birds, as you called them, can sense the direction of the positive or negative magnetic charge and move within their environment. Adepts are the same. They use extrasensory abilities, enhanced by nanites in their blood from the volumn they ingested, to move within and sometimes manipulate their environment."

With a bored expression, Masterson's own frustration was becoming clear, "But coming back to my original question, how are the Mundus different from the Cassidans and Dionans in the Genitor's service?"

Ningishzidda paused at the edge of the crevasse, looking over the side of the small wall that provided some protection from falling over into the abyss. "Their individual conception is not managed the same way as it was on Cassida or Diona. The famulim are not as engaged in the process of conception for the Mundusans as they were for the Cassidans or the Dionans."

Masterson stood an arm's length from Ningishzidda, "What do you mean? I understand the famulim and Cassidans were the first. But I don't understand why that system of controlled insemination was continued to Diona and not here on Mundus."

"The Cassidan technique of procreation, specified conception, is efficient and resulted in creating a vibrant, balanced civilization that served as the model of what would follow on Diona."

"And yet both civilizations collapsed in time." Masterson paused as he considered his next words. "The Cassidans flourished billions of years ago after the formation of the Sun and its planets. The Dionans flourished hundreds of millions of years ago, long after the Cassidan civilization had fallen. They didn't coexist in the Temporal Spectrum and were billions of years apart. I assume Cassida seeded Diona the same way it did Mundus, using their time travel capability. But why the change in procedure for inhabiting this planet with its laborers?"

"It was the Will of the Genitor," conceded Ningishzidda.

"Bullshit," blurted a now angry Masterson.

A surprised Lord Ningishzidda looked at Masterson with a confused expression.

"What happened to Diona to cause the Genitor to abandon their continued use of the Cassidan model of specified insemination that allowed for the Mundusan population to be created differently?"

"What do you mean, Lord Dumuzid?"

"Everything happens by the Will of the Genitor, right?"

"Yes, of course, everything."

"Then the creation of the Mundusans, the creation of the Igigi, even the formation of the Ejicerce, is by their Will?"

Ningishzidda stared at Masterson, not saying a word.

"To what end is the conflict between the Ejicerce and the Anunnaki?" continued Masterson. "Don't say the Will of the Genitor. I believe it's the failure of the Cassidan's, not recognizing the Will of the Genitor and extending their sovereignty beyond their time within the Temporal Spectrum. I believe that the Cassidan system was flawed on Dionan just as it is flawed here on Mundus."

"How dare you!" spat Ningishzidda. "How dare you spout such blasphemy to me."

"What is the makeup of the Ejicerce?"

"The Ejicerce are from the Dionan Clans, some fallen adepts, and servitor Cassidans from the Temporal Transports that have jumped too many times, with a few Mundusans from the Clan ships."

Masterson scoffed. "Your estimates are current or from the past, recorded based on encounters with them, or by information fed to you from the Genitor's famulim about the Ejicerce from the future. Doesn't that seem like a war you can't win or have already lost?"

Ningishzidda appeared awestruck. He furrowed his brow as he stared at Masterson.

Masterson continued, "The Genitor that selected me for service responded when I asked him who they were at war with, saying that they were at war with themselves. They are the only power that can threaten them."

A startled Ningishzidda spouted, "You mean that the Ejicerce ascension and the decline of the Cassidan Castes and Dionan Clans is the Will of the Genitor?" Ningishzidda stood amazed when he realized the entirety of what Masterson had said. "You spoke with the Genitor?"

"Yes, several times during my training. I was given the volumen by a Genitor."

That admission stunned Ningishzidda. "You were trained by the Genitor? Your perception and manipulation of the dimensions must be incredible."

"Then I have your support when Lord Enki petitions the surviving members of the council to appoint me as their new leader of the council?"

"You?" Lord Ningishzidda's surprise was apparent. "You are not Cassidan! You are a Dionan, a synthetic Dionan, and cannot be the judge of Cassidans." Lord Ningishzidda roared, "No. No, you shall not be, you cannot be a member of the council. You cannot be the leader of the Anunnaki Council."

"I have Lord Enki's support. I have Lady Inanna's support," responded Masterson. "They know I'm not a Cassidan and yet Lord Enki plans to petition the council to seat me as their leader."

"Lord Enki is a senior member of the council chosen by Lord Anu himself, but Lord Enki is incapable of leading with the firm hand needed to get the required results. Lady Inanna was a talented adept assigned by Lord Anu as a special assistant to Lord Enki. But she lost her way and stopped following the Will of the Genitor and was destroyed at Lord Enlil's order. All that remains of her is her essence, which will be committed to the famulim Temple of Wisdom."

"What part did you play in what happened to Lady Inanna?" hissed Masterson as anger filled his heart.

Lord Ningishzidda hesitated to answer Masterson, knowing now that he was trained by a Genitor in preparation to be the envoy to Lord Enlil. "I need not explain my actions to you, Lord Dumuzid. Not here, not now."

Masterson frowned as the Anunnaki turned to leave. "I will find out what your role was in what happened to Inanna, Lord Ningishzidda."

"You are a Dionan, a mere servitor. You forget your place in the scheme of things here in this world." The taller Cassidan spun on his heels, causing his robes to flare around him as he hurried through the domicile to the exit.

"Go with your master," Masterson ordered the two famulim as they reappeared. The two looked confused then turned in unison to scurry in the direction Lord Ningishzidda had gone.

Masterson sighed and moved about the first floor living area of the domicile. He flopped down on a lounger, pinching the bridge of his nose, trying to ward off exhaustion and cursing himself for not handling the confrontation with Ningishzidda better. He needed allies, not enemies. Masterson hesitated then stood to leave the domicile, head back to the surface, and rejoin the Igigi. With a low voice he said to himself, "I think I've done enough damage for one day."

Waiting for Masterson outside the domicile stood four armed Cassidan males. He recognized them to be Gallu, members of the Cassidan Citadel Guard. The Gallu were Cassidans that hadn't shown an aptitude for training as an adept despite the vaulted benefits of specified conception, so they were redirected to training as the security for those that could. Now two of them were facing off with Masterson while two held back. The Cassidans were leaner and taller. Their bodies adapted to the lower gravity and air pressure of the ancient Mars of several billion years ago, so they weren't as strong as Masterson was in his Dionan body. Diona, or Venus, was the same size as the Earth, a veritable twin world, or at least it had been seven hundred million years ago when Earth was a giant snowball and all that lived there were sponges.

The Gallu towered over Masterson at three meters in height and were armed with lethal power rods. Masterson was surprised that they only wore the gray belted tunic and slippers used in garrison or aboard ships. The power rod was an electrified mace that, at its tip, could deliver an explosive charge of energy that could shatter an enemy's melam armor or explode a man's head. Masterson took heart that they weren't wearing melam armor or carrying the even more lethal lancer power-staffs, the particle stream range weapons he himself had used in the Battle of Eidin at the end of the last Ice Age.

"Are you here to escort me?" Masterson asked, frowning as the two lead Gallu advanced on him.

"We are here, Dumuzid, to ensure you never leave Kur again," growled the nearest of the two.

In an instant, Masterson dropped to the ground supported by his left hand, kicking out with both feet at the left knee of the larger assailant, causing it to bend backward, then rolled out of reach of his opponent as he hit the ground. If the Gallu had been armored, the move wouldn't have worked. The leading Gallu howled in pain as he collapsed on his left side, clutching his injured knee. The second Gallu, surprised by Masterson's attack, halted and went into a hand-to-hand fighting stance. That hesitation wasn't wasted by Masterson, who leaped to the right side of the fallen Gallu, snapping the power rod that was almost as long as he was tall from the fallen warrior's belt. The Gallu moved to stop Masterson but was too late, and felt a charge from the weapon released into his side, disrupting the muscle and bone of his rib cage, killing him.

The other Gallu were outraged. All three drew their power rods with their left hands in unison, the weapons humming as the power settings were rolled up. Small electrical arcs on the tips of the rods sparked and crackled.

Masterson spun on his right heel in a twirling movement to slice into his nearest opponent's left flank. The Cassidan blocked Masterson's two-handed attack with his rod but had to step back to keep his balance because of the power of Masterson's attack. In that moment of hesitancy by the Cassidan, Masterson spun low to the right again but kept his rod's point down and drove it into the belly of the Gallu with both hands gripping his weapon like a spear. The Gallu before him stiffened from the intense charge as the point discharged electrical current into his stomach. Masterson side-stepped to the right to face the third Gallu as the stench of burned flesh surrounded them.

"Demon!" the Gallu shouted, bringing his rod in a downward sweep meant to crush the smaller Masterson from above.

Masterson went to his knee, raising the rod above his head parallel to the ground, gripping the handle in his right hand and the other end of the rod with his left hand, behind the live electrical flange, and blocking the brutal downward attack from the Gallu. As the infuriated warrior bellowed and raised his own rod again, Masterson stood and spun, shoving his back against the hips and belly of the larger attacking giant. He then shoved his rod straight up and back over his head to impale the head of his attacker through the neck with the tip of the rod, causing the Cassidan's head to explode from the electrical charge. He fell back with a loud thud as Masterson stood to his full two-meter height to face the last Gallu warrior.

The surviving giant's eyes traveled between the three corpses of his slain comrades, all taken in very short order by the single Dionan servitor standing before him. The stench of charred flesh filled the air. "Who are you?"

A feminine voice came from the long-abandoned dwelling behind him, causing him to turn, ready to fight more Gallu.

"He is Dumuzid the Bull, the Slayer of the Tiamat, and leader of the Igigi," boasted Chantico, flames dancing around her fingers as she stood while pinning the Gallu with her eyes. Beside her stood Shala, their jumper, with Marduk and Hamaliel behind them.

Shala spoke with a low voice, "Ishtar said you needed help."

Masterson grinned but didn't relax his stance as he returned his eyes to watch the remaining Gallu, "Ishtar?"

"Your watcher, Lord Dumuzid." Marduk walked from behind Chantico and Shala to stand beside Masterson, also watching the Gallu. "She is the prophetess that most often is farseeing you, as you ordered us to do."

Masterson looked back as the Gallu lowered the oversized rod offering, "Surrender yourself to us and your life will be spared." The warrior screamed with frustration and anger then charged him with his weapon again raised, only to be immolated by Chantico.

Masterson frowned as he turned to a smiling Chantico. "I had questions for him."

Marduk interrupted, "We must leave. This is not a safe place for us." The four Igigi moved together, placing their hands between them so all could be touched by Ishtar. Chantico waved toward Masterson to take her hand with her eyes down, not looking into his. Masterson took Chantico's hand. Ishtar smiled then closed her eyes, concentrating. In the blink of an eye, they were all teleported out of the Citadel of Kur.

Chapter 17: The War for Heaven on Earth

"We have to hurry. I think Ningishzidda will move against us." Masterson barked orders as soon as they appeared at their destination. "I want to see Rikbiel. Send for him." He turned to Marduk, "Get the word out to expect an attack from Ningishzidda. I don't know what he can attack us with." Masterson frowned, "He may use the laborers' guards like they were servitors. Find out if Ningishzidda has a temple of his own like the Anunnaki used to collect resources." Marduk shook his head in agreement then sprinted off to call the names of some surrounding villagers that had helped in the past. Masterson turned to Chantico, "Who do you have here that can defend this location?"

"We have organized the way you said to. I broke down our numbers into groups of ten, trying as best as I could to make sure each group had unique talents within it."

Masterson's growing frustration with Chantico was clear. He took hold of her shoulders and looked directly into her dark eyes. "How many are here right now?"

She grimaced. "Twenty to thirty, maybe less..." She bit her lower lip. "I think Jianiel has already left. Maybe there are fifteen here now."

"Go find out." He watched her run off. Then, to no one in particular, he mumbled, "Where is Rikbiel?" Masterson scanned over the heads of the surrounding laborers and few Igigi people, looking for the commander of their transports. "Rikbiel?" he shouted. Frustrated, Masterson turned, looking back and seeing Ishtar standing where they arrived. She looked exhausted. Masterson shook his head then moved to take hold of her by her shoulders. "We're not done. I need to speak with Rikbiel. Can you find him for me?"

She was tired. It was clear by the way she held herself with her arms dangling at her sides, her eyes heavy with fatigue. "I can try."

Masterson looked about the familiar village Marduk's group had been staying at since the destruction of the *Tiamat* which now seemed like ages ago, another lifetime. "We have to move," he said to himself before searching for Marduk or Chantico with urgency. Masterson found them in the middle of an argument. They became silent at Masterson's approach. Masterson sensed that he was the focus of their agitation. The remaining Igigi that had been closer to the arrival point followed Masterson to form a group around Marduk and Chantico. The last to arrive was Ishtar. She was now more alert than when Masterson had found her.

"Are these all there are here now?" Masterson greeted everyone standing with a quick nod before turning his full attention to Marduk.

"Yes. Jianiel left for the Yellow River Valley far to the northeast right after you left this morning. Hamaliel left with her team after the midday meal, for the Sindhu River basin, also to the east."

"This is your team, Marduk?"

"No, seven are going with Chantico back to Ganzir. The rest are staying here with me."

Masterson looked with surprise at Chantico, "You're going back to Ganzir? There's nothing left there."

She lifted her chin. "The laborers there are my people. I cannot leave them leaderless now that I know Lady Inanna is truly gone. I will lead them south, higher into the mountains there. As you said, Lord Dumuzid, we need to live in the high regions where the Anunnaki will not go."

Masterson tried not to show his disappointment with her decision to return to the Western Hemisphere and not stay in the Mediterranean basin. He smiled, nodding his head. "You're wise to do so. Your people will profit from your wisdom and courage." He turned to address the others, "My attempt to argue our case with the Anunnaki is in jeopardy. One of the Cassidan attendants who served the council and whom I thought was an ally to our cause is against us serving the Genitor directly, and may seek to replace Lord Enlil as the leader of the council." Masterson scanned the faces of the Igigi standing before him. He saw growing concern and confusion. "The name of the Cassidan adept is Ningishzidda. I don't know what forces he has under his control, but I believe some of them are Gallu and most likely have resources from the abandoned Anunnaki underground citadels."

Marduk interrupted, holding his right hand high in the air to get everyone's attention. Upon hearing the name of Ningishzidda, many of the Igigi seemed to panic more. "Quiet! Let us listen to what Lord Dumuzid has to say!"

Masterson continued, "We know Ningishzidda has some Gallu fighting for him, but they were easily handled and no match for our abilities and powers. Before we further divide into our separate teams, we'll take the fight to him, give them another example of our fighting prowess and abilities. I want us to hasten our response, but as one. Ningishzidda, I am sure by now, knows we can arrive in the blink of an eye. I'm sure he's planning on us attacking the same way we did the *Tiamat;* through infiltration and hasty attack using our abilities. We'll do something different this time. Everyone sit and listen; no questions until I'm finished." With that, Masterson and Marduk used hand gestures, signaling for the Igigi with them to take a seat on the ground and listen.

"The Anunnaki have been using the aggressive nature of Mundusan laborers to their advantage since the Great Deluge was released by Lord Enlil following the fall of Eidin. Doing so allowed Lord Anu to remove the attendants and servitors directly involved in the collection of resources on the surface back to *Nibiru Station.* You know that the laborers were initially led by priests and priestesses that worked directly with you, serving the Anunnaki as managers of the resource collection centers in the cities, the temples." Masterson stopped and scanned the faces of the Igigi men and women now listening to him. "We know that Lord Enki and Lady Ninhursag, known to some of you as Lady Ninmah, were ordered to use their specified conception techniques to create you, the Igigi, to assist in tasks that were originally done by the Anunnaki attendants and servitors that Lord Anu had withdrawn. I believe that Lord Enlil either didn't get permission to do this or the collection of the resources for Lord Anu hasn't been sufficiently collected to prepare for the return of the *Nibiru.*"

This revelation to the Igigi seated around Masterson and Marduk caused many of them to gasp. Marduk stepped forward, waving his hands, ordering them all to listen.

"I believe that either way, Lord Enlil isn't ready for the imminent arrival of the *Nibiru,* and that caused him to lash out at you and why he finds handing over the stewardship of this world to you, the Igigi, so repugnant."

One of the Igigi males, Sophocles, spoke up. "What are we to do then, Lord Dumuzid? If the *Nibiru* is here, surely we are doomed?"

"We use what resources we have to resist and survive. We have no choice. Earlier I said Enlil has used the aggressive nature of the laborers to manage their collection of the special minerals by having them war upon one another, then placed the spoils in the temples in selected cities. Enlil is the sponsor of the city of Nippur. The temple there is dedicated to him by the laborers. We take that city from him. We don't destroy it, but we claim it as our own."

One of the twin males called out, "And they will respond with another *Tiamat*! How do we fight a second *Tiamat*?"

"Our advantage is the laborers; we must show them that their survival rests with us, otherwise the fate of this world will be the same as the worlds of the Dionans and Cassidans."

The other twin, Apollon, brother of Apostolos, called out next, "Tell us, Lord Dumuzid, tell us how we are to do this!"

"I will show you tomorrow, Apollon. I will show you all." The Igigi around Masterson and Marduk suddenly cheered, jumping up and dancing in a circle around him. Masterson smiled, shaking his head and hugging those that needed hugs, laughing with those that needed laughter until it became too dark for them to continue.

Slowly, the Igigi dispersed, leaving Masterson standing with Marduk and Ishtar. He spoke to them in the darkness of night, "Ishtar, I need you to find the ruler of the city of Babylon. His name is Hammurabi. I want to speak with him. Marduk, send the two brothers, the twins, with her for her protection."

Marduk gently took hold of Ishtar's elbow, speaking gently to her, "Find Marina. She is familiar with the cities of this region. She may know the location of Hammurabi and save us some time."

"I already know where Hammurabi is."

Masterson frowned, "You do? How?"

Ishtar arched her right eyebrow as she turned to look up into Masterson's dark blue eyes.

"Lord Dumuzid, am I not a prophet like yourself?"

Masterson's frown deepened. "What do you mean?"

"I am trained to use my sixth-sense ability to see things others cannot. You have shown the same ability repeatedly in our battles with Lord Enlil."

Masterson stopped her, turning his attention to Marduk. "Prepare the others. We're going to Hammurabi this morning."

Marduk nodded in agreement then turned to rest before the sun rose.

Masterson turned his attention back to Ishtar. "I need to speak with Hammurabi. Can you take me to him now?"

"I need to fetch Shala. It is her gift to jump between two places, remember?" Ishtar moved close to Masterson with just a hint of a smile on her face as she looked up into his eyes. "I know who you are, Lord Dumuzid the Bull."

"Everyone knows who I am."

"You are Dumuzid, the consort of Lady Inanna." Ishtar's smile softened, "You are her lover and you will stop at nothing to have her back in your arms. Am I not right, Lord Dumuzid, the Protector of Inanna?"

"What else do you know? Why did you call me a prophet, like yourself?"

She pressed close to Masterson, her smaller, softer body pressing close to his. "I serve Lady Inanna. She often took me to the temple at Uruk with her, and she often, very often, spoke of you in particular, Lord Dumuzid."

Masterson snorted, "You little vixen. What is it you want from me, Ishtar?"

"I want to continue to serve Lady Inanna, my lord." She reached up to hook his neck and draw him down to her lips for a sweet kiss.

Masterson took her in his arms for a moment of sensual enjoyment then slowly separated them by holding the smaller woman by her hips and moving a step back. "What is the price for this service to Inanna?"

"You allow me to serve you. There is no need to bring Inanna back." The small woman looked up at Masterson with heavily laden eyes as she tried to pull him back into her arms.

Masterson forced her back on her heels, holding both her arms to her side, "How do you know I intend to restore Inanna to her physical body?"

"I am a prophetess, Lord Dumuzid, remember? I know what motivates you. But you cannot bring her back. No one can do that. You are not even an Anunnaki, you are Dionan!"

Masterson narrowed his eyes at Ishtar. "Go bring Shala then take me to Hammurabi. I'll wait here." Masterson's displeasure with Ishtar was clear on his face and the way he stood. She sensed she had overstepped her position in their small group and quickly left to search for the spirit walker, Shala.

As Ishtar melted into the darkness, Masterson looked up into the stars. The stars looked the same as they did to him in his previous life. They looked the way they always did. They never changed, yet so much for him had.

Masterson suddenly appeared in an open Sumerian field of grass. With him were the twin ergomancers, Apollon and Apostolos. Shala had also requested them when she found out where they were going. Between the twins and Masterson stood the two women, one on each side of him, holding his hands for the chain teleport. Shala had let go of him as soon as they materialized, but he had to release Ishtar's hand as she continued to grip his.

Masterson and his team had arrived on a small hill overlooking the main encampment of Hammurabi's coalition army. They were in eastern Sumer. In the distance, he could see the mountains of Elam, the future Persia. Behind them was the fertile river valley of the Tigris River. To the south, but out of sight, was the Southern Sea. The stench of humanity was quickly the next sense they experienced. Masterson felt he was in his element, surrounded by soldiers. He drew emotional strength from being back among soldiers as they were quickly noticed by the Babylonians. Runners were sent to their leaders to notify them that Igigi had arrived.

While they waited, Masterson turned to Shala and asked, "When you jump us, you're using your sense of how many dimensions to do it?"

"I am a trained adept using the seventh sense, my lord!" Shala smiled up at him; the fact that she was quite pleased with herself was clear.

"Can you jump into the future and the past like the Cassidan time ships do?"

"No, my lord, I can only jump to places I have experienced or experienced through the eyes and memories of another."

"How did you know Hammurabi was on this hill then?"

Shala blushed deep red, almost making Masterson laugh aloud. "I peeked, sir."

Beside them, Apollon burst into laughter. "The little girl sneaks into others' minds without them knowing, sir. She probably knows one or two of these laborers."

"Or more," chimed in his brother.

Apollon continued, "That is how she knew the army was here."

Shala surprised Masterson again when she turned to Apollon and acted like a small child arguing with its sibling, even to the point of balling her hands into fists as if she was going to fight him. Despite the Igigi being hundreds of years old, he was learning that their behavior was still that of an adolescent human child. He was beginning to believe they were designed or trained that way to make them easier to manage by the Anunnaki. That caused their downfall in the eyes of Enlil. It was the source of their chaotic and unpredictable behavior.

Masterson stood with his arms folded, watching the multitude of warriors watching them. He was surprised yet impressed that the unit commanders were already organizing their companies into loose formations. Not phalanxes as the Greeks would use nor legions invented by the Romans, but they were organized, and independent units were armed similarly with Bronze Age weapons just the same. He smiled.

Shala surprised him by grabbing his arm and pointing at a group of men that were riding through the formations toward him on wagons drawn by two horses each. She was literally hopping on her toes and giggling as she pointed even more precisely. "There he is! There he is, King Hammurabi. He is the older man in the second chariot."

Masterson watched with his arms folded over his chest as the wagons drew near and stopped. Several warriors dropped from the wagons that Shala had identified as chariots but looked like simple two-axle wagons to him. Once Hammurabi was safely on the ground, the elderly man turned toward Masterson and his Igigi. The warriors all went to one knee, including the two holding the leads of the wagon horses. At once, a human wave took shape as thousands of warriors in formation behind their king all went to their knees as companies.

Hammurabi stood then opened his arms wide as if to hug the entire group of Igigi before him. "I am honored that you watch us in our battle with the Elamites today." He lowered his eye briefly out of respect then looked up, smiling. "Lord, what is your pleasure?"

"You are engaging the Elamite army of *Siwe Palar Khuppak* to drive them from Babylonian and Laran lands, correct?"

"Yes," was all King Hammurabi said.

Masterson smiled. He was tired of excessive explanations and endless discussions about things. "We're here to help."

Hammurabi knitted his brow as he looked at the five gods, as if he sensed a trap. "Lord, I am thankful for the gift of your participation, but the gods have never helped in an actual battle before, other than giving us their blessing and keeping the other gods from interfering on behalf of our foe. Are you here to do more?"

Masterson was surprised by Hammurabi's question and the information on how the Anunnaki had performed their roles in the view of the laborers. He hadn't considered how the humans saw the Anunnaki and their Igigi other than aggressors when citadels were directly attacked by the servitor.

Ishtar stepped forward, brushing Masterson's elbow as she passed him, "Most honored King Hammurabi, may I speak?"

Hammurabi's eyes narrowed as the darkly beautiful Igigi woman stepped toward him. He turned his gaze toward Masterson, "Lord, does this one speak for you?"

Masterson crossed his arms over his chest as he gazed at the back of Ishtar's bowed head as she stood between him and Hammurabi. "She doesn't speak for me. No one speaks for me, King Hammurabi, as none do for you. She is a trusted advisor in the court of the Igigi."

Hammurabi nodded. "I will hear your counsel, goddess."

Ishtar's face was radiant as she smiled at King Hammurabi. "King Hammurabi, my gift from the Anunnaki is that of sight. I am a prophetess in the Court of the Anunnaki. I have the Seventh Sense and can see things that others have done or will do as a valued member of Lady Inanna's Court."

The King frowned, "You are?"

Ishtar, without batting an eye, replied, "I am."

Masterson chuckled before stepping forward to stand close to Ishtar, just off her right shoulder, "She talks like that." Masterson smiled, "Mysterious – all oracles are like that."

King Hammurabi chuckled at the remark.

Masterson's voice drew his attention back to him. "You march against King Siwe-Palar-Khuppak today?"

"Yes, but the warrior I am meeting on the field of battle today is King Sirukdugh. It is his army we fight today."

Ishtar interrupted, "The King of Larsa, King Rim-Sin, will not aid you today. He will withdraw his army toward his city as you move forward into battle."

A confused Hammurabi frowned deeply then looked to Masterson, wanting an explanation as Ishtar continued, "You will then wage war on Rim-Sin and deliver his people from his harsh rule into your realm of power, Lord Hammurabi." She stopped, her eyes not focused on the king any longer but at something in the distance. Her focus was so intense, Hammurabi turned to glance back over his shoulder briefly.

Masterson spoke quickly, "You'll expand your realm because I am behind you, King Hammurabi – along with my allies," Masterson gestured toward the three other Igigi standing behind him. "You're favored in my court, King Hammurabi. You'll complete your assault on Sirukdugh. But rather than pursue him into Elam, you'll turn your army to the south and take the cities of Uruk, Isim, Lagash, and start with Nippur. You'll collect all the gold and silver, and other precious metals and minerals not directly needed by the city's laborers, and bring them to Babylon to be kept in the city temples. Once you've done that, fortify yourself because you'll be the envy of the Assyrians, and they'll surely come for you." Masterson smiled, stepping forward to lay his hand on the shoulder of King Hammurabi of Babylon. "They shall come for you, but you'll prevail because we're with you."

Hammurabi looked into Masterson's Dionan face and saw the face of Dumuzid, the Bull of Heaven. "Captain!" he shouted, keeping eye contact with Masterson. When he heard the voice of his commander of troops, he shouted as loudly as he could, "Order the army forward into battle!"

Masterson quickly moved back to the Igigi, away from Hammurabi. Hammurabi mounted his war chariot to return to the place where he could best direct his army. Everyone watched as the Babylonian forces, comprising of allied contingents from the cities of Larsa, Kish, Sipper, and Barsippa, moved forward en mass to engage the Elamites. Masterson found the highest point of the small hill they were standing on as he watched. To the far east and barely visible rose the tall Zagros Mountains of what would one day be Persia then Iran. This was the Elamite homeland. King Siwe-Palar-Khuppak was the Elamite leader but wasn't present at the battle. The Elamites had been raiding the twin river valley for generations and had seized some of the smaller settlements along their common borders with cities allied with Babylonia, which included the Sumerian cities of Lara, Nippur, and Inanna's citadel of Uruk. Inanna's inactivity and probable fate were known to the laborers because of the Igigi. Masterson suspected it was the reason the Elamites were moving against Uruk and its allies. He bit his lower lip and frowned as he recognized how Anunnaki politics affected the short-lived Mundusans.

As the Babylonian army moved forward, the formations on the right slowed their pace. The main body continued to move forward toward the Elamites. Then, just as predicted by Ishtar, the right flank formation, which included Larsa and Borsippa, reformed and withdrew from the battle just as the Elamites quickened their pace then charged the Babylonians. The Babylonian troops, who were the bulk of their army, held together despite the Larsan and Borsippan troops abandoning them. The other allied troops from Kish and Sippar held their positions on the left as the Elamites were engaged.

As Masterson studied the battle as it unfolded before them, Apollon and Apostolos enjoyed the spectacle of person-to-person melee with schoolboy glee, shouting and cheering when they witnessed athletic prowess displayed by fighters from either side as the battle progressed. Both of the Igigi males begged Masterson for permission to join the fray on behalf of the Babylonians, despite his continual refusal. The two Igigi girls played tag. Then, when they became bored with that, they began constantly asking Masterson when they were leaving before becoming content with braiding each other's long raven hair. When it became clear that Hammurabi's army would carry the day, Masterson turned from watching the battle to call the four Igigi to him. It was time to go. Shala was happy to form them all into a line, holding hands before she herself took the hands of Apollon and Apostolos in hers, forming a small circle.

"Return us to the mountain."

Hearing Masterson's order, Shala closed her eyes, and when she opened them, they were home in the Grecian foothills at the base of a stub of a mountain near the eastern shore. Apollon, Apostolos, and Shala all quickly sprinted to friends while Ishtar remained at Masterson's side, smiling up at him. He waved her off, motioning for her to follow the others.

Marduk stood waving them into a large stone house. He introduced the newcomers to the meeting he was holding with the other Igigi. Once everyone was settled he excused himself to move to speak with Masterson privately. Shala, Apollon, and Apostolos joined the half dozen others that had been talking with Marduk. Apollon playfully tackled one of the other men, halfheartedly wrestling as Apostolos and Shala laughed, and soon was she chatting with others herself.

"Chantico, Hamaliel, and Jianiel all returned last night and want to speak with you." Marduk took hold of Masterson's elbow, leading him back outside the house to walk as they talked. Masterson noticed Marduk would lower his voice whenever a laborer moved near them, despite speaking to Masterson in Cassidan and not the regional Mundus language.

"Where are they now?"

Marduk continued, "They are waiting for us, but they have discovered that Enlil's servitors were not all destroyed when we destroyed the *Tiamat*."

The new information stunned Masterson only for a second. He nodded. "Actually, that makes sense. The *Tiamat* probably had its full complement of servitors, the entire Fourth Battle Order."

Marduk listened with uncharacteristic interest as Masterson continued to explain, "The Fourth Order, if deployed without the support of other Orders of Battle, would have at least three fully functional commands. Two of them, Support and Logistics, were most likely still operating completely from the *Tiamat*. We probably got the leadership and most of the servitors from those two commands." Masterson stopped and scratched his bearded chin. "But the third command is their tactical operations command, the combat troops. We know we took out the servitors that had assaulted the Ganzir citadel. There were several hundred servitors involved in that battle. They were probably using one battle group, around six-hundred ground combat servitors. Their transports were drone saucers. So it would be ground combat servitors only."

Marduk listened intently but was having a hard time keeping up with Masterson talking to himself, trying to figure out how many they may still have to fight. Masterson saw the look of confusion on Marduk's face and smiled. "We probably still have a lot to fight, even if Anu doesn't send more from the *Nibiru*. All the more reason to win the support of the Anunnaki, who are friends of the Igigi."

Marduk nodded his head quickly as he ushered Masterson toward a cleared field, out of earshot of the stone house they had just left. Sitting in a small, wooded area near a cleared field were several of the Igigi. The youthful-looking Igigi were unusually quiet and somber as Masterson and Marduk approached them.

Masterson looked around the group of men and women who remained seated as he joined them. "Who's first?"

Jianiel spoke first. "Lord Dumuzid the Bull, the citadel of *Sanxingdui* was laid waste. I found the city smoldering when I returned. I believe it was attacked by Lord Enlil's servitors at the same time as Ganzir."

"Why do you say that?" Masterson joined them by seating himself on the ground as part of their discussion circle.

Jianiel went slack jawed, looking at Masterson in disbelief, "The use of servitor's weapons was clear. Metal work was melted, and much of the city was destroyed by fire ignited by the servitors' astral weapons, the laborers said."

"How did they arrive?"

Rikbiel spoke up, "Surviving laborers from *Sanxingdui* resource collection center and Hamaliel's *Mohenjo-daro* resource collection center on the Indus River all verify the same thing, Lord Dumuzid. The servitors all arrived and left in flying houses using powerful weapons to destroy their homes and families."

Masterson was glad to see Rikbiel had rejoined them.

"In fact, they were hiding from me when I arrived on one of our transport saucers." Rikbiel looked at a visibly shaken Hamaliel for confirmation of his account of what had happened.

"We are all very lucky Rikbiel returned to check on us. I was afraid that the servitors would return and kill more of the laborers as they searched for us."

Masterson spoke over Hamaliel, "I don't think they were searching for you. I think they were purposely continuing their plan of attack that was decided before we attacked their main transport ship. I feel that a junior Cassidan or even a Dionan commander is continuing the mission that was launched against Ganzir, despite the *Tiamat* no longer being in control."

"What will you do to stop them?" Hamaliel questioned Masterson with a loud, almost shouting, voice. "We cannot allow them to destroy the laborers' homes and cities."

"I have spoken with a prominent leader of one of the Sumerian region resource center citadels. He's going to move against Lord Enlil's own resource center within days. I'm going to use an army of laborers to seize an Anunnaki-controlled city. The city of Nippur."

Marduk frowned, "We cannot wait. Enlil not only has his Anunnaki adepts, but he also has an unknown number of servitors at his command. The longer we put off this, the more Igigi and laborers that will die."

Hamaliel stood up. "We cannot wait. I do not want to use laborers as our fighters. We must fight for them, not they for us!"

Masterson nodded his head. "Agreed. The slaughter and destruction will continue so long as Enlil is in power." He stood up, surveying the looks in the eyes of the emergent leaders of the Igigi. "We must act."

Chapter 18: Eshumesha

It took a few days to organize, but the Grecian Igigi got many to respond to their call to arms and reassemble after Masterson, as Dumuzid the Bull, had told them to scatter to the four winds and conceal themselves. What the scattering had done was to build their resolve to take action. Surviving members of the *Tiamat's* combat force were making their presence known worldwide, raiding citadels that had been managed by Igigi adepts with quick strikes. Servitor attacks weren't directed at the underground storage vaults, those were left intact. They were destroying surface features of the centers and city infrastructure, and scattering the laborers to the countryside. The surviving laborers called the servitors carrying out these attacks demons; they were called the *Gallu* in Mesopotamia, the *Rakshasa* in southern Asia, and the *Tzitzimimeh* in Mesoamerica.

Marduk, Chantico, Hamaliel, and Jianiel had collectively decided, rather than trying to engage Enlil's servitors by ambushing them at one of the outlying Igigi managed citadels, to take the fight directly to Enlil himself after consulting with Masterson as Dumuzid the Bull. Chantico, Hamaliel, and Jianiel had each lost a city in their region to the servitor raiders.

In coordination, several Igigi appeared at all the gates to the ancient Sumerian city of Nippur. The Igigi were organized as Masterson had directed. Each group had adepts trained in different yet complementary skills, using the best they could from the Battle of Ganzir survivors. Not all Igigi wanted to fight the servitors one-on-one again after the horrendous bloodletting from the assault on the *Tiamat*. Of the Igigi still alive, twenty-seven answered the call to come fight once again.

Masterson had arrived with his team outside the massive main gate of the city of Nippur in a saucer transport piloted by Rikbiel.

Some teams had movers and had teleported to their targeted gate, and some had flown in on transports like Masterson's team had. Rikbiel was controlling the other three transport saucers from his ship. Once all the Igigi had left their transports, the ships took off and hovered above Nippur at high altitude, providing over-watch and early warning for the approach of servitor *Lightening* class tactical ships or troop transports.

Masterson looked to the Igigi standing on either side of him, "Shall we do this?"

They all smiled. The two brothers, Apollon and Apostolos, stepped forward. Both were adept at using Ergokinesis, the absorption and manipulation of energy. Apollon looked at the massive wooden and metal gate then turned to smile at his brother. They began doing an intricate dance to focus their full attention on the task at hand. They reflected each other as they moved in unison. The attention of the warriors on the wall and the other Igigi were on them as they moved. They came out of a pivotal spin facing the great gate of Nippur with their hands extended as if they were pushing the door together. A great force smashed into the heavy gate like it was hit by lightning, with a loud crack and the sound of rolling thunder afterward. The gate splintered, sending shards of wood and metal shrapnel flying, wounding or killing several warriors, horses, and laborers. The air was thick with dust as Masterson and his Igigi entered Nippur.

Several of the braver Nippuran warriors attempted to attack the small group of intruders with their swords and spears but were swept away effortlessly by Masterson's powerful escorts as they moved into the city. Their aim was Enlil's temple and its portal to the underworld city of Kur. Masterson noted that there were alarm horns being sounded in the distance. No doubt they were warriors at the other city gates calling for help as they too faced aggressive Igigi invaders. The Nippuran warriors surprised Masterson and the Igigi when the streets narrowed into alleyways winding between dwellings and small domesticated animal pens.

Ishtar stepped to the front of Masterson, holding her hand against his chest to stop him. She looked to the front as if searching for something. "It's not right. This is not right."

Masterson's eyes followed Ishtar's, looking toward the roofs of the cube-shaped, single-family dwellings packed closely together.

There was space between them, and some could be easily scaled. Most of the houses followed the Sumerian model of simply being one large room structure with access to the flat roof. There were a few more elaborate buildings that were two floors or adjoining rooms on the ground level. Most had crude windows that let the hot air circulate to cool the house in the evenings, with flaps of leather to seal them at night.

Masterson's attention was brought back to ground level when an arrow thudded into the chest of Apostolos standing next to him. The twin slumped and was caught by his brother, Apollon, who lowered him to the ground to lie on his back, screaming his name. A second and third arrow whizzed into the crowd of Igigi as they stood together in the tight alleyway. The sickening wet sound of the arrows impacting human bodies could be heard around Masterson, followed by the horrendous howl of the warriors armed with spears and bronze swords rushing them, following the volley of arrows. The Igigi were unarmed; they carried no personal weapons.

The first two of the Nippuran warriors reached them with their spears thrusting forward. Masterson sidestepped, grabbing the spear of the warrior before him and yanking it forward, trying to pull it from the aggressor's hands. Lefteris, a conjurer, stepped forward, gripping the second warrior's spear and shoving the point of the weapon into the stone wall of the house on the left side of the alley, snapping the spear as if it were a stick. Lefteris then smashed his elbow into the helmeted face of the attacking warrior, forcing him back into the fellows behind him. As Masterson wrestled with his warrior to control the spear, he could see that there were others armed with spears and bronze swords behind these two leading fighters. With a burst of strength, Masterson hoisted the end of the spear he controlled up and over his head, then twisting himself, turned under it and smashed it into the wall on the right side of the alley as Lefteris had moments before. Into this gap between Masterson and Lefteris stepped the smaller Katia, the mover.

Waving her arms before her in the cramped space between Masterson and Lefteris, she made intricate moves with her hands, like Apollon and Apostolos had at the gate. She suddenly pushed her hands forward. It was as if a tremendous gust of tornadic wind from the desert had swept through the alleyway from behind the Igigi, clearing the path of Nippuran warriors which were flung into the air or violently shoved against the stone walls of the alley, dropping them to their knees.

Stepping up and placing one large hand on the small shoulder of Katia to let her know he was there as she held her fighting pose, Omiros stretched his bloodied hand from an arrow protruding from his belly to send a wall of intense fire down the alleyway to clear it of any fighters still on their feet just as the desert wind gust had passed. The warriors battling Masterson and Lefteris dropped their weapons and ran from them in the direction the fire wall had gone, hopping over the burnt carcasses of their comrades as they fled.

Omiros collapsed to his knees after creating the fire wall, his hands clasping his wound where the arrow had penetrated him. Masterson quickly dropped the spear in his hands and went to his side, giving him support while surveying the group and looking for others wounded. Rania moved quickly between those wounded, assessing them then moving to the next. She kneeled beside Omiros, across from Masterson, closed her eyes, placed her hands on his bleeding wound, and took a deep breath before concentrating.

"Lefteris, I need you!" She applied pressure to Omiros' abdomen as Lefteris kneeled beside them, examining Omiros as Masterson laid him on his back on the trampled clay of the alleyway.

Masterson stood and looked up and down the alley. "Miliadis, put some people on the rooftops to look for approaching fighters." Then he waved to Sophocles, "Take someone with you and scout down this alley to see if they are reforming for another attack." Sophocles pointed at two of the new Igigi to join their group. The three of them sprinted up the alley toward the temple of Enlil. Little Katia and Apollon were attending to Apostolos, who was bleeding out from the arrow in the center of his chest.

Apollon looked up at Masterson pleading, "Do, do something, do something, Dumuzid the Bull!"

Katia reached over and touched Rania, gesturing for her to shift to Apostolos, resting her bloody hand on Rania's arm.

Rania gasped before reaching for Lefteris, pulling him to her side. "They have pierced his heart."

"No, no, it's one of his four trunks of life, not the heart itself or he wouldn't be alive." Lefteris moved over Apostolos, placing both hands on his chest but not pressing down as Masterson thought he was about to do.

Masterson's jaw dropped as he watched Lefteris closely. The blood stopped hemorrhaging from Apostolos' chest. Masterson thought he had died, causing his heart to stop pumping the blood from his wound and over Lefteris' spread fingers. Lefteris was breathing calmly as they all watched. Masterson blinked. The wound was gone. In an instant, it was just gone. Lefteris continued to press his hands against the wound until Apostolos' eyes fluttered open.

"What have I done now?" Apostolos groaned, causing everyone to laugh joyously.

Rania and Katia hugged each other tightly over Apostolos, who looked around with a truly dumbfounded expression on his face. Smiling, Rania and Lefteris turned back to Omiros' belly wound. Apollon stood, looking up at Masterson. He simply smiled as he gripped Masterson in a tight bear hug.

"Apollon, bring your brother and the others to Enlil's temple once Rania and Lefteris are finished healing them. I want Ishtar to remain with you, to warn you if another attack is coming. I'll take Miltiadis, Theofilos, Marina, and Louiza with me to the temple. We need to call out Enlil before this escalates to a full-blown battle like the *Tiamat*."

Apollon nodded then turned to organize the Igigi that were new to their group to explain what they were doing. Masterson called for the four veterans in their group to come with him. He stepped over to place his hand on Lefteris' shoulder asking, "How did you do that, what you did to Apostolos?"

"By following the Will of the Genitor and having faith in what I have learned." Lefteris smiled at Masterson then turned his attention to those he was tending. Masterson watched Lefteris move about the Igigi wounded. Fortunately there were few, and Lefteris' amazing power meant a quick recovery for those that were hurt by the unexpected volley of arrows.

Miltiadis and Theofilos stood by him to his left with the two women, Marina and Louiza, behind them. They were looking to

Masterson for orders. Their resolve was shaken by the attack by the laborers' warriors. Masterson knew that breaking his team into three smaller groups was risky, but he knew he had to get to the temple to gain control of the situation. He hadn't expected the city guard to defend against his uplifted Igigi. His Igigi were eager to fight Enlil's adepts and servitors, but he wasn't sure they had the will to fight the laborers, their own people. He needed to rally them at the temple.

The revelation of seeing Lefteris' volumn-enhanced abilities to alter reality, the way he had healed Omiros, had shaken Masterson's confidence. What if Enlil or one of his adepts had that power as well, or any of the Anunnaki for that matter? *Is warping or altering reality the power of the Genitor?* He wondered. That revelation was a potential game-changer in a way that Masterson hadn't considered before. Humans with the potential to alter reality in a moment the way Lefteris had with Omiros' chest wound, making it simply disappear, could easily challenge the power of the Anunnaki. But why hadn't Enlil just willed the Igigi away, or the whole human species, back at the Battle of Eidin? Masterson reasoned there must be limits to what they could or couldn't do with their power. Why had the Genitor neglected teaching him more about the volumn and its gifts? He quickened their pace to get them to the Ekur Temple. As they ran, their progress was slowed by laborers scampering to get clear of them or hurriedly running into their homes to hide.

The four of them trotted between the rows of nondescript dwellings as they made their way deeper into the city. The very top of the Ekur ziggurat could be glimpsed as they snaked through the endless maze of buildings. Masterson glanced to his side. "Theofilos, what's your volumn ability?"

The smaller Igigi male smiled as they trotted, "I, Lord Dumuzid," he panted as they ran, "I am a prophet. I can tell the nature of the use of a tool and about the person who uses it."

"What? How do you use that?" Masterson's surprise wasn't well hidden by his quick response.

"My Lord! My services are valuable. I can tell you much about a man or woman by the tools they use and how they hold them!"

Masterson nodded his head as they padded along, "And you Miltiadis? What's your ability?"

"Lord Dumuzid the Bull, I am a strategist!" Miltiadis was nearly Masterson's size and build. The Igigi male looked formidable.

"A strategist, how so?"

"Never play Miltiadis in a game of chance, Lord Dumuzid," warned Theofilos.

Miltiadis nearly shoved the smaller Theofilos off his feet and into the walls of the home they were passing. Miltiadis smiled at his friend who struggled to keep his place beside him as they continued to trot with three men leading the way.

"I am a prophet also, Lord Dumuzid. I can see alternative futures and what the outcomes will be through visions provided by the Genitor well before it occurs. I think that perhaps I have a similar power as your own, Lord Dumuzid the Bull."

"And they call you a strategist?" Masterson looked upward as they talked, searching for the four slightly glowing orbs that were the bottoms of the Rikbiel's saucers.

"Prior to the *Tiamat,* Lord Dumuzid, I was useful in determining where to plant seed or pasture animals. I was also very well liked for predicting the seasonal rise and fall of the rivers, or if the seas were about to unleash their fury." There was pride in the voice of Miltiadis as they ran.

The use of flame and wind was clear from the damage they found as they snaked their way through the alleys toward the temple. Masterson's concern about their ability to defend themselves was becoming clear as they neared the temple. Masterson was clearly regretting not keeping their ergomancers with him after their earlier skirmish with the Nippur warriors. He was confident that Lefteris and Katia could defend themselves and the others, but he had growing concerns about those he had sent ahead to the temple in case they were confronted again.

Masterson looked over his shoulder at the two Igigi women running with them. "What do you two do?"

Louiza shouted, surprising Masterson, making him smile, "I am an ergomancer, Lord Dumuzid, like the beautiful Apollon and Apostolos!" She pumped her muscular arms to emphasize her strength, a trait of the manipulators of energy Masterson recognized. He assumed it was from the muscular stimulation from the collection and discharge of the energy through their bodies.

"And you?" Masterson looked at Marina, a thinner woman, who seemed to handle their jogging the most comfortably.

Unlike her companions, she didn't smile while she spoke or seem excited to be with them. "I am Marina. I speak to those that have come before us and who will come after us."

Her answer startled Masterson, causing him to stop, surprising everyone. "You talk to the dead?"

His question brought a faint smile to her lips. "They are not dead when I talk with them, Lord Dumuzid."

"Explain."

"I visit them in their dreams. They are living when I speak to them. We have discussions."

"Do they know their fate or ours when you talk with them?"

"No, they do not know their own destiny, but sometimes they know what happens to us. Most of the time they are not aware of precise details."

"But you can glean information about how something will turn out?"

Marina bowed her head said, "Yes, Lord Dumuzid, I know you will be successful today."

"Of course he will be! We all will be!" Miltiadis was adamant in his belief in their success.

Masterson gave them all a sideways grin then motioned that they needed to continue to their destination. He pulled Louiza to the front to run beside him, displacing a very vocal Miltiadis as they closed with the base of the temple.

As they emerged from the maze of dwellings, they were again faced by a contingent of Nippur's guards. Louiza lunged to the front of their small group, taking up a steady pose as she moved her hands to prepare for manipulating energy against the warriors. The faint smell of ozone wafted through the air as the hair on the Igigi and Masterson's bodies stood, making their skin crawl. Masterson hadn't stood directly beside an ergomancer while they prepared to do battle before.

This time, the warriors didn't attack, but they stood ready should the word be given. There was a nervous tension as Masterson and his small team faced off with the guards. Miltiadis reached over to touch Masterson's forearm, pointing at a transport saucer from the *Tiamat* that was dropping off a team of servitors with lancer-staffs and in full armor. The Dionan servitors deployed quickly so Louiza couldn't take them out with a single attack. Masterson noted that some of them were oriented to the west, meaning that the other Igigi were near. From the east, he could hear the unmistakable sounds of fighting. He knew his Igigi needed immediate relief and could cause the servitors to use their advanced weapons or call in tactical air support to attack them on the ground. There they stood at the base of Enlil's temple in Nippur, the Ekur Temple.

Suddenly, there were four sequential explosions high in the sky over the temple, followed by two *Lightning* class gunships doing a quick flyover above the city toward the sounds of the fighting. Masterson immediately knew what had happened. The servitor combat force that had been deployed off the *Tiamat* during the transport's destruction had attacked citadel Yellow and the Indus rivers in Asia, commanded by either Enlil or Ningishzidda. The servitors had just destroyed Rikbiel's saucer transports high over the city. The flyover was to let the Igigi know they were here in force. They must have been called by Enlil or one of his adepts once their four saucers had landed. The *Lightning* gunships and transports were hyper-sonic, flying thousands of miles per hour. The *Tiamat*'s combat force was garrisoned within a few thousand miles of Nippur. Masterson guessed Elam or southern Iran, in his earlier life, was the best guess as to where their base was.

Masterson turned to see the rest of his team walking out of the maze of dwellings behind him. They were also looking skyward, searching for more evidence of the servitors' arrival. Drone missiles, small bright lights, foo fighters he had once described them as, zigzagging in the sky over the city, could be seen zipping about overhead. They could descend on Nippur and the cities to the east in an instant, like they had on Ganzir, once the order was given.

Masterson looked back toward the temple ziggurat looming before them. He crept forward to ascend the stairs leading to the top of the temple. The warriors of Nippur moved but were ordered to stand back by the chief priest of the temple. Emboldened by the priest's order for his warriors to stand back, Masterson picked up his pace. But when his followers moved to follow, the warriors assumed a combative stance. The message was simple – Masterson as Dumuzid the Bull alone could ascend to the upper levels of the temple.

Halfway up the stone stairs to the top of the ziggurat, Masterson stopped and gazed about him over the magnificent vista of Bronze Age Nippur. He pursed his lips, knowing that if he didn't do something quickly, the city would erupt into a battle between the Igigi and the Dionan servitors, destroying the city and the closure of the only portal he knew of that would give him access to the buried underground city of Kur. He sprinted up the remaining stairs of the ziggurat to the portal, not really sure of what he would do. He should have realized that Enlil would use his remaining servitors to defend his own temple from the Igigi.

Lightning flashed from the top of the Ekur Temple, arcing in several directions. The flashes of lightning lit up the morning sky with numbing light, and the accompanying thunder shook the earth, causing large swaths of the adobe dwellings and shops to crumble to dust. Masterson dropped to his knees on the stone stairs to avoid falling down the way he came. The sounds of battle between the Igigi and the combined army of laborers and servitors stopped. In the silence, Masterson looked up to see several tall figures standing atop the temple. Masterson slowly rose to his feet and crawled up the side of the temple to the top.

Lord Enlil, with a small entourage, emerged from the single structure at the top of the ziggurat. He stopped at the top of the stairs, looking down at Masterson. "So, this is how your Igigi show their stewardship of Mundus – by attacking my temple vaults?"

Masterson stopped a few meters from the Lord of the Sky. "Lord Enlil, the reason we're here is in protest of the continued destruction of the cities by the servitors." Masterson looked around at the panoramic view of a partially destroyed city, dust rising like clouds from the ruins of the crumbled adobe brick buildings. The scene reminded Masterson of the bombed cities of his previous life in the twenty-first century. It saddened him.

Lord Enlil turned to one of the two Gallu servitors standing behind him. The Cassidan stepped forward, closer to Lord Enlil. "Tell the servitors to make it known to the Igigi that their Dumuzid the Bull has been captured. They are to cease fighting immediately or forfeit his life." The Gallu nodded then turned to obey the command, leaving them to stand to the side using a communications suite within his armor to pass the order on to subordinate servitor commanders.

Lord Enlil turned his attention back to Masterson. "You will round up your group of misfits and take them to the Eshumesha temple complex beside this one to await my decision on the fate of your rebellion. If you do not comply with my instructions, Dumuzid, I will destroy this city and everyone in it while you watch. That will satisfy my promise to Enki and his followers to not destroy you." Enlil had used the name he himself had awarded Masterson when appointed to be Inanna's protector. Enlil ordered the second Gallu to take Masterson to the Eshumesha complex as he reentered the structure housing the portal at the top of his temple. The Gallu stepped forward, gesturing for Masterson to join him as he activated a teleportation portal for him to step through.

Masterson stepped out into the Eshumesha temple complex with the Gallu servitor right behind him. As the portal dissolved, Masterson looked around, realizing they were in a walled-off area that served as a collection point for harvested grain, grasses for weaving, and other agricultural produce. He quickly realized that the mineral and special metals vaults were in Enlil's temple, and this smaller site served as the collection point for the food and materials that the city's priests could use.

The Gallu servitor shoved Masterson to make him walk toward the temple building. Masterson took two steps forward then stopped. When the servitor shoved him again, he rolled with the push, spinning on his feet to the left, grabbing the pit of the extended arm of his opponent with his right hand while gripping the left wrist of the armored man. Using the leverage of his body weight, Masterson continued through the roll, bringing the surprised servitor to the ground, lying on his back. Masterson drove the tips of his fingers into the exposed throat of the servitor just above where his impact armor closed. Masterson held back, not delivering a killing blow. He looked down at the hooded and partially concealed face of the Gallu servitor. "Do not touch me again unless you intend to kill me." Masterson released his grip on the servitor's wrist and stood, walking into the temple's building on his own.

He turned, looking back out into the large walled courtyard he had just arrived in. Portals were appearing in equidistant points, bringing in his Igigi fighters, some wounded, and their servitor escorts. Slowly, the Gallu servitor stood and took charge of the arriving forces and their prisoners. Masterson watched the arrivals, searching for his team of Igigi that led the attack on the city. He quickly realized that not all the Igigi assaulting force had been captured. Marduk was not among the prisoners, nor were Ishtar or Shala. He smiled as he saw Louiza, Omiros, and Sophocles arrive, none of them worse for wear despite having been wounded earlier. The four fighters were separated immediately and moved to different locations in the courtyard, watching the servitors watching them as they did so. Theofilos and Miltiadis immediately rushed to Masterson's side as they emerged from the teleport portals. They spoke over each other as they asked him questions. Katia, Rania and the remarkable Lefteris held back their uncertainty at the way things had turned out, which was clear on their faces. Only Marina looked tranquil among the Igigi that were captured with him. Her silvery gray eyes met his only briefly, her calmness in the storm giving him unspoken support as they waited to see what would happen next.

They settled into their house arrest within the temple grounds. The accommodations weren't bad. The attending labored priests and priestesses served them well with food and drink, and the sleeping arrangements were as good as they had back at the mountain with their villager allies. After the sun went down, many of them were sitting around makeshift fires the priests had set for them in the walled courtyard. The Gallu had been replaced by Dionan servitors from the destroyed *Tiamat,* who had their Cassidan surveillance and targeting technology built into their impact armor suits. They carried their lancer-staff particle stream weapons and power-rods at the ready as they oversaw their prisoners. Both sides had lost members at the hands of the other, and both sides were tense and prepared for the other to attack first.

Marina came to Masterson as he sat on the small porch at the entry to the temple building from the walled courtyard. She lightly touched his arm. "Marduk wants to talk to you." She sat down beside him and cuddled in Masterson's arms. Many of the Igigi had already coupled up for the night to share body warmth while they slept. Most still walked together or sat talking. Masterson wasn't sure what Marina was doing as she moved close to his body to share her warmth with him. "Now we will go to sleep and I will meet you in your dreams, Lord Dumuzid. Together, we will visit Marduk in his dreams."

"I've done this before. It didn't go well." Masterson smiled and pulled Marina close to him, enjoying the warmth of her body. His eyes quickly became heavy and within no time, he was asleep.

Masterson was standing under an olive tree, in an orchard of olive trees. He smiled. Ancient Greece and Rome were his favorite topics of study in college. He would later teach them after his military career ended after being wounded in Afghanistan.

He was startled when Marina placed her arm in his. "I like this! Is this your home?"

Masterson smiled at her then noticed his arms were human, his hands scarred from his war injuries. His skin was not the Dionan ruddy hue as it had been when he fell asleep with her cuddled in his arms. They were human again. He smiled at her. "How do I look to you?"

"The way you always look. Are you alright?"

He frowned then looked back at his hands. The scars were gone; they were more muscular and the Dionan color. He flinched. They were standing at the Acropolis, still in Greece. He knew that, although he wasn't really sure how he knew they'd been in Greece before. "Can you control my dream? Things are changing rapidly and that's unsettling."

She reached up to caress his face. "Close your eyes and breathe, focus on my touch."

"I can't close my eyes."

"Yes you can. Close them and let me lead you to where Marduk is."

"When I close my eyes I see us in third person," said Masterson.

Marina looked surprised. "You can see yourself outside yourself?"

"Yes."

"Can you change where we are?"

"I can." Masterson smiled as his apartment in Boston appeared around them. "I can!" He moved around the apartment that he had called home, touching things, moving them. He walked to his desk, looking at the papers lying on it. He turned on his computer and smiled again.

"Your level of control is very high. Can you bring Marduk to this location in your dream?"

"I can try." Masterson stood still. From his perspective, his appearance flickered then became stable as his Dionan self. His skin was ruddy again and the scars on his hands were gone, replaced with the large, muscular hands and forearms.

"Dumuzid the Bull!" the voice of Marduk announced his sudden appearance, standing before Masterson and Marina. "Where is this place? I was in the village."

"Marduk!" Marina rushed into his embrace, smiling up at him and shedding her usual shyness and subtle avoidance of looking at the faces of people around her.

"Marina!" Marduk hugged the girl tightly as he looked around the exotic room. His frown showed that he was totally confused and was seeing what Masterson was seeing.

"This was my home when I was fully human." Masterson laughed and gestured around the apartment, "It's from five or six thousand terrestrial years in our future. Do you like it?"

"You are from the future, Lord Dumuzid? I had assumed you were from the past since you have the look of the Dionans and talk of Cassidans like you have been around them for ages." Marduk slid the smaller Marina under his arm as she hugged his torso.

Masterson moved to sit in his favorite reading chair, a well-worn leather recliner. He rubbed the arms of the chair then gestured for the others to take seats to begin their talk. "I haven't been trained as you, Marina, in the volumn-enhanced abilities within the dreams of others, yet you seem surprised at my control here. Why?"

"You have always been able to control what happens; the details and the time it takes for things to happen in your dreams with such precision, Lord Dumuzid?"

"No, I've had lucid dreams, and I've had dreams where I'm in third- and first-person or even someone else entirely. But no, I couldn't control specific aspects of my dreams like this before, nor with this clarity, this level of lifelikeness. I suspect this is because of the volum I was given on Cassida?"

Marina nodded in agreement with his belief that his control of their shared dream was because of the volum taken during his training. "I do. Lord Dumuzid, if I may ask, what is the talent that they trained you for?"

"They did not train me specifically for any volum-related skills or abilities. They seemed to be impressed with my aptitude for basic survival and combat. I was given the impression that I wasn't the original choice for the mission I was given, but I had impressed them during my early training."

"They were the Cassidans, the Anunnaki caste?" asked Marduk.

"No!" Masterson was enthusiastic in his response, "I was selected by a Genitor. A male Genitor. Then a second Genitor, also a male, very similar in appearance to the first. They could have been sibl..." Masterson realized what he was about to say was foolish. All Cassidans and Dionans were members of a brood of clones, specifically designed for the projected needs of their communities. Each were born as soon as their infantile bodies were capable of survival outside their incubation chamber then raised with their siblings, or brood brothers and sisters, in families to facilitate socialization and normal cognitive health as their bodies rapidly matured. "I have a question. The Anunnaki, don't they have greater volum powers than the Igigi? I don't understand why I haven't seen their powers being used more than I have by now."

The two Igigi looked at each other, surprised by his question. Marina answered after waiting to see if Marduk would answer. When he didn't, she spoke, "We were conceived in the traditional way of the Cassidans, as is the Will of the Genitor, Lord Dumuzid, because of our intended purpose. To assist the Anunnaki here in this world, we were taught that just as the Genitor and their famulim designed the Cassidans for their world, who in turn designed the Dionans for their world, we were designed for this world."

Marduk interrupted her, "That is why we are so confused by the Anunnaki wanting to destroy us now. To me it makes no sense – it does not fit the world of Cassida as it was described to us. We were taught that for us, the Will of the Genitor is that we participate in our communities and provide for the survival of all its members, and share in the prosperity and celebrate our collective success."

Marina spoke excitedly, "To ensure the harmony within the community, we were conceived with specific abilities needed by the community that we focus on during our formative training. The movers control the elements, helping to harvest the special minerals and production of food for the laborers."

"And build the underground citadels or the above ground spaceports," added Marduk.

Marina smiled, "The priestesses, like me, help coordinate the work or help the Anunnaki directly as messengers."

"Or help in the planning, determining the best path for a project to be completed," said Marduk.

Masterson nodded his head, "And Lefteris and Rania?"

Marina perked up as she spoke of her friends. "They are healers. They use their abilities to heal us by manipulating the energy generated by our bodies."

"No, that's not what I saw. I saw Lefteris completely remove the wound, as if it never existed. It altered reality. That's an amazing and dangerous power. The ultimate power that I would expect is welded by the Genitor themselves."

"No, Lord Dumuzid, we are all taught stringently to obey the Will of the Genitor. It took you to enable us to not adhere to our teachings and rebel. We can follow, but for us to lead, as you do boldly and without hesitancy, is impossible." Marduk looked to the carpeted floor as he made this admission.

"Even at the cost of your very lives and the lives of your friends?"

Both Igigi nodded in unison, affirming that their conditioning ran deep. "We look like the Mundus humans, but inside," Marduk pointed to his head, "we are as Cassidan as the Anunnaki."

"Perhaps that's why I was selected by the Genitor to deliver their message to Enlil, and why my training was so abrupt. I'm not controlled by conditioning, I'm untainted."

Masterson scratched his chin as he thought. "But why were Chantico and Ehecatl able to stand up to me, thinking I was a servitor in Ganzir? Doesn't that violate their training? They nearly killed me! We fought and destroyed the *Tiamat*. Killing adepts and servitors and destroying their ship violates the Will of the Genitor, doesn't it? In fact, how do servitors justify killing each other and laborers, and keep within the Will of the Genitor?"

Both Marduk and Marina looked at Masterson helplessly.

Masterson focused on Marduk, "I think it's an age-old problem. Perhaps a problem that first developed on Cassida billions of years ago. Power without accountability breeds violence against those without it. I've not seen evidence that the Genitor holds the Anunnaki accountable for their actions. In fact, I've seen no direct Genitor involvement since I left Cassida. The only thing I've ever seen Enlil concerned about is his power over the Mundus mission, and the return of Anu and *Nibiru Station*. The one with power seeks to protect and grow their power over others. Those without power resent and grow distrustful with every abuse. I think that's the reason Chantico, Ehecatl, and Aktzin could attack me when they thought I was a servitor in Ganzir. I think it's easy to justify harming servitors and laborers because they have literally no power."

"But we have power. You have taught us that, Dumuzid. We defeated them at Ganzir, and we destroyed the *Tiamat* with your leadership." Marduk reached across the small coffee table to touch Masterson's knee. "*You* have given us the will to fight back!"

Marina gasped hearing what Marduk had said, "We follow Dumuzid the Bull's will?"

Marduk was shocked at what he had just said. He looked down at the carpeted floor, ashamed.

Dumuzid the Bull stood, stepping around the coffee table to stand beside Marduk. "Not my will. I was sent here by Lady Inanna.

She believes in you. She believes in Mundus belonging to Mundus. I think she sees the flaws in the strict Cassidan system of directed conception as it applied to Diona and here. And that's what you must fight for, Marduk. You must convince the Anunnaki that the Cassidan system is billions of years old. It didn't work well on Diona, destroying their world millions of years ago. I believe the Ejicerce, the Forgotten, are Mundusans from the future, trying to stop this world from suffering the same fate as Diona."

Marduk was shocked, "What do you mean I must convince the Anunnaki? Why not you? That is what Lady Inanna sent you for, right?"

Masterson looked between the two of them then spoke to Marduk, "I am as Mundus as you are. But the body the Genitor gave me is Dionan. And besides that, I came to Mundus as a servitor in their Seventh Order. The only standing I have with the Anunnaki is that of a bodyguard for Lady Inanna. Although you and the other Igigi recognize me as a leader, the Anunnaki don't. After my conversation with Ningishzidda in Kur, I know they'll never see me as anything more than a Dionan servitor, a tool."

"But, I am not a leader. I am a keeper of records. My job was to report on the harvest of food, metal, and precious stones collected. I am pleasing to the eye and good at small talk, more pleasant company than a famulim, but not a fighter like the servitor, nor a laborer. Why must I be the one to issue a demand to the Anunnaki, to Enlil? He will destroy me. He will destroy us all."

"You are at ease around them. You know their ways better than anyone else and, more than anyone else, you understand what's at stake. Who can speak on this better than you?" Masterson reached out to take Marduk by his shoulders, standing him up to face him. "You must prove to Enlil that a Mundus can match a Cassidan man-for-man, that as a people, Mundusans are meant to be the stewards of this world because it is the Genitors' Will."

Chapter 19: The Nibiru Station

Masterson slowly climbed his way back to wakefulness. He smiled, feeling the warm, soft body of Marina curled up beside him, under his right arm. Masterson yawned and stretched carefully to not wake her, then he looked about where they sat leaning up against the wall of the temple. He hadn't been asleep long. He noticed his fellow prisoners were as they were when he had fallen asleep, so not much time had passed. Masterson gently eased Marina back onto the stone floor of the temple, trying not to wake her. She moaned a complaint but curled up and was quickly deep asleep again. He eased himself up and stood over her for a few minutes. He had learned more about the volumn-enhanced abilities of the Igigi and the Anunnaki in the last few days than he had learned during all his days on Cassida or his short time as a servitor of the *Erimna Sebu,* the Seventh Order.

He moved about his fellow prisoners. Their fate had disillusioned many. They had come at his call to overthrow Enlil's regime and take charge of their world. Instead, they had been led into a trap by Masterson as Dumuzid the Bull, the Bull of Heaven. Now Dionan servitors guarded them as they all huddled together in the courtyard and small temple of Eshumesha among the offerings of food and other perishable goods brought to sustain the "gods" and, by default, the priests and priestesses that served the temple complexes of Nippur. It didn't help that Masterson wore a ruddy Dionan body. He saw the growing distrust and fear that many of the gazes turned toward him as the morning light dawned over the Mesopotamian city's walls and over the face of the towering Ekur Temple.

The eyes of the Igigi weren't the only ones following Masterson as he moved. The servitors were keeping a close watch on his movements too. They were fully armed in their hooded impact armor with particle-stream lancer-staffs and energy rods. Their defiance of the power their prisoners could wield against them was clearly on display. Wolves watching lions was the image that flooded Masterson's mind as he watched them watching him and his companions.

Masterson continued to prowl as more and more of the Igigi woke from their slumbers. He took roll of those that were with him and those that had somehow escaped being rounded up by the servitors the day before. The team that had entered the city with him were all present. The two brothers, in fact, were still sleeping as peacefully as if they were back in the Grecian village. Only a third of his attacking force had been captured. He didn't know whether the others had been killed or had escaped, although he knew from the chatter of the night before that some had died during the initial arrival of the servitor transports and gunships. Masterson sighed. They should have easily overpowered the servitors, even with their gunships. The Igigi were more powerful. The only explanation he could come up with as he rehashed the events of the day before was the Cassidan programming. It was still strong in their minds. Ishtar smiled up at him when he found her. She sat with Shala, which surprised Masterson.

"You two could have left. Why didn't you?"

"You will be triumphant today, Lord Dumuzid." Ishtar cocked her head to the side as she waited for his reaction. Beside her, a sleepy Shala rubbed the sleep from her eyes.

"Today? What will happen today?" Masterson said as he looked beyond the two women to watch several servitors guarding the back gate to the temple courtyard.

"Yes," she seemed disappointed that Masterson wasn't more excited about learning that he would ultimately be successful. "You will see Lord Enlil today and your goal will be achieved, Lord Dumuzid."

Masterson smiled at Ishtar, "Why didn't you two leave when you had the chance?"

Shala spoke over Ishtar to answer Masterson's question. "Lord Dumuzid the Bull, we are as committed to this cause as you are. We are the ones being hunted down and murdered by the servitors. The laborers are being killed too, but the servitors are hunting us. Our cause is just and we must take a stand or this persecution by the Anunnaki will always continue."

Shala's quick response surprised Masterson. This was the first time Shala had expressed her commitment to the fight.

"Besides," Ishtar quipped, "My friend Shala and I can leave anytime we want to."

Masterson laughed at Ishtar's point. They could leave anytime they wanted to, so long as they stayed together.

"But if we did, who would watch over you, sir?" added Shala.

"Alright, alright. You've made your point. I'm thankful to have two such loyal protectors as yourselves." Masterson turned his attention to the courtyard back entrance as a detachment of servitors moved toward him.

The team commander presented himself to Masterson, "Protector Dumuzid, I have orders to escort you to meet with Lord Enlil." Masterson nodded then took his place with the servitors to be escorted from the courtyard. The presence of the servitors on the walls and standing at the gates of the temple courtyard muted any voices that were raised in protest as the small band of servitors guided Masterson out. As he stepped through the gate and out of the courtyard, he looked back at the faces of the Igigi that had fought alongside him against Enlil. He saw faces filled with support, loyalty, and sadness. He turned and followed the guards from the temple to an open area that served as a bazaar, or makeshift market, where produce from the temple that was no longer needed or wanted was available to the city laborers. They had cleared it for a small spherical shuttle to land. Masterson recognized the common utilitarian hull design similar to the shuttles used by the *Glorious Questor*.

This shuttle could comfortably carry half a dozen passengers. They designed ships of this type with two usable decks, with the electro-magnetic drive and avionics housed in the lower half of the sphere. Shuttles were robotic or flown remotely from a transport carrier or citadel control center. Access to the drives and the flight deck was through circular hatches at the center of the deck with a gravitic field which would enable a person to float up or down as desired. Masterson enjoyed flying in these crafts and looked forward to doing so again, despite not knowing where he was being taken.

As Masterson and his team of guards stood several feet from the shuttle, it glowed as a ramp extended down from the middle of the ship, leading to a circular opening that appeared on the surface of the ship. Nudged by one of his guards, Masterson walked up the comfortably-sloped ramp to enter the ship. As expected, there was no one aboard. The opening in the hull closed like the shutter on a camera and faded into the wall as if were never there. The circular hatches in the floor and ceiling weren't there. Or were, but hadn't been activated. Either way, he didn't have access to their use. The room was empty. The floor and walls were the whitest white. There were no seams in the pseudo-ceramic surfaces.

"I wish to sit," Masterson said aloud. Before his eyes, the pseudo-ceramic floor morphed into an ergonomic chair. "I'm hungry and thirsty." As he expected, a table rose from the floor within reach of the chair. Cassidan fruit rose from a small chamber in the center of the table with a cup of water beside it. "Now I would like to see outside." On command, the circular wall of the shuttle became clear, as if it weren't there. It startled Masterson. Despite the number of times he'd flown on Cassidan and Dionan ships, he was never quite ready for the visual impact of seeing just how fast they moved. He didn't feel the momentum of the shuttle's movement, he felt as if the ship was still on the ground. But it had already reached the upper limits of the Earth's atmosphere and sped up toward deep space. He walked to the wall and reached out to verify it was still there then leaned forward so he could rest his forehead against the invisible barrier, gazing down at his beloved home.

He turned his gaze upward toward the bow of the ship, the direction the shuttle was flying. Off to the right he could see the Moon peeking around the horizon of the Earth at an alarming rate because of the speed at which the shuttle was flying, now free of the atmosphere. Masterson still felt the sensation of normal gravity within the ship as it continued to climb. No feeling of acceleration, no weightlessness, just him standing next to the crystal clear wall, looking out into infinite space.

Masterson turned and walked back toward the table and chair the ship had provided him. He smiled and tossed a Cassidan apple into the air and caught it. He looked back at the clear walls of the ship;

Sea of Worlds: Gods and Men

there was no sensation of movement at all once the Earth and Moon were out of sight. The stars were so distant that they didn't appear to be moving at all, despite the speed he knew they must fly at. Masterson ate the apple and drank the water then sat and contemplated what was happening to him. Where was he being taken?

After considering his fate for some time, something outside the ship caught his attention. He stood and walked to the wall to look. The ship was diving toward what could only be described as a dark square floating in space. He didn't know how fast or how long they had been flying, but it wasn't uncomfortably long. He wasn't tired nor hungry after eating the Cassidan fruit. As the ship headed for the center of the square and descended, more details of the surface of the object became visible. It was huge, several thousand miles across, and dark. As the ship continued its trajectory toward the object, features became more and more apparent, as well as sparse illumination. Small trails of lights were lit on the surface, which became less and less flat. The shuttle streaked on, its flight path continuing to take it toward what appeared to be the center of the square. Masterson could now see that the small lights were buildings, sprouting out of the object's surface like city towers. The shuttle reoriented itself as it descended into the gargantuan square. Masterson was now looking at the square's surface as if the ship were landing on a planet, with the surface in the bottom direction of his ship. The horizon stretched into the distance as the shuttle lowered quickly but without the curve like that of the Earth. The horizon was a flat line. He stared at it until the ship was low enough for it to disappear. He noticed that as he got closer to the surface that there were two monstrous maws from which transports of many sizes and shapes were arriving and departing. Masterson reasoned that they were port facilities and were large enough to handle even the megalith ships like the *Leviathan* and the *Tiamat* class transports.

His shuttle knew exactly where it was going. Masterson definitely felt the sensation of being swallowed as the small sphere-shaped ship dove deeply into the massive maw. There were several layers of docking facilities handling many ships, from personal transports to large haulers, which he assumed were used for hauling resources or personnel. All basic geometric shapes were represented by the ships; spheres, rectangular prisms, pyramids, all of them.

Masterson marveled at how big the place was as his shuttle slowed then fitted itself into a socket or cup that was approximately its size. The entire ship was sucked into a tube and was whisked into the innards of the port facility with absolutely no sensation of movement at all. Masterson stood watching as the ship shot down a rollercoaster-like chute at what appeared to be breakneck speed, of which he still felt no sensations of momentum. The ship finally slowed and stopped. Masterson realized he was in a secure location by the number of Gallu and servitors visible from the ship before its walls went opaque and everything returned to white. He turned to watch the furniture that had been provided to him melt back into the pseudo-ceramic floor. A different section of the hull opened and extended a ramp for him to leave the ship. He took a deep breath.

    A team of Gallu met him as he walked down the ramp. They were in full Gallu melam armor with the heavy plates and horned conical helmets which showed the wearer's military rank. He could feel the electrostatic charge of the heavy armor as he walked down the ramp. Being in proximity of the heavy armor made the hair on his arms stand up. Masterson looked up at the tall Cassidan team commander and nodded. The commander turned and activated a personal teleport portal then turned back to usher Masterson through first. On the other side of the portal, Masterson recognized the usual settings of one of the Cassidan forums with the elevated dais in the center. He stepped through.

    The Gallu commander behind him urged him to continue to move forward into the great hall. Masterson hadn't expected this. The hall was immense, almost cathedral-like in appearance, with tall, vaulted obsidian ceilings. The size of the hall instantly reminded him of the gargantuan buildings of the cities of Cassida. As they moved deeper into the hall, he noticed how great a distance there was between people and tiered, open galleries on the multiple levels of the structure. Cassidans and Dionans moved about in small groups or independently, shadowed by cohorts of famulim, ever ready to assist those about them. It was like being back on Cassida. Then he remembered that this Cassida had existed over a billion years ago and was now nothing more than a desert wasteland buried beneath the windblown sands of Mars.

In the distance, Masterson saw what had to be a simulation of the Sun. Like everything else about this place, the size was over the top. It dominated the far side of the hall they walked through. As they continued to walk toward it, he noticed a delegation of Cassidans standing and waiting in his path. As he closed with the tall Cassidans, he realized that Lord Ningishzidda was standing amongst them. The two men stood stoically as they faced each other, Gallu to his back and Cassidan adepts and attendants behind Ningishzidda.

"Your impulsiveness has brought you here to this moment, Dumuzid." Ningishzidda towered over Masterson as he spoke. "You are chaos incarnate."

"Where is this place?" Masterson asked.

Ningishzidda shifted his gaze from Masterson to look about them. His appreciation for where they were was clear on his normally stoic face. "We are in the Temple of Anu, on *Nibiru Station*."

"This is *Nibiru Station*?" Masterson paused, "I expected something different."

Ningishzidda's head snapped back, looking down at Masterson. "You are always saying or doing the unexpected, Dumuzid, but that will not serve you well here." He half turned then added, "I think today your story ends."

Ningishzidda led the way to their audience with Supreme Commander Anu. As with everything Cassidan, Commander Anu's audience hall was massive. The distances between small groups moving about provided security in the hall between those seeking to meet the commander. The chamber provided an excellent view of the hydrogen fusion event at the center of *Nibiru Station*. Masterson was in awe as he realized they had a nuclear fusion furnace in the middle of their ship to supply power. His appreciation of Cassidan engineering prowess grew.

They approached an elaborate, oversized dais. Upon it sat an ancient Cassidan whom Masterson immediately realized was Anu. Flanking Commander Anu were a bevy of adepts, attendants, adjutants, servitors, and famulim, the full range of the Cassidan specified conception caste system. Individuals conceived, pruned, and placed in positions they were created for according to the community's master plan.

A raspy, ancient voice boomed throughout the cavernous hall. "So, this is the one?"

"He is." Lord Enlil stepped forward from a small group of advisors toward the Supreme Commander Anu and approached the elder slowly, showing deference to the leader. "He is the envoy dispatched to the mission commander of Mundus. He delivered his—"

Commander Anu interrupted a surprised Lord Enlil with a dismissive wave of his hand. He waved for Masterson to approach him. As Masterson did, his Gallu guards remained where they stood. Masterson stood within arm's reach of the Supreme Commander of the *Nibiru Station*, a remnant of the vast Cassidan civilization. "I have heard from others that you have been called Filio Domini, Dumuzid, and Dumuzid the Bull by Cassidan, Dionan, and Mundusan, respectively. Who and why were those names given to you?"

Masterson thought before speaking, "With great respect, Supreme Commander Anu, I was given the name of Filio Domini by the Genitor that selected, tested, and trained me. The name of Dumuzid was selected for me by Lady Inanna and awarded to me by Commander Enlil when I was released from service with the Seventh Order of Battle at Lady Inanna's request. The name of Dumuzid the Bull was given me by the Igigi following the Battle of Ganzir, sir."

"How is it that a hastily created synthetic servitor with an implanted memory instigated a rebellion against the Will of the Genitor?" Commander Anu cocked his head ever so slightly as he gazed with interest at Masterson.

"The Will of the Genitor, Supreme Commander Anu?"

Commander Anu scoffed, "It is no wonder Lord Enlil petitioned me to end your existence, servitor."

Masterson straightened his back and raised his chin, realizing the reason he now stood before Commander Anu. "May I speak, Lord Anu? As you said, I am an envoy of the Genitor. I was sent by the Genitor to inform Lord Enlil of a strategic aspect of the Battle of Eidin. I have fulfilled that purpose, and yet I am here, standing before you. I submit again that it is the Will of the Genitor that I provide you with strategic information too."

Lord Anu stood, listening to Masterson. He didn't silence Masterson but listened, much to Lord Enlil's dismay.

"My Lord Anu, may I petition that someone else be permitted to speak on my behalf before you to argue my case?" asked Masterson.

Masterson's request resulted in a hint of curiosity in Commander Anu's ancient eyes as he squashed an attempt by Lord Enlil to protest with a wave of his hand. "You may."

"Supreme Commander Anu, I request that Lord Ningishzidda contact the Igigi being held in the Eshumesha Temple in the citadel of Nippur. The Igigi chief scribe, Marduk, will present himself to serve you by speaking on my behalf."

"Blasphemy!" shouted Lord Enlil, "A Mundus cannot come to *Nibiru*!"

Slowly, Commander Anu turned his gaze on Enlil. "Commander Enlil, are there Dionans serving the Will of the Genitor within the walls of this station?"

Lord Enlil became flushed, his skin turning a deeper shade of blue.

"Lord Ningishzidda," called out Commander Anu.

"Yes, Supreme Commander?"

"You will go to the city of Nippur and bring the Mundus attendant named Marduk to this proceeding."

"Yes, Supreme Commander." Lord Ningishzidda turned and left quickly.

"Lord Enki warned me you would be a surprise, Servitor Filio. He did not misrepresent you."

Commander Anu turned his attention to several attendants and famulim standing at a respectable distance around him and Masterson. "Make Envoy Filio comfortable. Give him an opportunity to speak with the scribe he requested. We will continue this conversation in two cycles. Envoy Filio has unrestricted access to the accommodations and facilities of our home during his stay."

Masterson watched as Commander Anu turned and walked away with several of the attendants and famulim immediately following him. He turned to look at Lord Enlil, who stood seething. Masterson smiled at Enlil, sending him into a rage, eyes glowing cobalt with a sudden surge of bio-kinetic energy.

"That would not be wise, brother." Everyone turned as Lord Enki approached his brood brother.

At seeing Enki, Enlil abruptly turned and walked off. He was clearly not happy to see his brother, and left with his attendants and adjutants joining him after they showed their displeasure with Enki's intervention.

Enki stood beside Masterson, watching Lord Enlil and company move out of sight in the great hall. Slowly, Enki turned and silently looked at the Gallu guards before offering, "Supreme Commander Anu has given this former servitor access and use of *Nibiru's* facilities. Your services are no longer required. You are dismissed."

Masterson and Lord Enki stood for a while, simply taking in the majesty of the many oversized structures around them. The most impressive was the view of the miniature fusion reaction orb that was suspended at the center of the *Nibiru* and visually dominated everything.

Masterson nodded at the orb and finally asked, "How is that even possible?"

Lord Enki smiled as he turned and looked down toward Masterson. "How is anything we do possible?"

"Consciousness."

Masterson's response surprised Lord Enki, "Very good, Dumuzid. Your insight into things is indeed impressive. And that you are untrained, a servitor and not an adept makes you even more impressive."

"I finally realize what the Cassidan castes are really about." Masterson looked up at Lord Enki. "They aren't about heritage or social dynamics at all. They're about dimensional perception and adaptability to training to master aspects of detection and manipulation, and possibly transcendence."

"Very well done, Dumuzid, and you came to this realization on your own without instruction or access to the accumulated wisdom of the famulim. I am very impressed. It will be unfortunate if Commander Anu ends your existence with you having come so far on your own."

Masterson looked down at the obsidian tiles they stood on.

"Shall we walk, my friend? I enjoy our strolls together." Lord Enki gestured in the direction Commander Anu and Lord Enlil had walked in.

"You have served the people of Mundus well, and you have served the Lady Inanna well. What more can be asked of a servitor?" Lord Enki smiled sideways at Masterson as they strolled together.

"You speak as if the decision about my fate has already been decided and is known among the elite."

"We both know it has been," replied Lord Enki.

"And the Lady Inanna, she is an Anunnaki, one of the elites herself. Is her fate sealed, too? As you yourself have pointed out, she is a Cassidan elite, an accomplished adept, meaning she is skilled at dimensional manipulation. Surely she's too valuable to the community to be discarded?"

Lord Enki whispered, "But she is not being discarded, she is transcending to join the Genitor."

"But her value to the Mundus people is still important. Her method of empowerment versus Enlil's tendency to destroy viciously is better suited for reaching the goals everyone wants."

"You make a good argument for her re-installment in the Anunnaki Council, but is that not someone else's task now?"

Masterson didn't respond to Lord Enki.

Chapter 20: Revelation and Judgement

Masterson had been provided a dwelling and the customary service of three famulim while the Anunnaki council gathered on the *Nibiru Station*. He had thought the return of the *Nibiru* meant that the station actually came to Earth's orbit to collect valuable resources from its Mundus colonies governed by the Anunnaki. He remembered that during the Battle of Eidin, when the Ejicerce were on the verge of taking the eugenics complex, Lord Enlil had ordered the Cassidan and Dionan adepts, attendants, and servitors to evacuate all ground facilities to the orbiting *Nibiru* using Atmospheric Reentry Couriers, or ARCs. Masterson was surprised to learn that the *Nibiru* didn't really need to orbit the Earth. The station could dispatch auxiliary ships to its Mundus colonies to collect the precious resources it required as it made a near pass on its never-ending meanderings through the Solar System.

Masterson sat wondering more about the purpose of the *Nibiru Station* when his attention was drawn to the entry into his dwelling. One of the famulim triplets interrupted to announce Lord Enki. It then stepped aside as Lord Enki stepped into the room. "May I entertain you with more conversation, Lord Dumuzid?"

Masterson stood smiling, "Of course, sir, particularly if it's about what's happening with the council and Lord Marduk's efforts on my behalf." Offering Lord Enki a seat at the table he was using would be awkward because of their different sizes, so he simply dismissed the pseudo-ceramic chair and table to melt back into the floor.

"That is precisely why I have come to speak to you. I am withdrawing my offer to nominate you to be the mission commander replacing Enlil." Lord Enki said. "The Igigi delegate you had requested, Marduk, masterfully presented the case for the Igigi to serve as the stewards of Mundus." Lord Enki paused, "But in doing so, also built a powerful case against you replacing Lord Enlil as the mission commander."

Masterson nodded while scratching his beard, "So Commander Anu will consider awarding stewardship of Mundus to the Igigi?"

The tall Cassidan smiled. "Oh yes. In fact, the Supreme Commander seemed enthusiastic about the idea when it was breached by Marduk quickly in his petition." Lord Enki pinched his lower lip in thought before continuing, "Was that your intent all along – to liberate the Igigi entirely from Cassidan rule?"

It was Masterson's turn to consider Lord Enki before responding. "No, Lord Enki, I believe it was yours. Yours and the Lady Inanna's intent from the moment the Mundus mission was conceived."

"And why would we do that?" Lord Enki paced as he listened to Masterson's words.

"May I ask a question first?"

"Of course you may, Lord Dumuzid." Enki stopped pacing almost as quickly as he had begun. He turned to face Masterson, waiting for the question.

"What is the fundamental difference between the Cassidans and Dionans, and the Mundusans?"

"Why, I suppose it is that they reproduce erratically based on hormonal reactions in their biological makeup. That erratic coupling of genetic material does not guarantee optimal performance in their preparation for the positions they are to fill in their communities." Lord Enki looked dismissive as he continued, "There is a lot of waste in preparing Mundus for their community roles. The variance of success in the preparation seems to grow with the population, which is out of control."

Masterson interrupted, "Out of control?"

"Well, yes," Lord Enki smiled unexpectedly, "Or so Lord Enlil has claimed to the Supreme Commander."

"But you disagree?"

"Have you studied the history of Dionan, Lord Dumuzid?" asked Lord Enki.

"I haven't had the opportunity. I know they are organized into clans and families instead of castes and orders like in the Cassidan fashion. But I know little beyond that. Most of my experience with the Dionans was serving as a servitor in the Seventh Order and traveling with the Dionan crew of the Temporal Courier *Glorious Questor*. I assume the choice of a Dionan body to place my consciousness and memories in was to provide me with believability when working within those groups."

Lord Enki arched his eyebrow. "That is an astute observation." He gathered his thoughts before continuing, "Diona is the second planet in this system. It is a terrestrial world as were the first, third, fourth and fifth worlds, the rest being hydrogen and helium protostars that failed to generate enough gravitational force to ignite. The fifth terrestrial world from the star was obliterated when the Genitor arrived in this system to be used for the creation of this station, and the famulim in the early stages of the colonization of the fourth planet, Cassida."

"Or Mars," said Masterson.

"Or Mars," yielded Lord Enki. "The Cassidan civilization was created immediately after the creation of this system. It flourished under the guidance of the Genitor but consumed the easily accessible resources of their world. It was the Genitors' Will that the Cassidan people seed a second world within the system. Diona, the second planet from the star, was chosen based on habitable conditions on its surface."

"Ah." Masterson sighed, "But Cassidan physiology wasn't optimum for the new planetary conditions. So the population of Cassida was left to become extinct."

Lord Enki ignored the question and agreed with Masterson's assumption about Cassidan physiology. "Exactly. You have made a very astute observation once again, Lord Dumuzid. So, under the guidance of the Genitor and the help of the famulim, technology was constructed that enabled Cassidans to travel the temporal spectrum through dimensional manipulation to seed and nurture the fledgling Dionan civilization billions of years in Cassida's future."

"But there was a problem, wasn't there? Every time a Cassidan or Dionan changes their location on the temporal spectrum using dimensional manipulation technology, there is a deterioration of the integrity of their physical body, which affects their essence as well."

"You know more than you would lead us to believe, Lord Dumuzid."

"Because of the mentorship of Lady Inanna. She was a catalyst that enabled me to fulfil my mission, sir."

"Which has cost her dearly, Lord Dumuzid," said Lord Enki.

"She sent me here to this spot on the temporal spectrum. I'm here because she wanted me here," explained Masterson.

"That is why she is bodiless, her essence separated from her physical existence. That was her act of betrayal, according to Lord Enlil."

Masterson frowned and bit his upper lip as he concentrated on the facts and not his surging emotions concerning Inanna's fate. "She sent me here because somehow she had knowledge that this was the exact time for the Igigi to move to secure their stewardship of the Earth." He paced under Lord Enki's watchful gaze. "The only way she could have that knowledge is by someone providing it to her since Anunnaki and high ranking Dionans don't time travel often because of the damage it causes." He suddenly realized the actual relationship between Inanna and Captain Valarus of the *Glorious Questor*. Masterson turned to face Lord Enki. "The Dionan civilization reached its zenith hundreds of millions of years ago in Earth's past, correct?"

Lord Enki nodded his head, watching Masterson.

"Then Captain Valarus and the *Glorious Questor* have to be from the Earth's past, too. They can't be from the future. But the Ejicerce are from the future, aren't they? So any knowledge of the future that Inanna had was provided by someone from the future or at least had visited the future. Valarus was from the past, but he's been to the future. I know that as a fact. I've taken part in trips to the future with him! My memories are from the future as well. The consciousness placed in me isn't native to Cassida or Diona; it's native to a point thousands of years from now."

"Lord Dumuzid, the Ejicerce are from the past and the future. They are who they are because they time travel using Cassidan technology. They are from the future and the past." Lord Enki nodded his head. "Your point is valid, however. Lady Inanna sending you here to this exact point on the temporal spectrum was an informed decision on her part. As to your consciousness being from the future, that could simply be a manifestation of the volumn ability in you as a form of precognition. You are a prophet."

Masterson scoffed, "Aren't you curious who her source was?" Masterson stepped closer to Lord Enki. "Who was feeding her information about the Igigi and the events at this point on the temporal spectrum? I don't think it was Valarus. He doesn't strike me as a strategic thinker. He may have been the conduit for the information, but not the source."

"What are you suggesting – that the Ejicerce have a strategy for their behavior? They are chaotic, they are motivated by revenge and a desire to regain the freedom to travel as they want. Most of them are restricted from time travel, which is enforced by the Orders of Battle."

"Could it be one Order of Battle that is controlling the Ejicerce? The Third and the Seventh were fighting each other for control of the eugenics center at the Battle of Eidin, weren't they?" Masterson saw that his line of argument held little chance of influencing Lord Enki, but he had to try. "Lord Enki, if you don't know who or what her source of information was, don't you think it prudent to bring her back? That's the only way you can determine where she was receiving her information about the future from."

Lord Enki laughed, "You still want to bring Inanna back to life, have her in her physical body. That is not possible. Her body was destroyed by the Gallu under Lord Enlil's direct supervision."

Masterson reacted quickly, without hesitation. "The Genitor, or someone, placed my essence in another body. I was placed in this synthetic one on ancient Cassida, apparently over billions of years ago. Can't the same be done for her?"

"You were created by the Will of the Genitor for a specific purpose, Dumuzid."

Masterson shook his head, showing he disagreed. "What if this is the purpose I was meant for, to root out the source of the Ejicerce rebellion? Do envoys continue to deliver messages repeatedly?"

"Sometimes. There have been envoys in the past that have delivered several messages during their allotted time."

"Then my continued insistence that Inanna be forgiven and brought back to the physical world, it could be the Will of the Genitor." Masterson's claim surprised Lord Enki. The surprise then shock showed clearly on his face. The Anunnaki lord was speechless.

Masterson turned away from Lord Enki. "Consider what I'm saying. I remember, if the Ejicerce weren't part of the Will of the Genitor, how could they continue to operate or even exist?"

The tall Anunnaki silently turned and departed Masterson's dwelling, leaving Masterson alone to wait until summoned by the Supreme Commander and the council.

Several watch cycles had passed when Masterson woke from a fitful sleep then rose from the sleeping pallet. Sluggishly discarding the blanket, he staggered to the hygiene cabinet of the dwelling to refresh himself, just as he had done so often since coming to the *Nibiru*. He was pulling the ubiquitous gray servitor tunic over his head when two melam-armored Gallu entered unannounced through a teleport portal near his dwelling's door.

"It is time."

Masterson nodded, hearing the welcome announcement. He finished dressing, slipping on soft soled ankle-boots then the empty utility belt, and joined his escort to be taken to learn his fate and the fate of the Igigi. They stepped through the teleport portal, arriving outside the Supreme Commander's audience hall. The grand imagery of the *Nibiru Station* no longer impressed him. He knew exactly where he was heading and didn't wait for the Gallu escort to step from the portal behind him. Supreme Commander Anu sat in his chair as several attendants and famulim scurried about him. The other members of the Anunnaki Council sat stoically in their chairs to Commander Anu's left and right, listening to a Cassidan adept petitioning them. Masterson was surprised when one of his Gallu escorts guided him to the side to stand with attendants rather than present him to the seated council, many of which had their eyes on him during his entry into the great hall.

Lord Enlil stood from his seat on the council and moved to stand before Supreme Commander Anu, signaling for the speaking adept to move aside. "Supreme Commander, members of the Council of Judges, I call before you an envoy of the Genitor, appointed protector of Inanna, Dumuzid, and his advocate Igigi Adept Marduk." Immediately, Lord Enlil returned to his seat. The Gallu retrieved Masterson and moved him to stand before the seven judges joining Marduk, who had taken the previous adept's spot. Both men stood together without looking at each other, their eyes focused solely on the Supreme Commander.

Commander Anu spoke from his seat, his voice resonating through the great hall, "We have considered the petition placed before us by Dumuzid, Protector of Inanna, and Envoy of the Genitor." Commander Anu motioned for Lord Ningishzidda to step forward from his position, standing behind the row of seven chairs and off to the side.

"The Council of Judges, in agreement, has decided that the Anunnaki Mission to Mundus will be suspended for one solar orbital cycle of the *Nibiru*. Commander Enlil and his adepts and attendants will withdraw for that period and will serve at the pleasure of the Council of Judges here until we return. During the period of withdrawal, the Igigi will serve as the stewards of Mundus on behalf of the Genitors' Will."

Commander Anu interrupted, "Adept Marduk, your declaration of Igigi innocence to the Council of Judges was most persuasive. You indeed were correct that you did not start a rebellion against the Will of the Genitor. The Igigi simply but effectively reacted to conditions as they existed that were created by outside influences generated by others. For that reason, the Igigi now have complete stewardship of Mundus for 3,600 Mundusan years, to show what your people are capable of. The next time the *Nibiru Station* passes this way in its solar orbit, the Council of Judges expect to be overwhelmed by the successes of the Mundus people in achieving the Will of the Genitor." Commander Anu gestured for Lord Ningishzidda to continue.

Lord Ningishzidda nodded to the commander then resumed where he had stopped. "The Council of Judges has awarded the stewardship of Mundus to the Igigi while inviting the Anunnaki mission to serve the Will of the Genitor on *Nibiru Station* for one solar refueling cycle." Lord Ningishzidda promptly turned and returned to his spot standing behind the seven chairs of the Council of Judges.

"Lord Dumuzid," Commander Anu's voice thundered through the great hall, commanding everyone's instant attention. "Lord Dumuzid, your role in the destruction of the Temporal Transport *Tiamat,* and losing the crew of adepts, adjutants, servitors and famulim of the Fourth Order has not been forgotten or forgiven by the Council of Judges. There was much debate over your fate amongst my esteemed member judges as to exactly what to do with you. Only your status as an envoy of the Will of the Genitor and your insight into events around you have stayed our hand in ordering the harshest of punishments to be rewarded for your chaotic actions. Being a synthetic, we have determined that since the Genitor created you, only the Genitor can end you."

Masterson shot a quick glance at Lord Enlil at hearing the word *chaotic* used to describe him.

"You are no longer the protector of Inanna, a task you failed. Therefore, you lose all privileges associated with that position. I cannot revoke your status as an envoy of the Genitor, though if I could, I would. My fellow judges have argued that the Council of Judges must have access to you, and you to them. I decree that you are therefore ordered to remain on the *Nibiru* as special advisor to the Council of Judges. You are to be properly incorporated into the station community, and serve the Will of the Genitor in the service of all the people of the Domain and not just those of Mundus. This is my decision and the decision of the Council of Judges. It is final and non-revocable."

Masterson was led from the presence of the Council of Judges and from the audience hall by the Gallu. He had questions, but no one was in the mind to answer them as they walked. He was taken to an administration center near the audience hall where he was left for the reminder of the day. Masterson wasn't in custody, but he had nowhere to go, no one to call for help. He felt truly alone for the first time since his life as a Cassidan servitor had begun. Masterson understood the rationale for being treated this way. He was sure that his new status as being insignificant was the purpose behind his being ignored. It was the way things were done, whether it was being psychologically isolated in a dungeon of the mind, or physically isolated by being left alone in a public building without instructions on what to do next. But he was used to knowing nothing about what was happening around him.

The *Nibiru Station* didn't have a day/night cycle. He had already observed that the ship was organized into three watches of 24 hours each, a full day on either Earth or Mars. Each shift required roughly one-third of the crew manning their work stations. Masterson didn't know how much personnel it took to operate the *Nibiru,* but he estimated it was in the tens of thousands, if not hundreds of thousands, possibly millions. He stood and looked out the window of the administration center's lobby. The station was a city unto itself, a lattice of bubble car tubes running through or between monstrous suspended blocks of onyx, dotted with illuminated spots that were, in fact, windows of inhabited floating buildings. The construct made the Grand Canyon on Earth look like a streambed because of its size and complexity. Masterson immediately compared the gargantuan innards of the *Nibiru* to a human brain, with neurons firing and synaptic pathways within the brain, to the bubble car tubes filled with passengers. Masterson sighed and stepped away from the window.

"Lord Dumuzid?"

Masterson looked up to see his three assigned famulim standing before him. He was taken aback because they had approached him without his seeing them until they were standing before him within arm's reach. Masterson frowned and rubbed the back of his neck with his right hand.

"Sir, we were alerted that you were to return to your dwelling. When you didn't, we came in search of you. Were we correct in doing so?" asked the lead famulim.

"That cell is to be my home?"

"Yes, sir. For now, it is your current designated dwelling. It is not satisfactory?"

Masterson looked at the three famulim for a long time in silence. Then he smiled, "Come, my new amigos, let's see if we can find a better place to call our home. Seems I'm going to be here a while." Masterson put his arms around the hips of the two taller famulim, hugging the two of them close to him in a friendly embrace as he walked toward the exit of the administration center, leaving the third famulim standing, staring at their backs before moving quickly to catch up. "What are you guys called, by the way?"

"I am Cadmualion," said the famulim to Masterson's right.

"I am Atabanus," responded the famulim to Masterson's left.

"I am Ron," chimed in the famulim following them.

Masterson smiled, "Come on, Ron."

As they walked, Masterson asked them questions, like a child walking between two adults. First he asked about what they knew of his status on the *Nibiru*. They informed him he was now identified as a member of the *Nibiru Station* and designated as an advisor to the Council of Judges. This information led to him asking about what that meant as far as his movements and access. He had attendant status, meaning he was to be treated as a staff member of the Council by the servitors and famulim. But it also meant he had access to information. That pleased Masterson.

"Am I to report to anyone?" Masterson asked as they entered a nexus area, a place where multiple bubble car tubes could be accessed. It was a pleasant place, sculpted entirely from ubiquitous pseudo-ceramic material that permeated Cassidan constructs. The nexus had an excellent view of the fusion power plant as the center of the station. Masterson used that as his compass when he was moved about the station by the Gallu, from his arrival to the declaration of his punishment at the Council of Judge's audience hall. The hall was very close to the power plant. His residence appeared to be more distant.

Looking down at his hands as he sat on a bench, he looked up at Ron asking, "How are the residences organized on *Nibiru*?"

"What do you mean, sir?"

"How are dwellings assigned to personnel living here? Are they organized by status or job?"

Ron looked down at Masterson with a sudden realization of the meaning of Masterson's question. "The station is divided into four cube-shaped quadrants. Each quadrant has two access channels that facilitate the comings and goings of the station's auxiliary vessels. The channels are large enough to dock and refit an Order of Battle Temporal Transport and service many auxiliaries. Order of Battle personnel are assigned dwellings close to those channels when a

Leviathan-class Temporal Transport is being refitted or repaired. At the point of intersection of those four quadrants is where the station's fusion power plant is located." Ron gestured toward where the great orange-red orb was suspended, dominating their field of view.

"Make sure we stay away from where the *Tiamat* and the *Leviathan* are usually docked then," said Masterson. Looking up at Ron, "I have some history with the crews of those transport ships."

"We know, sir," said Cadmualion matter-of-factly.

Masterson scowled at Cadmualion, "Continue, Ron."

Ron nodded. "Within each quadrant, there are four sectors. At the center quadrant where the four sectors intersect, is where the temples are located. The station temples are where the famulim are housed. Each famulim lives there when not engaged in work with their designated tasks."

"So that's where you three are at when not with me?" All three famulim nodded in unison, making Masterson smile. "Do you sleep?"

"Yes. The Genitor review our daily observations as we meditate in chambers," said Atabanus.

"You meditate? Do you mean upload information?" asked Masterson. Long ago he had learned that the famulim download their observations into a central database housed in their temples on ancient Cassida. They shared a hive-mind that they regularly updated. Although their bodies only had a twenty-year service life, their consciousness could be rebooted into another body from their last upload. Theoretically, these were the same famulim consciousnesses that once walked the grand halls of Cassida billions of years ago. Masterson hoped that was true. He had met some amazing famulim he wouldn't mind meeting again.

All three of the famulim cocked their heads to the side together as they processed Masterson's question. Cadmualion was the one to answer, "Yes."

"Continue with your explanation of where folks live on this station, Ron."

"At the center of each sector, four within a quadrant, there is a Center of Wisdom, or the community center. Four distinct communities radiate from the Center of Wisdom as the sectors do from the quadrants."

"Why is the community center called the Center of Wisdom?"

"The community center serves not only as an administrative center for the quadrant but is also the location where all training and preparation of replacement personnel occurs, sir," said Ron.

"I want a dwelling close to one of those Centers of Wisdom."

Cadmualion spoke up, "I will arrange that immediately, sir."

Ron continued, "Adjutants oversee the management of the subdivisions of the station. The seniority of an adjutant compared to another is determined by the level they are managing. A sector adjutant holds more management authority than a community adjutant does. A quadrant...."

"That's fine, Ron, I understand." Masterson turned his attention to Cadmualion, "When I served aboard the *Leviathan*, there were training rooms shared by combat teams on the temporal transport. These rooms had a virtual training ability. We could create an environmental facsimile of various locations and situations the combat team might operate in. Could I have one of those in my dwelling?"

"Yes," answered Cadmualion.

"In the Center of Wisdom, I was given consciousness on Cassida. There was a room where I could interact with a facsimile of people I had known from memory. Can I have that too?"

"Yes," answered Cadmualion again.

Masterson suddenly stood and clapped his hands together with great enthusiasm. "Let's get to it then! Ron, you stay with me. Cadmualion, ah I can change your name, right? Cadmualion, you are now named Larry." He turned to Atabanus. "And you are now named Curly. Right, got it? Now, Larry and Curly, you two go arrange for my new dwelling with a facsimile room." Dismissing Cadmualion and Atabanus, Masterson turned his attention back to Ron, who appeared to be confused. "Now tell me all you know about volumn."

Chapter 21: The Morning Star

Masterson sat naked on a towel, enjoying the high-definition facsimile of a beach as he gazed out at the sun rising over an aquamarine sea. He smiled and looked over at Ron, who had perched himself on a pseudo-ceramic rock, also to observe the facsimile sunrise.

Ron cocked his head to the side, paused then announced, "Someone is arriving, sir."

Masterson stood, wrapping the towel around his waist. The amazingly realistic scene disappeared, replaced by a large domed, windowless room. Masterson padded shoeless from the facsimile room into the larger team bay. The sleeping alcoves had been converted to special purpose rooms by his three famulim, at his request. They had converted the training room into a very spacious and functional dwelling for him in a very short time, thanks to the programmable nature of pseudo-ceramics.

"To what may I attribute this visit to?" Masterson asked as he stopped before two Cassidan servitors wearing knee-high tunics.

"Lord Enki has summoned you. We are to escort you to his location."

"Ron, bring me some clothes." Masterson turned his attention to the two servitors. "It's been several watches since I was dismissed from the Council of Judge's audience hall. Why does he want me to come to him now?"

"Lord Enki wants you to meet someone," said one servitor.
"Who?"

The other servitor spoke, "It is not for us to say, Lord Dumuzid."

Masterson furrowed his brow as he pulled the knee-length tunic over his head. Masterson turned to gesture for his famulim to accompany him, but the two servitors intervened. "You alone are to come with us, sir."

Masterson nodded and waved off his famulim. Then, without further delay, he stepped forward to follow the two servitors into the teleport bubble.

Masterson emerged from the teleportation bubble into what reminded him of the tactical command center of the *Leviathan*. Early in his tour of duty aboard the Temporal Transport *Leviathan*, he had met the *Sebu Erimna* or Seventh Order of Battle's commander, Michail. But this room was much larger, accommodating more adjutants and technologists. There was one large central console with a facsimile of the Earth suspended over it. Then there was a ring of eight smaller, similar consoles ringing the large one. All the consoles were well staffed and active, each with a facsimile of human Mundus bronze-age warriors either marching, standing or digging what appeared to be trenches.

"You did this!" Masterson recognized the voice instantly. He turned to see Lord Enlil moving toward him. Masterson braced, preparing to receive Enlil's attack.

"Hold!" boomed the command of the Supreme Commander. Lord Enlil stopped in his tracks, his piercing gaze still locked on Masterson.

"Bring Lord Dumuzid to me," the voice of the Supreme Commander again boomed. Everyone in the command center was quiet. The two servitors guided Masterson by his elbows to stand before Supreme Commander Anu.

"Dumuzid, you continue to surprise. Was this attack on Lord Enlil's temple city your plan? Are the Igigi using the Mundusans against the Anunnaki?" Supreme Commander Anu asked as he looked down at Masterson with expressionless eyes.

"Yes," responded Masterson, looking back up at the taller Cassidan leader.

"Why, Dumuzid?" asked Supreme Commander Anu.

"The Anunnaki divorced themselves from the Mundus generations ago. They rely on the Igigi to supervise the Mundus laborers more and more. Yet, they seem to have forgotten that. They launched an attack on the Igigi by targeting specific Igigi leaders, arresting them and killing those taken. This began with the disappearance of one of the Anunnaki Council members on Mundus, Lady Inanna. The situation escalated when the servitors of the *Tiamat* openly attacked the citadel of Ganzir, razing it to the ground. Ganzir was favored by Lady Inanna. The Igigi responded by attacking the *Tiamat*."

"Led by you, you traitorous demon. You led the Igigi in a murderous attack that destroyed the *Tiamat*, killing tens of thousands of servitors and their leaders!" screamed Lord Enlil, now beside himself with anger.

Masterson continued with a calm voice. "The Igigi used their volumn-enhanced powers and their training to board and engage the servitors directly. As a result, the ship's synthetic consciousness destroyed the ship to keep it from falling into the Igigi's control."

"Liar!" screamed Lord Enlil, "Liar, you destroyed the *Tiamat*."

Masterson furrowed his brow as he turned his dark blue eyes on Lord Enlil. "How? I have no enhanced volumn powers. I have no training in the technology or instrumentation of the servitor battleships. Nor do the Igigi. Who else could have destroyed the *Tiamat*? Only its crew or the ship's own synthetic consciousness."

"And now you turn your Igigi against my temple to destroy it?" Lord Enlil's eyes flashed cobalt blue as he moved toward Masterson again.

Supreme Commander Anu spoke, "Dumuzid has not been on Mundus for several watches. He has been under surveillance by the famulim since his arrival. He has not even been given access to his Igigi advocates during their petition to the Council of Judges on his behalf. I find his argument that he lacked the abilities or training to have destroyed the *Tiamat* during the uprising compelling. This attack by the Mundusans on Lord Enlil's temple I see as the direct result of their management by the Anunnaki Council. For generations, laborers were not directly managed by either Cassidan or Dionan adepts and attendants. That task was left to the Igigi, whom now holds jurisdiction over them by my decree."

Lord Enlil turned on Supreme Commander Anu hissing, "That is your fault! You kept my servitors on the *Nibiru* following the fall of the eugenics center at Eidin. You denied me use of the *Salsu Erimna* and held the Third Order on the *Nibiru,* forcing me to continue management of Mundus with a reduced contingent of adepts and attendants, not to mention adjutants and servitors, knowing the Ejicerce had played a major role in the loss of the Eidin citadel as proclaimed by the Genitors Envoy!" Lord Enlil pointed an accusing finger at Masterson.

"Judgement on the Envoy has been declared for his part in the loss of the *Tiamat* because of his service to the Genitor and us at the Battle of Eidin." Supreme Commander Anu glanced back at Masterson momentarily before continuing to address Lord Enlil. "The stewardship of Mundus has been awarded to the Igigi. You will continue to withdraw your personnel from Mundus to the *Nibiru Station.* What happens at the Nippur Citadel is not your concern."

Lord Enlil pointed his finger at Masterson before turning to leave. "We are not leaving Mundus permanently, Envoy. The Igigi have only one *Nibiru* solar cycle before we return. Then Mundus will be mine again."

"You will return to your dwelling, Lord Dumuzid. I will speak with the other Judges about Lord Enlil's behavior concerning you."

The Supreme Commander was about to turn away and return to the central console when Lord Enki spoke up from one of the subordinate consoles. He had watched the display of Lord Enlil's anger quietly. "Supreme Commander, I would like to speak to the Envoy if that is permissible. I realize your attention is focused elsewhere, but I would like some clarification that only he can provide about what is happening on Mundus."

Supreme Commander Anu nodded then continued back to the central console surrounded by his adjutants and attendants.

"Come with me, Lord Dumuzid." Lord Enki addressed the two servitor escorts, "I will take custody of Lord Dumuzid. Return to your team, adjutants." Lord Enki said nothing as he led Masterson from the command center to board a bubble car. They were soon whisking through the *Nibiru's* tunnel network at high speed to a destination of Lord Enki's choosing, passing through several of the station's sectors as they moved from one quadrant to another.

Masterson likened it to riding a roller coaster. "Can I ask where you're taking me?"

Lord Enki turned, smiling down at Masterson in a friendly way, "To meet someone."

Masterson frowned but asked no further questions. They arrived at what, to Masterson, appeared to be very similar to the hospital or what his first set of famulim had called an *Inhaero,* the place where he had become conscious in his Dionan body. There were many famulim interacting with both Cassidan and Dionan *curandus,* or charges. He felt both dread and curiosity then a sense of anticipation built as they walked deeper into the facility. Masterson quickly noticed that no one was paying attention to Lord Enki despite his high rank as a member of the Anunnaki Council of Judges and the council overseeing the projects on Mundus.

"Do you come here often, Lord Enki?" Masterson asked as they moved between the floors of the facility on wide ramps.

"This is my place of work, yes, when aboard the *Nibiru.* Does this look familiar to you?"

"Yes, it does. It looks like the facility I first became conscious in on Cassida."

"It is the place where conception for so many begins, just as it was on Cassida and later on Diona." Lord Enki smiled and turned to look at Masterson, "And eventually on Mundus, once it is ready for the transition."

"Transition?" Masterson questioned. "The plan is for Mundus to have specified conception like the other worlds do?"

"Yes, of course." Lord Enki ushered Masterson into a small clinic just off the main corridor of the floor they had arrived on. The clinic was lavishly equipped with several technicians and famulim standing by as they entered. As they moved deeper into the suite of rooms, Masterson recognized Ishtar, the Igigi that had been his primary helper in organizing the Igigi, besides Marduk.

"What's she doing here?" Masterson quickly rushed to her side. She was unconscious, covered only with a light sheet.

"Wait," was all that Lord Enki said as he nodded to an attendant standing by.

Masterson focused on Ishtar as the technologists in the room became busy. They reminded him of the Valarus' crew aboard the *Glorious Questor,* operating their consciousness and amplification transference system equipment, the technology they used to enter the body of a holder on an excursion mission. Masterson quickly looked up at Lord Enki. Masterson seized Ishtar's soft hand as Ishtar's eyes fluttered. She slowly opened her eyes. It seemed like it took forever for her to focus then she looked at Masterson. She smiled, *"My Dumuzi."*

About the Author

Robert is an avid reader of science fiction, writing short stories and drawing pictures in his school notebooks as a child. His favorite novel as a kid was Jules Verne's 20,000 Leagues Under the Sea. Robert served as a navigation specialist in the U.S. Navy in the 1970s. He decided at the end of his fifth patrol on a Fleet Ballistic Submarine that Navy life was not for him. He reentered the service in 1980, joining the U.S. Army Infantry to ensure he would be outdoors, serving at various posts in the U.S., South Korea, and Western Germany. Following retirement from the Army, Robert earned his Bachelor of Science in Early Childhood Education, and his Master of Educational Science degrees at Western Kentucky University. He is now a retired schoolteacher living in Central Kentucky, enjoying grandparenting with his wife of over 30 years, Jiwon.

Printed in Great Britain
by Amazon